GETTING HIS WAY

SAPPHIRE FALLS

ERIN NICHOLAS

ABOUT THE BOOK

Bryan Murray always planned to settle down back in Sapphire Falls, and Tessa Sheridan was part of that plan— even if she didn't know it.

But fate has a funny, and sometimes painful way of working things out.a not-so-little tumble off a mountain while biking has turned Bryan's life upside down and landed him back in his hometown ahead of schedule, changing everything.

At least one thing hasn't changed-- Tess is still the same sweet, kind and beautiful girl he left behind.

Tessa has been saving herself for Bryan in every way. And dreaming about an exciting life. Somewhere else. But now Bryan's messing up all of her plans. Not only has he come home, but he's decided to go from the hot, sexy playboy of her fantasies to a sweet, romantic boyfriend type. Who wants a happily ever after with her. In Sapphire Falls.

What's a girl gotta do to have an adventure or two? She's going to have to make it happen for herself. Which means leaving home. Which means avoiding falling in love. All while being romanced by the only man who's ever had her heart.

Getting His Way

Copyright 2016 by Erin Nicholas

All Rights Reserved.

ISBN: 978-0-9973662-0-4

Editors: Kelli Collins and Heidi Moore

Cover by Qamber Designs & Media

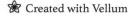 Created with Vellum

1

Tessa Sheridan was sweet. Super sweet. Possibly the sweetest girl in Sapphire Falls. She was so sweet, she made her *own* teeth ache.

Which meant everyone was going to be very surprised when she stormed into the Come Again and chewed Bryan Murray's ass.

She pushed open the door to Sapphire Falls' only bar and stomped inside.

But her entrance was barely noticed. The music was loud and the place was full, especially around the bar, where she expected to find Bryan, the owner.

He was there behind the bar all right, but he was blocked from seeing the door by three gorgeous women and four of his adoring fans. The women didn't bother Tess. Two were married, and the single one was interested in the town cop—even if she wouldn't admit it. The fans were men who thought Bryan was the coolest, funniest, most inspirational guy they knew.

And the thing was, Bryan definitely was cool, funny and inspirational.

In fact, Tess was about to yell at the guy who had inspired *her* and made her try something that had changed her life.

But she wasn't going to tell him that. Because Bryan Murray already had a hard time fitting his big head through doorways. And a lot of that was her fault.

She took a deep breath and marched to the bar. She squeezed in between Ty and Tucker Bennett. Being squeezed in between those two was no hardship, but she kept her mad face fully in place as she leaned on the bar and pointed at Bryan.

"I need to talk to you."

"Tess."

Bryan's face actually lit up when he saw her, and for just a second, she felt her heart flip and her frown ease.

No. She couldn't do that. She couldn't go all mushy over that smile—the way she had for about twenty two years. She'd fallen for him when she was five. She hadn't gotten over him until she was about twenty seven. Two and a half years ago.

"Can we talk?" she asked, keeping her voice firm and low.

Of course, the people right around them—including Bryan's adoring fans and the women with them—heard her.

And they all focused on her with rapt interest.

Bryan seemed to notice she wasn't overjoyed to see him and glanced around. "Actually, uh, I have a lot going on right now. Maybe later?"

She looked around too. The bar was busy, but everyone seemed happy. "Derek's here," she said of Bryan's main bartender. "I'm sure he can handle whatever comes up. It will only take a minute."

Maybe less. All she needed to tell him was to stay out of her love life.

Could that wait until later? Maybe. Would it be better without an audience? Possibly. But she had come straight over after she'd heard he had warned off yet another guy from asking her out. She was ticked, and she needed to confront

Bryan when she was ticked. And she needed to do it fast, before he wore her down and made her laugh and reminded her why she'd had a crush on him for as long as she'd known him.

This was the fourth guy Bryan had told hands off. Which was not just incredibly intrusive in her life, but also completely rude. Because *he* wasn't asking her out either. He'd been home for a year and seven months and hadn't so much as bought her a beer.

Okay, he'd given her a couple of free ones. As the owner of the Come Again, he could do that. He gave away free beer to people on a nightly basis. It wasn't like it was some big gesture.

Five years ago, if she'd heard that Bryan was keeping the other guys in town from dating her, it would had given her hope that he wanted something from her besides friendship. If he'd done it ten years ago, she would have assumed they were going to get married and live happily ever after. Of course, ten years ago—and fifteen years ago and twenty-five years ago on the first day of kindergarten—she figured they were destined to be together forever.

Now she knew better.

She had grown up. She had matured. Finally. She was done waiting for Bryan Murray. She was no longer pathetically in love with him.

She had been young and naïve and starry-eyed over the guy from age five to twenty-seven. But no more.

And considering Bryan knew she had been pathetically in love with him all that time, she needed to fill him in on the fact she was done with it. Apparently soon.

"Not later," she said. "Now."

He was leaning against the counter on the backside of the bar and shifted to rest his elbows on top, putting his face directly in front of her. She moved back, not able to handle having his face only inches from hers.

"Tess, let's do this after closing," he said, his voice almost soothing.

Soothing. Yeah. Then why did she feel like she'd just touched a live wire?

After closing, with no one else around, was *not* a good idea. If they were alone, she would revert to thirteen-year-old Tess— the girl with braces and oily hair and a big butt who would swoon every time he made a joke in math class. He could do no wrong in her eyes.

Back *then*. Definitely back then. Now she was smarter and more mature and knew that smiles and compliments didn't mean true love. Sixteenth-birthday kisses didn't either. Nor did marriage proposals. Evidently. Of course, he'd been nine when he'd informed her that he was going to marry her.

Fortunately, she'd moved beyond the romantic ideas she'd had when she was nine. And sixteen. And twenty-five.

They'd been twenty-five when he'd told her he knew he'd never meet another girl like her. He'd also been drunker than she'd ever seen him. But her stupid heart hadn't cared.

Tess lost her patience—something she never did. She slapped her hand down on top of the bar, making the beer in Ty's and Tucker's mugs jump. "You're messing with me, Bryan, and it's got to stop."

He'd been messing with her as long as she'd known him. It wasn't his fault. It was hers. But she was probably going to take it out on him.

He didn't look shocked. Or contrite. He cocked an eyebrow, looking almost impressed. Or something. "I'm messing with you?" he asked. He gave her a slow smile. "I really think I'd remember that."

That. That right there was the reason she couldn't be alone with him. Because one flirtatious sentence in his low voice, one mischievous twinkle in those deep-green eyes, and that slow country-boy grin, and she was on the verge of sighing happily.

4

And he knew it.

"Very funny," Tess told him, narrowing her eyes. "You need to stop. You're starting to piss me off."

There was a beat of silence, and then Bryan laughed out loud. And he wasn't the only one. Ty, Tucker, Kyle Ames, the town doctor, and Derek Wright, the main bartender, all laughed too.

Tess crossed her arms and waited for them to sober up.

Finally, Bryan looked at her, still with a big grin. "That's cute, Tess."

Her eyes widened. Her being pissed off was *cute*?

So she didn't get pissed off much. She was a very forgiving, kind, *sweet* person. Overall. But she *could* get pissed. Probably.

Okay, pissed was pushing it. She was irritated—and confused—by Bryan meddling with the guys who wanted to ask her out. But, yeah, probably not *pissed*.

Still, Bryan Murray needed to back off. He wasn't the guy she wanted. Not anymore. She wasn't even sure she wanted a guy at all. She'd found herself in the past just-over-two years and she liked herself, a lot. She was content. For the first time in her life.

And now Bryan was suddenly inserting himself into her bliss?

No.

It was true that she owed him. Her life had changed two and a half years ago when she'd read one of Bryan's blog posts for the first time. But he didn't know that. And she intended to keep it that way. Mostly because of the years of pathetic-over-him that he *did* know about.

But, yeah, she couldn't be *totally* pissed at him. Bryan wasn't the reason for her bliss, but he was the reason she'd found it herself.

Bryan had been the head coach to Ty Bennett—a world champion and Olympic medalist in the triathlon. He'd also coached several other high-level running and biking athletes, and he'd written a regular blog about training including nutrition and stretching and warm ups and such. But most important to Tess had been the inspirational posts. Bryan was a die-hard optimist, a guy who could never stay down. He was driven and hardworking and joyful about it all. And his outlook and attitude had all been severely challenged and proven, without a doubt, when he'd been involved in a mountain-biking accident twenty-six months ago.

Yes, she knew the exact date the truck had crossed the center line on the mountain road and forced Bryan and Ty off the edge. Because it had happened four months after she had started running. Ty had messed up his knee. Bryan had messed up his spinal cord. He had a partial spinal cord injury that now required crutches for most of his mobility and a wheelchair for long distances.

She'd first read his blog before the accident but she'd been glued to it after the accident so she could follow his recovery. He'd blogged throughout his hospitalization and rehab. He hadn't wanted visitors while he was in the hospital and rehab in Denver and she'd respected those wishes. Barely. But she'd been right there with everyone else who gathered around him when he'd come home for the first visit after his injury. Until then, the blog was the only connection she'd had. But the whole thing had proven he was every bit as driven, hopeful and amazing as she'd always thought.

His posts about finding your inner strength, motivating yourself and appreciating the moment you're in had impacted her most, even before the accident. When her friend Peyton had wanted help getting healthier, Tess had suggested they try running. Peyton had lasted about a month—and the last week had been almost constant bitching—but Tess had fallen in love.

And now she was able to run ten miles, bike twenty, and she was ready to see the world.

Also because of Bryan and his travel diary that he'd kept as a page on his blog. He'd traveled to races around the globe with Ty and always taken time to enjoy wherever they were for a few days. He'd documented hiking, biking, running and boating all over the country and world, and Tessa wanted to see it all for herself.

But she also wasn't going to tell him *that*. Just because he'd inspired her didn't mean she was in love with him. Anymore. He was just the source behind some of the words and ideas that had made her want to be better and try new things. She just liked his philosophies. He was like...Maya Angelou. Or Oprah.

Yes, Bryan Murray was like her Oprah.

She looked at Ty. "May I?" she asked, gesturing to his chair.

He grabbed his beer and stretched to his feet. "Please," he said with a grin.

Tess put a boot up on the rung of the bar stool and boosted herself up onto the seat. Then she got to her feet. The stool was made to swivel, and it did so slightly until Tucker grasped the back of it, steadying it for her. And *then* she realized she had a skirt on.

Well, crap.

She smoothed it down, pressed her knees together and straightened her back. Ty and Tucker wouldn't look up her skirt. Not with their wives, Hailey and Delaney, right there. As for the others... She needed to get this over with.

"Excuse me," she said loudly.

But not loudly enough. Conversation, music and laughter continued around her.

Dammit.

She took a deep breath. "*Excuse me!*" she shouted.

That did the trick. Everyone in the room stopped talking

and turned toward her. The jukebox continued to play Eric Church, but she didn't mind. Eric was one of her favorites.

"I just wanted to make a quick public service announcement," she told everyone.

She wasn't used to being the center of attention. She was the woman *behind* the people who were the center of attention. She had been Hailey's assistant for three years while the other woman had been mayor, and Tess now worked for the current mayor, TJ Bennett, Ty and Tucker's older brother. Her other jobs also put her behind the scenes most of the time. At the bakery, she stayed in the kitchen. When she helped Delaney with her home remodeling jobs, Delaney was the front woman. Tess taught yoga at Hope Bennett's studio, but being in front to lead a group through yoga poses wasn't the same thing as standing on a bar stool in the midst of the Come Again on a busy Friday night.

"It has come to my attention that some people have been misinformed about my dating habits," she said, feeling her chest and throat flushing pink. "I just wanted to clear up the misconception that Bryan Murray is in no way in charge of my relationship status, and if anyone has questions about what I'm doing socially on any night of the week, you should contact me directly."

She breathed deeply and started to lean over to get down but realized just in time that if she bent over, her skirt would pull up in the back and give Bryan an eyeful. She squatted instead, and grabbed the back of the stool. She felt a hand at her waist and she gave Tucker a grateful smile as he helped her down. Tess smoothed her skirt, licked her lips and headed for the door to the bar.

There was a moment of silence—except for Eric—in the room. Then...

"Grab her."

Tessa heard Bryan's grim command, but she kept walking.

"I don't know if that's a great idea," Ty told him.

She kept walking.

"Dammit, Ty. *Someone* fucking grab her," Bryan said.

She turned back to tell him that he could go *grab* himself, but he was busy grabbing his forearm crutches and moving from behind the bar.

The starch went out of her spine instantly. He was coming after her, but he couldn't do it on his own because he had his hands full with his crutches.

She was amazed whenever she watched him move around, whenever she thought about what he'd overcome. For a moment, she forgot she'd been trying to leave.

Of course, Bryan's life had been the one most impacted by his accident and injury, but he honestly seemed less affected by it than the people around him were. Tess knew that his sister, Caitlyn, and his mother had had their lives turned upside down by it. She knew that Ty had changed his whole life after the accident, though he hadn't been as seriously hurt. She knew that all of the people in Denver who had trained with Ty and Bryan missed them both a lot. She knew Bryan's clients were feeling a huge loss.

But Bryan had continued to smile and laugh and inspire people through it all. He'd worked his ass off in rehab to the point where he could leave his wheelchair behind and get around on one crutch most of the time, and he could go without anything occasionally. All the while being the same happy, optimistic, live-in-the-moment Bryan she'd always known. And loved.

He really seemed to be looking at the whole thing like just another challenge to be met, and he was meeting it head-on with a new life plan.

She really was quite proud of herself for *not* still dreaming about marrying Bryan Murray. Because he was definitely pretty great.

But now she had her *own* bliss. She thought he'd be proud of her actually. He was all about finding your "inner genesis", as he called it. The thing that made you start every workout, that got you going at the beginning of every run, that reason for doing what you were doing. She had that inside her now.

Kyle was beside her a moment later, his hand on her upper arm. "Come on, Tess. Give him a chance," he said. "Don't make him hobble down the street after you."

That right there was part of this whole thing. Kyle mentioning Bryan hobbling was said so matter-of-factly because Bryan had encouraged that. He never shied away from talk of the accident or his resultant injuries and his permanent disabilities. He talked about them candidly and with humor and encouraged others to do the same. Everyone was very respectful, and no one felt uncomfortable around him. She admired that too.

How could she walk out on him now?

She sighed. "Fine."

Bryan came up beside Kyle a moment later. "Does he need to carry you into my office?" he asked her with a frown.

Bryan frowning was about as unusual as Tess standing up on a bar stool and making a public announcement about her personal life.

"No," she said shortly.

"Then let's go." He turned and started for his office door.

Tess had no choice but to follow. And because she was behind him, and a red-blooded, heterosexual female who had loved him most of her life, she couldn't help but notice how wide his shoulders were and how hard his arms were and how not being able to run and bike like usual didn't seem to have taken one iota of tightness from his ass.

It was a partial spinal cord injury, so that meant he still had muscle activity in his lower body. From what she could see, it was an impressive amount. She knew he was doing a lot of swimming and working with what weights he could to improve and maintain his strength. He used the crutches, but he took fairly normal steps and moved quickly and with surprising grace. Using the crutches and wheelchair were no doubt a great workout for his upper body, but his butt and legs in the fitted, faded blue denim were certainly worth appreciating as well.

At the door, he stopped and turned the knob, pushed it open and stood to the side, waiting for her to pass in front of him.

She did, reluctantly.

She did *not* want to be alone with him. Even if there were fifty people on the other side of the door, being closed in his tiny six-by-six-foot office was a bad idea.

Because thirteen-year-old Tessa was never *that* far below the surface, and that Tess still loved Bryan Murray deeply.

———

B ryan spent almost zero time in his office. A bartender's job was behind the bar. Sure, owning the place meant a few duties besides bartending, but he liked to do his paperwork and phone calls out in the bar as much as possible as well.

Besides, the tiny office was not ADA compliant. He couldn't get his wheelchair inside, and even the forearm crutches made the fit tight.

But at the moment, he was thrilled that his office was essentially a storage closet the prior owners had shoved a desk and a filing cabinet into.

It meant he'd have to get nice and close to Tessa Sheridan.

And even if she was ticked at him, she smelled damned good.

He followed her in and pushed the door shut behind him.

She got as far across the room from him as she could, putting the desk between them, and then turned, her arms crossed. With her arms like that, her amazing cleavage got even better. Tessa was a curvy girl, and her breasts were downright glorious.

"You have to stop telling guys they can't ask me out," she said without preamble.

No, he didn't. "Can't do that, Tess."

Her cheeks were pink, and he didn't think it was from anger, even if she wanted that to be the reason. They hadn't been in this close proximity in a long time, but Bryan knew it affected her. Every time they'd been alone in a car, alone in a room, hell, even in a room or car with other people but within a few feet of one another, there had been chemistry.

She wanted him, and he was addicted to her wanting him.

Tessa had been his girl since that first day of kindergarten. Bryan had seen Tyler Bennett talking to her and had decided he needed to intervene immediately. He'd walked up to Ty and Tess and told her he liked her hair, then he'd asked Ty to be his best friend.

Ever since then, Ty and Tess had been permanent fixtures in his life.

At age five, he hadn't known that the bro code decreed that once Ty was his best bud, Tess was off-limits for Ty. But when he had figured that out, he'd been even more impressed with his decision that day.

Bryan hadn't dated Tessa. But he'd kissed her. A few times. After she'd broken her arm when they were eleven. On her sixteenth birthday. New Year's Eve their senior year. And when she'd been drunk as a skunk at the festival when they'd been twenty-one, and when *he'd* been drunk as a skunk when they were twenty-five.

Hell, he'd proposed to her when they were nine.

But he *hadn't* done a lot of the things he'd wanted to do with her over the years. Because she was sweet. She was a forever kind of girl, and he'd always known, in the back of his mind, that he would eventually end up in Sapphire Falls, with Tessa. Until it was time, he couldn't do anything about his feelings for her except be her friend.

Now it was time.

"You *can* do that. I know you feel kind of big brotherly toward me, but you have to stop. You're messing around and it's not funny," she told him.

"I do *not* feel big brotherly toward you," he said firmly. Jesus. "And I'm not messing around. You don't want to date any of those guys." Tessa had loved *him* since they were five.

Exasperated, she let her arms drop. Which really didn't change how great her breasts looked in that sundress.

"You don't know that. And even if you *did* know that, you don't get to tell them what they can and can't do when it comes to me, Bryan. You're not my...whatever."

She pressed her lips together.

But he *was* her whatever.

He moved around the edge of the desk. "I'm here now. I'm ready."

"You're ready for what?"

"For...you know. Everything..."

He trailed off. He didn't have a great excuse for why he was just now telling her how he felt even though he'd been back in Sapphire Falls for over a year. All he could say was that he knew the moment he told Tessa he wanted her, it would mean the end of, well, everything else. So he'd waited.

That didn't sound great in his head, so he was pretty sure out loud it would sound like he was a jackass.

It wasn't that he didn't want to be monogamous. It wasn't that he didn't think he could be very happy with Tessa forever. It wasn't that he thought he'd ever regret being with her.

It was just that it would be so different. A completely new life. And he'd had a lot of different and completely new over the past two years or so since his accident. He'd wanted to get a little stable first. Or something.

He'd always known he'd settle down with Tessa. He'd just figured he would get to *choose* when that happened rather than having fate or destiny or the universe or whatever decide for him.

But his injury and disability and move back to Sapphire Falls had decided a lot of things for him, and Tessa getting asked out and dating other men had decided the rest.

He was settling down. With her. Now.

"What is *everything*?" she asked, watching him with narrowed eyes and a definite tension in her spine that hadn't been there a minute ago.

He moved in closer, propping a crutch against the desk and bracing a hand on the desktop. "I want you." There. Straightforward was always the way to go.

Except now she looked confused.

"You want me to do what?"

Well, there was a loaded question. The first several things that jumped to mind were probably too graphic. He'd been thinking a lot about Tessa Sheridan and her delicious curves though.

Bryan cleared his throat. "I want you to date me."

Her eyebrows climbed up her forehead. "Excuse me?"

"I'm asking you out. I want to date you. How about dinner tomorrow night?"

She just blinked at him.

"Tess?"

"You want to *date* me? You're telling other people not to ask me out because *you* want me?"

He moved in closer, making her tip her head back to look up at him. Her big brown eyes would have made it hard to remember what they were talking about if it had been any other topic. But they were talking about him wanting her. That was never far from his mind.

"Yes. I'm ready to be everything you need."

Her eyes widened. "So now you're ready? *Now*? For whatever reason, you're finally ready and you thought I'd just be here waiting for you?"

Bryan blinked at her. She looked angry. About him wanting to date her. That didn't quite compute.

She *had been* waiting for him. That had been their deal.

"You told me you were," he finally said.

She frowned. "What?"

"You told me you were waiting for me."

"I—" Her puzzled look quickly morphed to astonishment. "That was *nine years* ago. And I was completely wasted on Booze!"

"Booze is like truth serum," Bryan said. It was. The homemade moonshine that Mary and Tex sold in mason jars with handwritten labels was potent stuff, and it made people speak their minds.

"It was during the festival," she said, as if that explained everything.

And it kind of did. People threw caution to the wind and lived like it was their last days on earth during the annual summer festival.

"Uh-huh." He wasn't buying it.

It was true that the festival made people happy and carefree. But it did not make people suddenly fall in love. Tess had already loved him.

Then again—Bryan thought about a number of couples who had gotten together during the festival. And not for hookups. Forever.

But, he reasoned, that just meant that if Tess had said it during the festival, Booze or not, it would stick.

"You still said it," he told her with a shrug. "I've been counting on it."

"That was *nine years ago*." She looked even madder.

Which was fascinating to him. Tess had never been *mad* at him before.

"Five years ago, I told you I knew I'd never find another girl like you," he reminded her.

"Yes. And that time *you* were drunk on Booze. And that seemed more a statement than a declaration of intent," she said.

He grinned at that. Sometimes Tess got downright prissy. "Well, Tess, I definitely had some intent. And I did it on the Ferris wheel." That was as good as telling all the other guys in Sapphire Falls hands-off. It was long-held tradition that if you kissed a girl on the Ferris wheel, you were declaring yourself committed to her and only her.

"You were drunk."

"I remember every minute of it."

She blushed when he said that, and Bryan grinned. He'd *kissed* Tess that night. That had been no peck on the cheek or quick buss on the lips on New Year's.

"So you think that carries weight for five years?"

"Yes." He wasn't sure anyone had ever challenged the statute of limitations on a Sapphire Falls Ferris wheel kiss, but he didn't think Tessa was going to ask for a public opinion on it anyway.

She huffed out an exasperated breath. "And now you're here. In Sapphire Falls."

He frowned. She definitely didn't sound thrilled. "Yes. I'm here to stay."

"What about your travels?"

He shook his head. Tess was a homebody. Born and raised in Sapphire Falls, she'd never lived anywhere else. He was ready for that with her. He'd gotten to see the world, and now he was ready to settle down. Yeah, so his accident had determined some of that for him. But just because this wasn't going exactly the way he'd planned, didn't mean he wasn't okay with how it was turning out. "No worries. I'm here for good. I'm all yours."

She shook her head. "I'm sorry, Bryan. I'm not interested."

He felt his eyebrows pull down and he leaned in. "What did you say?"

"I'm not interested in dating you. I'm sorry."

Bryan stood looking at her for several seconds. Then he shook *his* head. "No."

"No?" She frowned. "No what?"

"That's not right. You've *always* been interested in me." Okay, that made him sound like a jerk. But it was true, dammit.

She blushed at that but straightened her spine. "I *used to* be interested in you that way, but not anymore. Things...change." She swallowed hard after that.

And maybe if she hadn't—or maybe if she hadn't stumbled over the word change—he would have believed her. Maybe.

But he didn't.

He dropped his crutch, grasped her chin, tipped her head up and kissed her.

Her lips parted on a surprised gasp, and he swept his tongue inside, needing a taste, just for a moment. She tasted like bubblegum, and he was sure it was her lip gloss. Or maybe she'd been chewing some on her way over to the bar. Or maybe it was just her. That wouldn't be out of character. That's what he loved about her. In a world where things went to shit on a fairly regular basis, Tess was a constant source of sweetness and light and happiness.

He didn't care *why* she tasted that way, only that she did.

He needed her sweetness. He needed her to be the same girl he'd always known. The one who looked at him with hearts in her eyes.

Unfortunately, the girl in his arms was holding herself stiff. She wasn't fighting him, but she wasn't melting into him, wasn't running her fingers through his hair, wasn't pressing close as if she couldn't get enough of him.

Bryan lifted his head and looked down at her. Nothing? Really?

He felt a flutter of panic in his stomach. *No.* He could *not* lose Tess.

She was the one thing about his future that he'd been *counting* on, that had been a ray of sunshine in the midst of all the other dramatic changes in his life that he had been handling like a fucking champ, thank you very much.

She was the light at the end of the tunnel, the rainbow after the storm, and a bunch of other awesome metaphorical stuff.

He was *not* going to handle losing Tess. Not well. Not at all.

Then he saw it.

She pressed her lips together.

"You okay?" he asked.

"Ye—" She stopped and cleared what sounded like gravel from her throat. "Yeah."

And Bryan felt a huge grin stretch his face.

She was affected.

He didn't know why she was denying it or fighting it. But she was affected. And that was really all he needed to know.

"So," she said, crossing her arms again, even though it was incredibly awkward with how close their bodies were. She insisted on getting her elbows up between them though, and Bryan leaned back to give her a little room. But only a little.

"So," he said agreeably.

"You can see that the kissing does nothing for me."

"Is that right?"

"There's just no spark," she said, almost pulling off sounding apologetic about it.

"Tess," he said evenly, not even trying to resist the urge to run his thumb over her lower lip. "You know me really well."

She nodded. And Bryan thought she might be holding her breath.

"So that means that you know the *best* way to keep me coming after you is to tell me that I need to try harder. I do love a challenge."

She blinked up at him and then started shaking her head quickly. "No, I'm not challenging you. That's not what I meant."

"It's okay," he said, giving her a big, friendly smile. "I'm totally fine coming after you. You deserve that. After all, you've been there for me all this time."

She shook her head again. "You do *not* need to do that."

"Oh yeah, I do. After everything you've done to show me how you feel and make me feel special, I definitely do."

"I've never—" She cleared her throat and her gaze dipped to his mouth. "I've never done anything that big."

She hadn't needed to. There was something about Tess—no doubt her sweetness and ability to see the best in him no matter what—that had made him feel special just being the object of her affection. And she had actually gone big for him at one time. "Really? A year of love notes and gifts? That was pretty big."

Tessa stilled, and her eyes widened. "You knew that was me?"

"My secret admirer in seventh grade?" he asked. "Of course. Everyone knew it was you."

There had been notes about how great he was, how cute he was, how talented he was, how funny he was. Then there had been cupcakes on his birthday. Balloons when he won the state track meet in his event. A giant stuffed bear on Valentine's Day. And lots of other things throughout that entire school year.

"I didn't know you knew," she said, her cheeks bright red.

That was because he'd threatened all of his friends if they dared say a word or tease her, he'd beat their asses. They'd then threatened anyone else they thought might make a big deal of it.

It had been sweet, and he'd known she would have been horribly embarrassed if she'd known he knew. And she might have stopped. He'd loved those damned notes and gifts. Even more after he'd known they were from her.

"Don't be embarrassed. It was amazing. I was bummed when it didn't continue in eighth grade."

"Yeah, I got smart and got a *diary* in eighth grade."

"You wrote in your diary about me in eighth grade?" he asked, loving that.

She tipped her head back. "I realized that a lot of people knew those notes came from me. But I thought they'd kept it from *you*." She righted her head and opened her eyes. "Who told you?"

He chuckled. "No one told me, Tess. I knew your handwriting."

"You knew the *whole* time?"

Bryan grinned widely. "The *whole* time."

"Well, that settles it," she said. "No way can we date."

She slipped around him so quickly he couldn't react fast enough to stop her. By the time he'd turned, and wobbled a little, she was at the door.

"Why does that mean we can't date? It proves that you've been crazy about me for years."

"Because every time I look at you, I'm going to be thinking about those stupid, sappy notes where I spilled my guts."

Bryan started toward her and took a step before remembering that he didn't move very fast without crutches. He never knew if his ankle was going to be there for him or not. Fuck. He couldn't grab her and hug her and reassure her.

"I wanted to be the person you spilled your guts to, Tess. I never told a single person what those notes said." He might have bragged about being Tessa's one true love, but he'd never shared her actual words. "You don't know how important those notes were to me."

The notes, even though they had been so long ago and from a thirteen-year-old girl, had made him feel like a king. Tess had had some big self-esteem issues and had struggled with who she was and what she wanted. Bryan had known that on some level, most thirteen-year-olds dealt with similar issues. But he never had. So having that insight into her heart and mind had made him feel great. Special. And he knew the notes had been a part of him wanting to be someone who could encourage and inspire people even now. Those notes from Tess, telling him how much she admired how hard he trained in track, and how much he made her look forward to algebra class because of his jokes and goofing off with Ty, and how special it made him feel that a smile from him could make her whole day better, had helped form him into the person he was today.

It was funny to him—then and now—that she'd really thought she had been keeping her identity a secret. He smiled at a lot of girls every day, but only one had ever lit up like a Christmas tree for him.

She met his eyes from across the five feet that separated them and took a huge breath. "Bryan, that's sweet. You've always been sweet to me. But I don't want sweet. And I don't... want...this."

Bryan watched her slip out the door and it bump shut behind her. He let her go this time.

There would be other chances to be with Tess. If nothing else, this was Sapphire Falls. It was impossible to avoid someone indefinitely. Besides, he had a better plan than trapping her in his office and kissing her until she saw things his way—though that certainly had merit. But remembering those notes from seventh grade and watching Tess try to deny how she felt, he knew just what to do.

He really did love a challenge.

2

Tess got to the parking lot before she swore.

Dammit. Hell. Shit.

She leaned against her car and took a deep breath of the humid night air. Well, this sucked.

She needed to get out of Sapphire Falls.

It was time. She'd been planning it—more or less—for about a year now. She was going to Denver to train with Jake Elliot. Jake specialized in taking runners from casual to competitive. While she didn't consider herself a *casual* runner exactly, she had only done a couple of 5ks in all the time she'd been running. And she was ready for more. She didn't need or want the medals or trophies, but she needed something to keep pushing her. Competing against other runners seemed like the obvious way to measure if she was getting better.

She had stumbled across Jake's name and information incidentally through Bryan's blog. She'd followed a link about shoes, which had led to another about shoes, which had led to one about hydration, which had led her to Jake.

Tess had been running for two and a half years now. She was almost up to half-marathon distance, and she was ready to get more serious and run in places that weren't flat and surrounded by corn. She was ready to push herself. And to get out of her tiny hometown.

She'd started saving up a year ago, not just to move, but for race fees, travel and to pay Jake. She was a few hundred short of her goal, but it was time to go. Obviously.

Bryan Murray wanted to date her.

She couldn't do that. She'd risk falling head over heels for him. Again. She'd get drunk and tell him that she'd wait for him forever. Again. Hell, she might even start writing him love notes again.

She shuddered. Putting a few hundred miles between them seemed like a good idea. Her pride would thank her.

And leaving didn't seem so difficult. Once the festival was over, she could move on. Bryan kissing her just now had helped her see that.

The kiss had been sweet and romantic and...*nice*. And he'd done it that way on purpose. The kiss on the Ferris wheel all those years ago had been hot, wet and out of control. Because of the Booze, but still something that could make her warmer just thinking about it. Fully sober, Bryan kissed her *nicely*.

She wanted more of the hot, wet and hungry ones.

Thankfully, she had never put *that* in one of the notes she'd sent him. Surprisingly. She'd put just about every other thought and feeling into those notes. The notes that Bryan had known were from her all along. She rubbed her forehead. How embarrassing. But she'd been thirteen, for God's sake. She couldn't believe Bryan still thought that all meant something.

That had all been so stupid. But, at the time, it had been so therapeutic too.

She'd been able to say things to him that she so wanted him to know but that she hadn't been brave enough to say in person. Like how wonderful she'd thought he was when he'd rescued the dogs that were being left outside in the cold. Or how amazing he'd been to the new kid who had moved in and didn't have any friends. Or how much she'd loved watching him with his mother because he was so sweet to her. That's how the notes had started. Just little I-think-you're-great notes left in his locker. Over time, as she'd felt more secure that he didn't know who she was, they had become longer and more and more about *her*. Her thoughts and feelings and dreams. Somehow Bryan had unwittingly become the friend she needed—the one who just listened, never laughed and never judged.

She'd had a close girlfriend growing up, but Kacey had moved away the summer before their seventh-grade year. Tess supposed that was part of why she'd needed to write everything down. Why she'd given all of the thoughts and feelings to Bryan was still kind of a mystery. Probably because she'd *wanted* to be close to him, and having him know things no one else did felt good. Even if he didn't know who she was. Except he did—had—*did* know.

Great. Bryan had always known about her crush, but now she knew that he knew about so much more.

"Hey, you okay?"

Tessa jerked upright as Hailey Conner Bennett came around the front of the car parked next to Tessa's. "Hey."

"Are you all right? I tried to stop you on your way out, but you were moving like you were on a mission," Hailey said, settling her butt against the side of Tess's car.

Yeah, on a mission to get the hell out before she ruined every *sweet* image anyone in Sapphire Falls had of her. "Bryan just...upset me."

Hailey nodded. "Got that. What did he say? Or do?"

Tess focused in front of her instead of on her ex-boss and kind-of friend. Hailey had been the queen bee in Sapphire Falls all her life. She'd always been this cool, put-together, gorgeous, in-charge woman who had intimidated the hell out of Tessa.

Hailey was two years older than Tess, Bryan and Ty, and that hadn't helped the intimidation factor either. Tess had taken the job as Hailey's assistant when she'd been mayor because Tess was awesome at being the behind-the-scenes girl, making others look good, while Hailey was awesome at being in the spotlight and looking good. They had worked perfectly. Plus, the job had been flexible. And easy. Well, flexible in that she could take off in the middle of the day for her other jobs because she could do a lot of her work at night at home. Easy in that Hailey had taken care of almost everything on her own anyway. The beautiful blonde loved being in charge, and Tess had taken care of the tiny details that drove Hailey crazy.

Now Hailey headed up the tourism and business development in town—the things she loved and handled almost entirely on her own. The other nitty-gritty detail things she hated fell to their new mayor, TJ Bennett.

Tess's job had gotten more demanding since TJ had taken over. Now she actually had to be an assistant. TJ not only didn't have the time for everything Hailey had done, since he was still farming and had a new wife, he also didn't have the patience for the little headaches that popped up on a daily basis.

Tess had needed to get really creative with juggling her other jobs. Fortunately, Hope, the woman who owned the yoga studio and natural healing shop, was TJ's wife. So she was happy to work around Tess's other job responsibilities. Delaney Bennett, one of TJ's sisters-in-law, was Tess's other boss, and she was great too. She did home remodeling and furniture refinishing, and Tess could do a lot of those projects on weekends if needed.

She sighed, thinking about all of the balls she was juggling, and looked over at Hailey. "I miss working for you."

Hailey smiled at her and tucked her long hair behind her ear. "I was a peach," she said drily.

"You were easy."

ERIN NICHOLAS

Hailey laughed. "I'm so telling Ty you said that."

Tess chuckled. She doubted there was anyone else in the world, including Hailey's completely head-over-heels husband, Ty, who would use *easy* as a word to describe Hailey. But she had been in many ways.

"I also have to tell Ty what Bryan said or did. He wanted to come out here too."

Tess shook her head. "It's nothing Ty needs to be upset about."

Although...it might be good for everyone to know Bryan had asked her out and that she'd turned him down.

Everyone knew she'd pined for Bryan all this time. It might be good for her reputation if they knew she'd moved on. As she'd proved by *not* melting into a little puddle at his feet when he'd kissed her. Her knees had *maybe* wobbled, slightly. But if that was how he was going to kiss her, she was safe from making an ass of herself.

Sweet might describe Tessa, but that was not how she wanted to describe her love or sex life.

She looked at Hailey. Somehow, she thought she could tell the other woman what she was feeling. They hadn't really been *friends*, but when Hailey had last run for mayor—and had lost—a lot of things had come out. Like the fact that Hailey could be vulnerable and sweet. And that she had ADHD, which explained a lot about her personality and habits. And that she did actually know how to ask for help. Tessa had been happy to pitch in on the campaign, and since then, they'd had more of a friendship than before.

It maybe also helped that Tess didn't work for her anymore. Now they worked *together*. A lot of Hailey's projects, like her most recent campaign to expand the size of the annual town festival in Sapphire Falls and bring people in from a wider radius, needed extra hands and heads. Tess was the one Hailey always asked first. Yes, because Tess and Hailey both worked for

26

the town, specifically the mayor's office, which was ultimately in charge of the things Hailey was doing and developing. But also because they made a good team. Hailey was the visionary with the big ideas and enthusiasm and gumption to get things done. Tess was the detail girl who made sure all the I's were dotted.

"If it helps," Hailey said. "I think Bryan really does like you. I agree he shouldn't be telling other guys they can't ask you out, but I think it's because he has feelings for you."

"Actually, that doesn't help at all. That's the entire problem," Tess said with a sigh.

"It is?" Hailey turned toward her.

"He does have feelings for me," Tess said. "At least that's what he said in his office just now."

Hailey's eyes went wide in the parking lot light. "He did? That's great."

Tess shook her head. "No. It's not."

"But..." Hailey frowned slightly. "I thought you...haven't you been in love with him like all your life?"

"Yeah. Up until a couple of years ago."

"Yeah, you were even his secret admirer that one year—"

Tess groaned. "*Everyone* knew?"

"Yes."

Tess groaned louder.

"But," Hailey said, "it was sweet. I think he really liked it."

"I know he did. I'm part of the reason Bryan has such a huge ego," Tess said.

Hailey laughed. "That's true. But that's not a bad thing. That ego helped him through some tough stuff over the past couple of years."

Tess liked that idea. Maybe her sad crush hadn't been all bad then. And Hailey knew Bryan. Hailey was now married to Ty Bennett. Bryan's best friend. They'd only been married for a little over a year, but Ty and Hailey had carried on a secret affair for years before anyone had even known they were dating. Except for Bryan. Hailey would go out to Denver to visit Ty without anyone in Sapphire Falls knowing, but Bryan had lived in Denver *with* Ty. He'd known all about it. No doubt Hailey knew Bryan pretty well.

"He kissed me."

Hailey came around to face her fully. "In seventh grade? Really?"

"Tonight. In his office."

"Oh." Hailey's face relaxed into a smile. "That's awesome."

"No. It was...just okay."

Hailey just blinked at that. Then she asked, "*Where* did he kiss you?"

It was Tessa's turn to just blink. And catalog all of the places she *wished* Bryan would kiss her. Because some of *those* would have saved the kiss in his office from being sweet and friendly.

"Like on the cheek or the forehead?" Hailey prompted.

Oh. Right. Cheek or forehead. Sure. "Um, no. Lips."

"He kissed you on the lips. And it was bad?"

Tess sighed. "Well, not *bad*. There just wasn't..."

"Wasn't what?"

"Heat."

Hailey frowned. "Really?"

"Really. It was very nice. Sweet." She stopped and thought about it. "Yeah, nice. It was nice."

"And you wanted heat?"

"Definitely." Tess decided to let it all out. "That was the kiss I would have wanted back in high school when I was romantic and innocent. But now..."

"The books," Hailey said.

Tessa couldn't deny that the hot romances she read were a part of her new fantasies. "And I've had nice, romantic kisses. That's not what I expected from Bryan."

Hailey actually nodded. "I have to say, that surprises me too."

"It does?"

"Well, I've been...around," Hailey said.

Right. She'd been around in Denver. At the house where Bryan lived. Which meant that Hailey would have witnessed Bryan bringing girls home on occasion. Or all the time. "I'm sure he wasn't *nice* and sweet to all the other girls. He even kissed *me* hotter than that a few years ago during the festival. But he was drunk then," Tess said. "This is because he's stone-cold sober and it's *me*. *I'm* sweet, and Bryan's known me all his life and can't bring himself to kiss me the way he kisses the other girls when he's really thinking about it."

"But maybe—"

"But it's a *good* thing," Tess went on.

"It is?"

"I don't want to date him. So it's good that the heat isn't there and that he can't deliver for me on the fantasy."

"You don't want to date him?" Hailey asked. "Why not?"

She couldn't tell Hailey about Denver. No one in Sapphire Falls knew about Tessa's big plans. No one knew that she'd been saving every little bit of extra money from her three jobs for the past year so she could move to train for competitive marathons.

"Because after that kiss, I realize he would want to...make love. He'd be sweet and gentle and *nice*. And that is *not* what I want, Hailey. I really think it would be better for Bryan and I to be friends. He clearly doesn't feel the heat."

Hailey chewed on the inside of her cheek.

"You know I'm right," Tess said. "I'm sweet. Everyone knows it. No guy in this town, maybe especially Bryan, thinks of me as someone he wants to nail on the hood of his car or go down on behind the Come Again or use toys with or tie up. They want to romance me and light candles and make love to me."

Hailey nodded. "You might have a point."

"So there you go," Tess said, even as her heart fell with Hailey's agreement. Tess needed to head to Denver. And not just to run. There were other hot guys in the world who *would* do the hood-of-the-car thing. Probably. She assumed.

"I'm sorry, hon," Hailey said, pulling Tess into a brief hug. "All those years you were waiting. And then it fizzled."

Tess shrugged. "Now I know. And I don't have to wait any longer."

That thought made her stomach flip. But not necessarily with excitement as she might have expected. It felt a little like nerves.

"Right," Hailey said. Her smile didn't quite reach her eyes, but she didn't tell Tess she was crazy or wrong. "You can have any guy you want."

"Thanks."

But Tess didn't think that was quite true. Bryan might have been warning guys off asking her out, and she might have yelled at him about that, but the truth was, all the guys in Sapphire Falls thought of Tess as the sweet-little-sister, girl-next-door type.

Probably because Tess *was* the sweet-little-sister, girl-next-door type.

To these guys.

In this town.

She hadn't had a hot date with a guy she wanted to sleep with in—ever. She'd been *stupidly* saving herself for Bryan for years. She hated thinking about it now. It had been so naïve and *pitiful*, but at the time, it had seemed romantic. Then she'd discovered herself. That she was strong and hardworking and capable of being more than she'd ever thought. So she'd stopped letting her life revolve around him, stopped *waiting* for him, putting her life and dreams on hold. And she'd dated other guys. And not once had she dated one she wanted to have sex with. Maybe it was the idea tucked in the back of her mind that she was leaving. Maybe it was the romance novels that set the bar super high for chemistry and sex and love. Or maybe she just wasn't programmed for hot, casual sex. But it still sucked that she hadn't found anyone to get down and dirty with. It made her want to scream. Or run.

She really loved night runs.

Tess pushed off the car. "I should head home."

"Good idea," Hailey said. "Some ice cream therapy should help."

Yeah. So would a dirt road and a Miranda Lambert playlist.

Tess drove home, making a mental checklist of things she needed to get lined up for her move.

Like contacting Jake and finding an apartment and packing. And telling her mother.

She was going. She could be someone new in Denver. She could be the woman she'd been slowly becoming over the past two and a half years. The woman ready for more.

And now that Bryan had kissed her and it hadn't curled even one of her toes, she could leave Sapphire Falls without any what-ifs.

———

"Hey, TJ, it's Bryan Murray."

"Hey, Bryan, what's up?"

A plan. A brilliant plan that had come to him last night as he'd watched his office door close behind Tessa.

"I was wondering about the festival committees. Are there any that need some additional help?" Bryan knew that the festival and the committees were more Hailey's thing than TJ's, but he couldn't call Hailey. She'd tell Tess.

He also knew that Tessa was involved in every bit of the festival. She might not officially be Hailey's assistant anymore, but TJ would have given Tess to Hailey for festival time simply to keep Hailey out of TJ's hair.

There was a pause on the other end of the phone. Bryan leaned against the bar and noted that he needed to fill up the orange juice and check his stock of olives in the back room. TJ was Ty's older brother. Ty was Bryan's best friend. Surely as someone who had spent lots of time in the Bennett household growing up, who had left his home and family to go to Denver with Ty, who had coached Ty to multiple triathlon wins, not the least of which was an Olympic silver medal, Bryan could ask a favor from TJ?

"Are you calling me about mayor business on my cell phone?" TJ asked a moment later.

"Uh, yeah. I guess I am."

"Man, I'm on the farm. I'm elbow deep in shit out here. Literally. You need to call Tessa about this stuff," TJ told him tersely.

Bryan knew that TJ was on his farm working today. That was why this was the perfect time to call him. He could get Bryan hooked up with a committee without Tessa overhearing.

He just needed some time with her. Time where she couldn't walk away from him and time doing things that would show her he was more able than she maybe thought. He didn't think his physical status and occasional wheelchair use was an issue for Tess. She was way too nice a person to let something like that bother her. But it wasn't a *bad* idea to show her how physically able he still was. Just in case she was wondering. And the more time he had with her, the more time he would have to romance her and remind her that she loved him.

"Yeah, well, there's a little issue with that," Bryan said. "I can't ask Tessa about this."

Bryan winced slightly and waited. TJ was the oldest Bennett and a genuinely great guy. But he was not easygoing and fun-loving like his three younger brothers. He was the eldest son of the most beloved family in town. He was well respected because he was no-nonsense and loved Sapphire Falls as much as anyone. People loved him as mayor.

But there was a reason TJ had an assistant.

He didn't like to deal with the little details.

He'd *rather* be elbow deep in shit on the farm. Literally.

Bryan heard TJ's heavy sigh. "Why can't you ask Tessa about this?"

"Because she'll try to keep me from helping out," Bryan said.

"And why would that be?" TJ was clearly feigning patience.

"It's a really *long*, complicated story," Bryan said. "I guess it started back in kindergarten."

"Never mind. I don't care," TJ said, as predicted. "As far as I know, *all* of the committees need help. You want to help build the pen for the petting zoo?"

"Uh, is Tessa helping with that?"

TJ laughed. "Doubt it."

"I was thinking something more along the lines of..." Bryan thought through the various activities and booths and stands that were a part of the festival over the years, "...maybe the craft show?"

There was another pause on TJ's end. "Did you say craft show?"

Bryan infused his voice with enthusiasm. "Sure. Why not?"

"Because you don't know applique from assholes," TJ told him. "What's going on?"

What the hell was applique? And how did TJ know what it was? "I just want to help."

"Bullshit. What do you want?"

"I want to be a part of the festivities. I missed the festival for a few years, and now that I'm home to stay and feeling good, I want to help out."

"Bryan, tell me what's going on or I'm hanging up."

Dammit. There was a downside to having spent a lot of time around TJ growing up. He knew Bryan pretty well. "Okay, fine. I want a chance to work with Tess."

"And you don't think Tess will want this same chance to work with you?"

"Something like that."

"Well, considering I'm not at my desk at the moment," TJ said drily. "All I know off the top of my head is that Tess is heading up the kids' talent show."

"Perfect, I'll do that."

TJ sighed again. "They'll need help constructing the backdrops and things like that."

"Perfect. I'm in."

"And Tess is totally in charge. Don't give her a hard time."

"Perfect. I mean, of course not," Bryan told him, grinning widely.

"Totally in charge," TJ said again. "You have to do what she tells you."

Bryan honestly had no problem with that. "As long as she can't kick me off. You put me on this committee and you're her boss, so she can't get rid of me, right?" Bryan asked.

"Oh for fuck's..." TJ muttered something. "You really have a thing for her?" he asked, louder.

"I do."

"And you're going to treat her well. Be romantic and sweet and shit, right?" TJ asked.

"Absolutely."

"Then if you don't do anything stupid, I won't let her take you off the committee."

Bryan breathed out in relief. "Thank you, man. I mean it."

"Fine, fine. But, Bryan?"

"Yeah?"

"If you hurt her, *you'll* be in deep shit. Literally. And it won't be just up to your elbows."

Bryan grinned in spite of the threat. He loved that TJ was taking care of Tess. Even though he didn't need to anymore. Bryan was here now. "I got it. I'm not going to hurt her," he promised.

Hell, he wanted to marry her and make all of her dreams come true.

"Okay, then be at the rehearsal tomorrow at three," TJ told him.

"I'll be there."

———

Tessa read the list again. There were three people signed up to help with the talent show. Her, Mandy Jenkins, one of the moms who had three kids in the show, and a name that had been scrawled on there by someone other than Tessa between yesterday at four o'clock and now.

The name looked like it started with a B.

She knew exactly whose handwriting that was.

"TJ?" She knocked softly on his office door.

He looked up. "Hey, Tess."

She crossed the room and set a cup of coffee next to him. "Did you add someone to the talent show committee list?"

He nodded and looked back down at the papers in front of him. "Yeah."

"Did you *mean* to add that person to that committee?"

"Talent show. Yep."

The fact that the big, straight-shooting, gruff-but-honest mayor wouldn't meet her eyes made her certain whose name that was on the bottom of the list. She crossed her arms and waited.

He'd look up eventually.

TJ was almost five years older and towered over her at six

feet and five inches of burly grumpiness. But he didn't scare her.

Finally, TJ sighed. "He begged." He glanced up.

"He begged to be on the children's talent show committee?" Tessa asked. No way.

"He begged to work with *you* on something, and that was the first thing I could think of when he called me," TJ said.

Tessa's heart dropped. God, Bryan was pursuing her. What she wouldn't have given to have that happen a few years ago. "TJ—"

"I made him swear to behave," TJ said quickly.

Tess rolled her eyes. Behave. She actually wasn't afraid of that. She was pretty sure Bryan was going to be a total gentleman. Great with the kids. Charming with the moms. Sweet and considerate of *her*.

He'd been charming and sweet and considerate ever since he'd moved back.

That was the whole problem.

Bryan Murray had been sweet and considerate to her all her life. She wanted him to be...inappropriate. Sexy. Naughty.

No. No, she didn't. She was leaving. She could leave sweet considerate Bryan behind. She wasn't so sure about sexy, naughty Bryan.

"I'm sure it will be fine," she said, trying not to show her frustration. That would be very difficult to explain.

"Work his ass off," TJ said. "He said he'd do anything as long as he could work with you."

Was that right? Suddenly, Tess had an idea.

She just needed to be sure he hated every minute of his time with her. Because if she spent too much time with him, she might forget how to spell Colorado. If history was any indication of Bryan Murray's influence on her. Which it was. There was the time she'd forgotten how to spell *contagious* in the fourth grade because he'd smiled at her. And the time she'd messed up solving for X because he'd winked at her.

"I'll take care of it," she told TJ.

"You let me know if he gets out of hand," TJ told her.

She smiled at her boss and headed back to her desk. She pulled another list out of a folder and picked up her phone.

"Hi, Mandy. It's Tessa."

"Hi, Tess. What's up?"

"Wondering if you could call all of the moms of the talent show kids. We need to move rehearsal. The Blue Brigade's fashion show needs to practice at that time."

"No problem," Mandy said. "I'll call everyone. Should we move it to six or so?"

"Six will be great," Tess agreed. "Thanks."

Her next nine calls were to the ladies of the Blue Brigade, the group of ladies aged sixty-eight to ninety-four, whose mission was to spread goodwill and happiness throughout the town. They sent Just-Because and Thinking-of-You cards to people randomly. They handed out gift-wrapped packages of cookies for no reason other than to brighten someone's day. And they gave out goodwill assignments. At any point, someone could pass a member of the Brigade on the street and be handed an assignment card. That person then had to carry out the task on the card as soon as possible. The assignments ranged from giving someone a hug to buying someone a cup of coffee to telling someone a joke. PG-rated, of course. Unless you were telling one to Pastor Michaels. He liked the R-rated ones.

They also did a few fundraisers throughout the year to raise money for their cards, the arbitrary singing telegrams and balloon bouquets they sent, and the five scholarships to summer camp they gave annually.

The fashion show during the festival was one of their fundraisers.

And they would be beside themselves to have a man under the age of sixty as a judge. Heck, maybe Tessa could suggest Bryan be the emcee in her place. She could sit at the table with the three other women and two men who had signed up to judge.

Yes, Bryan would be an excellent emcee.

And twenty minutes later, every member of the Blue Brigade had agreed.

3

Bryan arrived at the Community Center at ten minutes to nine. He punched the button beside the door with the end of his crutch and it swung open automatically. He headed inside with as much bounce in his step as possible. Though, really, having a bounce was more a mindset than anything else, in his opinion. He was happy to be a part of the committee. He loved kids and he loved his hometown. But he was especially excited to sweep Tessa off her feet. Metaphorically, of course.

She was standing to one side of a stack of two by fours and chatting with Delaney Bennett. Delaney was married to Ty's brother Tucker and was the town's handyman. Handywoman. Contractor. Yes, he'd stick with contractor. He knew Delaney and knew she was laidback and not likely to get riled up about gender stereotypes, but Bryan wanted to show Tessa his good-guy side. Not that he'd ever mean to insult a woman doing any job, but he'd put his foot in his mouth before when he hadn't been careful. Sometimes both feet. Around Tess, he wanted to be completely respectful, maybe even chivalrous.

Unless that was chauvinistic. He remembered some friends

of his bitching because women didn't want them to hold doors open anymore.

Damn. He was going to need to check with someone on that. His sister, Caitlyn, would know. Or Lauren or Hailey—also both Bennetts now—would definitely know.

Bryan pulled his phone from his pocket and started to dial Hailey, but just then he heard his name. From Tessa.

"Hi, Bryan."

He turned, his best charming grin in place. "Hey, Tess."

"We're all so happy you signed up to help with this."

He narrowed his eyes. He wasn't sure he believed that at all. "Are you now?"

"I am. TJ said you were very adamant about being a part of this."

"Yes. Of course." He looked around. "What do you need from me?"

"Oh, so much," Tess said.

But she was already walking away from him by the time he debated making a suggestive comment to that. It was his nature to be flirtatious and a little naughty. He loved to make women blush and maybe even stammer. But this was Tess. Sweet, forever-girl Tess. He needed to behave.

"I'm all yours," he told her, following with one crutch. This was a full standard crutch today. For one thing, it was early. He didn't generally need both crutches until later in the day when he got tired. And, while he preferred the forearm crutches in the bar because they stayed connected to his arms even when he was using his hands, he liked the full crutch otherwise.

"Oh, I know," she said. "TJ told me."

TJ had told her Bryan was all hers? He liked the sound of that.

"You can sit right here," she told him, stopping next to a wooden armchair sitting in front of the stage. At the moment, the chairs for the audience had been removed and there were sawhorses and building materials scattered through the room, but Bryan knew at some point they'd have to move all the padded folding chairs back in and arrange them in rows.

He looked around. "I don't need to sit. I thought TJ said something about building some backdrops?"

"Oh, Delaney's got that handled," Tess assured him. "We need you right here. You need to be able to see everything clearly."

"See everything? The talents?" It just occurred to Bryan that there weren't any kids in the room. That was strange, considering it was a kids' talent show.

"Talents?" Tess laughed lightly. "I guess you could call them that. The girls refer to them as *assets*."

"Assets?"

But Tess had already moved off toward a group of ladies who were gathered on the far end of the stage. Bryan knew every single one of them, and not one was what anyone would call a kid.

Unfortunately for him—and fortunately for Tess—he couldn't go running after her. So he took a seat. Though tentative definitely described his mood now more than excited.

He sat and tapped his thumb against the arm of the chair, trying not to stare at the group of women thirty feet away. Of course, that was an impossible task, considering he was incredibly interested in what was going on, and considering Tess was one of them.

He let his eyes wander over her profile. She had long blond hair that hung in soft waves to her mid-back. The first time he'd touched it had been when they were five. He remembered her hair was the first thing he'd noticed about her. It had been long enough to touch her lower back and had been the color of sunshine. Which he'd told her when he'd been standing behind her in line to go out for recess. And he'd run his hand over it. Soft as silk. He'd never forgotten that. He'd taken advantage of the chance to touch it again two nights ago when he'd kissed her in his office. It was the thick, lush kind of hair that made a man want to bury his hands in it and run it between his fingers.

Following her hair down her back, of course, led to the sweet swell of her ass and the curve of her hips. The kind of hips that made a man want to take them in his hands and squeeze while he—

Bryan coughed and shifted in the chair. He had to stop that shit. Thinking Tess was beautiful and looked nice in the simple white sundress and sandals she wore was one thing. Thinking about putting her up on the edge of his desk and gripping those gorgeous hips while he thrust into her was something else altogether.

Tess wasn't one of his typical girls. She wasn't overtly sexy, she wasn't a flirt, she didn't wear revealing clothes and she didn't get up on the edges of desks. At least not for sex. In fact, she barely dated. Which was part of the reason her chewing his ass for telling guys not to ask her out was funny. She typically turned them down when they did ask. Why did she care if Bryan told them not to?

But that was even more reason for him to just chill the hell out, take his time, court her even. She was the type for courting. And she deserved it. God knew, she'd been waiting for him to come home long enough.

Which made him frown again. He really thought she had been waiting for him to come home, but she certainly hadn't acted happy about his proclamation that he was ready to be her boyfriend.

Maybe she just didn't believe him. He could understand that. He'd been waiting until all of his rehab was done and things were going well at the bar, until he was settled in his own place and not needing his mom and sister's help. Things had been on track until he'd gone to Texas to see Eli play ball with the minor league Kilby Catfish. Bryan and Ty had gone out on the town and Bryan had gotten cocky. That cockiness had ended up with him on his ass with a broken hip. That had certainly set him back. Hell, it had almost prevented his sister, Caitlyn, from pursuing a relationship with Eli.

Thankfully, Bryan had convinced her he was fine—or was going to be, anyway—and she'd ended up going to California with Eli when he was called up to the Majors.

But Bryan really was fine. He was the strongest he'd been since the accident, he was settled into his new life in Sapphire Falls, and he was ready to move on with everything else.

Besides, if something did happen again, like the fucking broken hip, there was no better person to be helping him out than Tessa. She was sweet and kind and caring and every bit the nurturing type. He hated other people fussing over him, but Tess made him consider faking a pain or two. Tess had been the cherry on top that he'd most been looking forward to.

Finally, she headed back in his direction.

Sweet. Kind. Pretty. Bryan repeated the words in his mind as she approached, rather than letting himself take in the gorgeous breasts filling out the top of her dress or the smooth, tanned expanse of her legs under the skirt. But he couldn't help taking in the great muscle tone in her legs. Tess had always been cute and curvy, but he thought maybe there was more muscle definition in her quads and calves now. He wondered if she'd started a workout program of some kind. She looked tighter and more confident, and no matter how much he tried to keep his thoughts on her smile and her pretty brown eyes, below the belt, he responded to everything else.

"Okay, I think we're ready," Tess told him. "Here's the script. You can read along while the ladies rehearse and we'll make sure everything matches up."

"Why would *I* be reading the script?" Bryan asked, taking

the pages from her. Maybe he was just filling in while they practiced.

"Because you're the emcee," Tess told him, as if it should have been obvious. "The ladies are thrilled. Jack Morgan did it the past three years, and they're excited to have someone young and new."

"I'm the *what*?" Bryan glanced over at the older women. They were all watching him and smiling and a couple of them waved when they saw him looking.

"The emcee."

Tess's big grin told him that she knew he was *not* thrilled.

"I thought I was helping with the kids' talent show," he said. Not that he wasn't great with older women—okay, all women. But he was great with kids too, and he had kind of thought that would be a good way to soften Tess up. Guys who were cute with kids were attractive, right?

Plus, he wanted to show her that he could handle construction projects and other physical activities.

"Oh, that rehearsal got moved. And when TJ put you on the schedule and said you were so enthusiastic, I figured you would be up for whatever we needed."

Bryan sighed. What he'd signed up for was to work with *her*. Which this was. Okay, fine. He'd charm all of their socks off. And maybe Tessa's panties...

He shut that thought down and focused on the script. He needed to stop thinking about Tessa's panties. Especially getting them off.

He shook his head. No. He needed to stop thinking about them altogether. Because even if she had them *on* he would still—

Dammit. He cleared his throat and focused on the script, reading out loud.

"Ladies and gentlemen, welcome to this year's fashion show. Over the years, we've brought you evening gowns, summer wear, swimsuits—" Bryan coughed. He hadn't been aware that the lovely older ladies of Sapphire Falls had been modeling swimming suits in the past. He had missed the last three fashion shows. "This year," he continued. "We're excited to bring you linger—" He broke off and looked up at Tessa. "Seriously?"

"What?" she asked innocently.

He looked around and dropped his voice. "Lingerie? Really?"

"Yes," she said, as if that was the most normal thing for a bunch of women, the youngest of who was pushing seventy, to be modeling lingerie.

He took a deep breath and went on, though he was sure she could hear the hesitation in his voice. Because there was a lot of hesitation there.

"We're excited—" he thought maybe he'd edit that word, "—to bring you lingerie for women who know what to do with it." Okay. So this was not what he'd been expecting.

That pretty much summed up his entire life right now.

Not the least of which was the blond with the nice legs standing next to him. She was supposed to be falling into his arms. He had no idea what was going on there.

But he was the master at handling the unexpected.

Tess lifted an eyebrow. "If you're not interested in helping out with this committee, it's okay. I understand." She started to reach for the script.

Bryan pulled it out of her reach. "Hang on. I didn't say I wasn't interested." Though *interested* was maybe not the right word to describe how he felt about seeing Cora Munson in a teddy. Cora was a lovely person. He had always liked her a lot. Cora was also eighty-six and used a walker. But, hey, if Cora wanted to wear a teddy, she should wear a teddy. Who was he to say she shouldn't?

"Well, you signed up really late. This is the only thing we

have left that we need someone for." Tess almost succeeded in sounding apologetic about that.

But she didn't *quite* get there.

"You're trying to run me off," he accused.

"What? No. Don't be silly." She reached for the papers, and he pulled them away again, causing her to lean over him slightly.

"Tess," he said softly, and with definite warning in his tone. "Are you trying to get me to quit this committee?"

She braced her hand on the arm of the chair and looked him directly in the eye. "Yes."

"Why?" Bryan was very proud of himself for not letting his gaze drop below her chin. Because her cleavage was *magnificent.* Thankfully, his peripheral vision worked perfectly.

"Because you're only doing it to spend time with me."

He nodded. "And do you know why *that* is?"

"Because you think you want to be my boyfriend." She said it with a touch of annoyance.

That almost made him smile. He simply could not wrap his brain around the fact that Tessa Sheridan was annoyed by the idea of him being her boyfriend.

"I'm doing it because I'm *going to* convince you to be my girl-friend. If it's not this, it will be some other way."

"So me saying no doesn't matter?" she asked.

"If I thought you meant it, it would," he told her honestly.

She frowned at him. But she didn't deny it. Instead, she straightened. "Are you ready?"

Bryan wasn't so sure as he read the next words on the page. "Ruby Patterson" and "see-through nightie" should not be put in the same sentence. "Of course," he told her. "I'm always up for a challenge. You should really start believing that."

"Okay, ladies!" Tessa called instead of replying.

Bryan chuckled and sat back in his chair.

The first woman to walk onto the stage was Ruby. Ruby was

probably sixty-six or seven, tall and thin, with bright white hair. She was wearing blue jeans and a Come Again Bar T-shirt.

"Hey, Ruby," Bryan said with a grin as she came to the middle of the stage and put a hand on a hip. He glanced down at the paper in his hand. "Where's your sheer pink nightie with the black bra and pantie set underneath?"

Stella Carson laughed from the side of the stage. "This is just rehearsal. You're gonna have to be here for the show if you want to see the goods!" she called out.

Bryan relaxed. So they weren't modeling the lingerie today. Got it. He nodded. "Sounds like I've got a front-row seat."

Ruby gave him a wink. "Isn't it nice that you're special to Tess?"

Bryan looked up at Tess. She stubbornly refused to take her eyes off the stage.

"I can honestly say that being special to Tess makes me feel very...nice," he said, a million other words than *nice* going through his mind. All of which would scandalize these nice ladies.

Okay, seventy percent of these ladies.

But he couldn't say the things he was thinking to them, or to Tess.

"Okay, Dottie, you're up!" Tess called, ignoring both Bryan and Ruby.

Dottie owned and did most of the cooking at Dottie's Diner on Main. She was a lifelong Sapphire Falls resident and, though a bit gruff, was as sweet as her famous chocolate pie.

Dottie strutted to the middle of the gazebo and executed a one-eighty as Bryan read from the script. "Dottie is showing off her sass with this black and white polka dotted—" Bryan broke off and looked up. "*Dottie* is wearing polka dots?" he asked with a grin.

"Who better?" Dot asked.

"You got me there," he agreed.

"Susan!" Tess hollered. "Your turn."

Dottie moved off, and Susan Leonard made her way to center stage. But unlike Ruby and Dottie, Susan didn't look like she was having fun with this.

She actually looked nervous.

Bryan looked down and read out loud, "Susan shows her stuff in this baby-blue ruffled camisole with French-cut panties."

He saw Susan blush bright red and her shoulders slump.

"Susan proves that—"

Bryan broke off when Susan took a deep breath and blew it out, then another, and another. It looked like she was practicing Lamaze breathing.

"Uh, Tess?" he asked. Susan didn't look so good.

"Yeah?"

He glanced up and saw that Tessa was watching Susan as well and looked concerned.

"I don't—"

Suddenly Susan bolted off the stage.

Bryan watched where she'd disappeared with wide eyes.

Then he heard it. They *all* heard it. The distinct sound of someone throwing up.

"Oh, my God." Tessa hurried off in that direction. "Just keep going," she tossed over her shoulder to him.

Sure. Okay.

Bryan cleared his throat. "All right, that puts Cora up next."

Cora came shuffling onto the stage. And the slow, almost hesitant steps didn't seem to be because of her walker. She actually looked a little miserable.

Bryan gave her a big smile. "So you're going to rock the leopard print, huh, Cora?"

She gave a big sigh. "What do you think?"

"What do you mean?"

"I'm eighty-six, boy. Do you know how longs it's been since I rocked anything?"

Bryan gave her a smile. "Oh, come on, Cora, rocking is all in the attitude."

"My *attitude* is that eighty-six-year-old women shouldn't wear leopard prints."

Okay, so Cora wasn't excited about this. She wasn't nervous like Susan. Cora just seemed depressed about the whole thing. It was one thing to not want to do something. That was fine. But it was something else to think you *shouldn't* do something.

Bryan pushed up from the chair and walked the short distance to the front of the stage. "Okay, ladies, gather 'round," he said loudly.

All nine women came forward and formed a half circle in front of him.

"Here's the deal," he said. "Every single one of you should be wearing whatever you want to," he told them. "You should all feel *good* up here. And far be it from me to talk anyone *out* of wearing lingerie—"

"Oh, I'm guessing you've talked lots of women out of their lingerie," Linda Kelson said.

The women all laughed.

"And out of lots of other things," Stella added.

Bryan felt his smile stretch wide. "Yeah, yeah, okay. Let me rephrase. Far be it from me to keep a woman from wearing lingerie, at least for a short period."

They all loved that and laughed again.

"But," he went on. "A woman's beauty and sexiness isn't about what she's wearing." "It's about what she's *not* wearing," Stella said.

Bryan shook his head, though he was still grinning. What had he gotten into here? "The most beautiful thing a woman can wear is *happiness*," he said. "Women are beautiful when they're playing with their dogs, holding their children, laughing with their friends, dancing, cooking, yelling at a football game, reading a good book—whatever it is that gives them that soft look and that glow of happiness."

Bryan looked around at the group, startled to find nine pairs of eyes staring at him. A few mouths were even open.

"So," he went on, carefully. "If Ruby feels good in her lingerie, she'll be beautiful in it. But if Cora doesn't want to wear the leopard print, we need to find something she *will* feel good in. But, Cora, it's not about your age or anything else. You can rock whatever you choose to wear, I promise."

Cora seemed to be thinking about that. "The color green makes me happy."

Bryan nodded. "Then you should definitely wear green."

"I want it to cover my ass," Cora added.

Bryan snorted. "Whatever you want."

"And I should bring my cat," Cora said. "She definitely makes me happy."

Bryan nodded. "I think—"

"Oh! I'll bring Pudding," Linda said.

"Pudding?" Bryan asked.

"My dog. She's so sweet. I could put *her* in a leopard print!"

They all laughed.

"That's a fun idea," Stella agreed. "I could make a little nightie for Cher that matches mine."

"Cher?" Bryan asked.

"My black lab," Stella told him.

Of course Cher was her black lab. Bryan got the inkling he was losing control. Then again, he *had* wanted to help the women relax and have fun with this.

"I like my polka dots," Dottie said. "But it *would* be funny to put Pepper in polka dots too. I'll bet I could find a polka dotted sock or something."

"A sock," Bryan repeated. "Because Pepper is a..."

"Ferret," Dottie said. "I think a ferret would look pretty funny in a nightie."

Right. But a black lab would look totally normal in one.

"Well, I don't have a pet, but if we're talking about ways to make this happy for me, I'll be wearing long johns and carrying a book and a cup of tea," Mary Simpson said.

"Oh for Heaven's sake!"

Everyone turned to find Tessa standing stage right.

"Tess—" Bryan started. She must have walked in late and didn't know what was really going on here. A pet lingerie show would be... Yeah, okay, that was maybe a bad idea.

"You all know this isn't really happening," she said to the women. "No need to get all worked up."

"But a pet fashion show, Tess," Stella said. "That would be a lot of fun."

Tessa took a deep breath. "Okay, we can think about that for next year. But we've already got everything set up for this one."

Bryan tried to intervene. "I was just helping the women—"

"I know what you were doing," Tess said, looking at him with a combination of exasperation and, if he wasn't mistaken, affection. It was a tiny bit, but he was pretty sure it was there.

"You ladies can go. Thanks anyway," Tess told them.

Bryan frowned as the women dispersed, still talking about pets in pajamas. "We weren't finished."

Tess crossed to the edge of the stage and jumped to the floor. "There's not going to be a lingerie show, Bryan. I talked the ladies into playing along for this. They got caught up—in you, big shock—and kind of forgot."

He wasn't sure what to say to that. Actually, he wasn't sure he should say anything to that. "There's no show? But I thought you did this every year."

"There's going to be a show, just not a *lingerie* show."

Ah, he suddenly got it. "You were trying to scare me off."

"Yep."

She was clearly unapologetic, and that almost made Bryan smile. He wasn't used to Tessa being anything but completely accommodating.

Well, they'd already established that she'd been trying to get him to quit, but the rest didn't make sense. "The show is off? Because Susan got sick and Cora doesn't want to do it? I really think I talked them into it."

"Of course you did," she said, crossing to his chair where he'd left the script.

"What's going on?" He made his way to where she was standing.

She handed him his crutch. "We're having a fashion show, but it's summer wear—shorts, tees, summer dresses. All the women are in it and more than happy about it."

He narrowed his eyes even as he felt like smiling. He liked Tessa. She was funny and maybe just a bit sassy. He didn't know she could be sassy.

The other night when she'd stood up on the stool at the Come Again and announced to the town that he wasn't in charge of her love life, and then in his office when she'd faced him about the whole situation and turned down his boyfriend offer, it had been the first time he'd really ever seen Tessa raise her voice or be spunky. And he'd liked it. A lot.

He loved her sweetness. He'd been counting on that sweetness. But he really liked this spark too. He dated sassy women. He liked them and was very attracted to that type of confidence.

Of course, that had been when he was a pretty confident himself. Cocky even. For a guy like him, a woman needed more than a little self-confidence to not get rolled over by his own. He liked women who would tell him to shut up and fuck off when needed.

But he wasn't that cocky guy anymore. He was confident. He was sure of himself and what he wanted and could do. But the cockiness had been knocked out of him on that mountainside.

He wasn't invincible after all. So now he liked to think of it as a softer, deeper confidence than he'd had before.

Before the accident and rehab, his confidence had come from the things he could *do* and the way he could push the people he coached to do more. Now, he'd learned that sometimes *he* needed to be pushed, and that he couldn't *do* everything just because he wanted to. He couldn't run a 5k now no matter how much he wanted to. He couldn't mountain climb like he did before no matter how much he wanted to. He had most definitely gotten a lesson in humility during his hospitalization and rehab, and now his confidence came from somewhere even deeper than it had before. Because now he didn't just know and believe in his strengths, he knew his weaknesses too.

That was why he could be with Tessa *now*. She had always been too sweet, too kind-hearted, too...well, frankly, too in love with him before. He would have broken her heart. But now he was more mature, still confident but less cocky. Now he could appreciate her and her quieter, softer ways.

But that didn't mean the moments of sassy from her didn't stir him.

"You made this into a lingerie show today for rehearsal to try to get me to quit," he reiterated.

"Yes, but somehow, I stupidly forgot about the part where you can't be pushed out of your comfort zone because *everything* is in your comfort zone," she said, clearly irritated. "You took this situation and not only went along with it and were charming and kind, but you even gave the women a pep talk about modeling lingerie in front of the whole town."

"Well, to be fair, they were more excited about their *pets* modeling," he said.

"You took a situation that was supposed to be uncomfortable for you and turned it into something fun and happy and upbeat." She frowned at him. "You're impossible."

ERIN NICHOLAS

Impossible? Was that really the adjective she wanted to use there?

"You do know that impossible is not a synonym for charming, right?" he asked.

She crossed her arms. "Yes, Bryan, I do know that."

"Just making sure."

In spite of her obvious ire, Bryan couldn't help grinning. She was riled up because he'd made the best of the situation? That didn't make sense, but she was cute when she was riled up.

His gaze dropped to her chest, where a flush of pink was climbing up her throat. Then, because he was a *guy*, his attention went lower. Over her beautiful breasts, down the front of her dress to where her hips flared, then down the expanse of her legs to her pretty feet with the pink toenail polish and the white sandals. She was curvy in all the right places and soft and feminine. He loved every inch.

His reaction to her was the strangest response he'd ever had to a woman. He wanted his hands and mouth on every single part of her. He wanted to feel her moving against him, feel her body heating and tightening around his, hear her moans and gasps as he made her feel every ounce of the heat and need he felt.

That wasn't the strange part.

It was all the other stuff he was feeling that was weird. At the same time he wanted to ravish her, he also wanted to take care of her. He didn't even know what that really entailed. Chocolate-covered strawberries? Love notes? Silk sheets? Marvin Gaye? What he did know was it didn't involve vibrators, doggie position or words like "suck me".

When his gaze returned to her face, the words "suck me" in Tessa's voice still echoing in his head, she was looking at him with both eyebrows up.

Dammit.

54

She didn't say anything. She seemed to be waiting for him to say something.

"I—" he started. But he couldn't make himself add that he wanted to bend her over and flip that sweet skirt with the pink flowers up over her back while he took her from behind. Nope, definitely not something he could say to Tess. "I'm sorry," he said instead.

Her eyebrows actually went higher with that. "You're sorry?

"Yeah. I got...distracted there for a second."

"By looking at my breasts?"

Bryan felt his own eyebrows shoot up. "Um..."

She tipped her head and gave him a look that clearly said she couldn't believe he was going to try and deny it.

"Okay," he said. "Yes. I shouldn't have...checked you out like that."

"Because you were thinking insulting things while you did it?"

"Um..." Was bending a girl over a chair *insulting*? Not in his world. The girls he knew would have all been quite pleased with it. But he wasn't used to dating girls who had collected teddy bears well into their teen years or who didn't have a favorite color, but instead preferred a rainbow of colors, from the covers they put on their textbooks to the clothes they wore. He definitely wasn't used to dating girls who thought he hung the moon.

Women liked him. The ones he dated *really* liked him. He'd even had a couple who claimed to love him. But none of them thought he was without fault. *That*, actually, was another reason why he could only now date Tess. She'd had very high expectations of him all along. He was only now capable of actually measuring up to them.

"No," he finally answered. "Not insulting." He thought she was amazing and beautiful. And the bending-over-a-chair thing was just one of the manifestations of those feelings. But he was going to have to work on some missionary-position fantasies. And maybe figure out what you said in bed to a nice girl. "Put your leg over my shoulder" probably wasn't on the list. For sure "you feel so fucking good around my cock" wasn't.

"Good. I don't consider you liking my breasts an insult either. So no need to be sorry."

That was the second time Tessa had said the word breasts to him, and he couldn't figure out why he felt turned on and discomfited by that at the same time.

"You look really nice," he said. He sounded like an idiot.

"Nice?" she repeated.

"Yes. You're beautiful and that dress looks great on you."

"Okay, well thanks."

"Sure. And I'm sorry that I—" He waved his hand up and down, mimicking how his eyes had gone up and down her body.

"And you want to be my boyfriend." Suddenly, she turned on her heel and headed out of the room.

"Wait. *What*?"

But she kept walking.

"Tess! Hey, Tess, hang on!"

He started after her, but after about six paces, she stopped and swung back. "What?"

He stopped, surprised. "I just—" Shit, he just wanted to be with her. "I'm sorry."

"For what?"

"For whatever is making you leave."

"You being you is making me leave, Bryan," she said. "You're sorry for being you?"

"I..." He really didn't know what to say to that either. "I didn't mean to make you uncomfortable. You're gorgeous. And you have..."

"Breasts," she said with a sigh when he trailed off. "They're called breasts, Bryan. And they're not exactly new."

"I know. I just haven't let myself look at *yours*."

She nodded. "Thanks for clarifying that. Thing is, if you feel bad just looking at my breasts, banging me on your desk at the bar would be really difficult."

She turned and started to walk away again.

Bryan was so overwhelmed by her words—and the vivid pictures they created in his imagination—that she got to the doorway before he recovered.

"What are you talking about?"

She turned back. "You said you want to be my boyfriend, but I can promise you that if I'm not getting some on top of your desk at the Come Again, I'm *definitely* not interested."

There was that extremely graphic image of her on his desk again. It wasn't his fault that it took him nearly five seconds to think of something *other* than that. It was biology's fault.

"Where are you going?" he called after her.

They could go to the bar. Derek might be there, but Bryan could get rid of him easily. The lunch crowd wouldn't trickle in until about eleven. They had almost an hour...

"Want to head over to the Come Again?" he called louder. Jokingly. Kind of.

She stopped abruptly and swung around. "That's not funny."

Yeah, it probably wasn't. "Sorry."

"And for the love of God, stop saying you're sorry!"

"Okay. Sor—right. Got it. No saying sorry and no joking about sex on my desk."

She looked as if she wanted to say more, but she pressed her lips together.

"For the record," he added. "It wasn't the idea of looking at your breasts that made me feel bad."

Again, she opened her mouth, then shut it without saying anything and shook her head. She pivoted toward the door.

"Where are you going?" he asked.

She paused with her hand on the door. "For a r—out. To do...some stuff. That's not here. With you."

Yep, she was cute when she was riled up. And not making sense.

"Hey, Tess?"

She sighed and didn't move. "*Definitely* somewhere you are *not*," she more or less muttered. Loud enough for him to hear. She also didn't turn around. "What, Bryan?"

"Good luck with the avoiding me thing."

She didn't say anything, but he thought maybe he could hear her grinding her teeth.

———

S tupidly, Bryan was still grinning when he walked into the Come Again ten minutes later. He was riling her up. That wasn't the same thing as kissing her or dancing with her or taking her out on a date. But it was actually more fun in some ways. Well, maybe not more fun than kissing. But fun in a different way. Now riling her up *by* kissing her...yeah, he could go for that.

But this was Tess. *Could* he go for that? She was the type of girl that made a guy think of flowers and chocolates and moonlight strolls. None of that said *riled up*.

And wow, Bryan liked riled up.

"What's with you?"

Bryan realized he'd been whistling as he looked up to find Derek watching him with an eyebrow arched.

"Nothing. A guy can't be happy?"

"You're always happy. But you're usually grinning-and-giving-away-drinks happy. This is whistling happy. So...you won the lottery or you got laid."

Bryan round the bar. "Ha. Neither."

Derek narrowed his eyes. "Right. You've got money and

you've had girls since I've known you and you didn't whistle."
Derek continued to study him.

"What are you doing?" Bryan asked as he moved down the
length of the bar. Suddenly, he was uncomfortable with the
whole having-girls thing. It had been a while. Well, it had been
a few months. Like three. But now his full focus was on Tess.

"Trying to figure out what could happen that would make
the most optimistic guy I know even happier than usual."

Bryan thought about lying or putting Derek off or just
ignoring him. But then he turned to the other guy and said, "It
is a girl."

"Ah-ha!" Then Derek frowned. "But you having a girl isn't
new."

"Me having *this* one is new."

Derek shook his head. "Thought you had a thing for Tess."

"Yep."

Derek's eyes widened. "*Tess* is the reason you're whistling?"

"Yep."

"So she changed her mind."

"No." Now Bryan frowned.

"So what's with the whistling?"

Bryan thought about that. It was because he was feeling
hopeful.

Why was he feeling hopeful?

It seemed that he should be less encouraged since she'd
tried to get him to quit the committee and had needed to get
away from him after it was all over. But damn, he did feel
happier.

Feisty. She'd been a little feisty.

And if he was *totally* honest with himself, feisty was more in
his wheelhouse than sweet. He'd mellowed, for sure. He knew
what was important. He had made some major life changes and
was ready to make more. But there had been brief, fleeting
moments he'd been trying to completely wipe from his mind

where he'd wondered if he really could hang out with a sweet girl long-term.

There was a glimmer of hope now that Tess wasn't *too* sweet. Hell, she'd used the word breasts and had talked about him *banging* her on his desk. In fact, she'd laid that down as a *requirement*.

He was *definitely* hopeful.

"Tess is coming around," he finally told Derek.

"So you haven't..." Derek trailed off meaningfully.

Bryan frowned at him. "No." And why did *that* question annoy him? He wanted to...with Tess, and this was exactly the kind of conversation he had with his friends. But now, talking like this about things he wanted to do with Tessa, seemed wrong. "And this is *Tess*, Derek. We're not talking about her like she's some hookup from last call, got it?"

Derek actually looked relieved. "Yeah. Got it. Good. I was hoping you felt that way about her."

Bryan turned fully to face his bartender. "What do you mean? Tess is the girl I intend to spend the rest of my life with. You know that." Everyone knew that. Bryan wasn't a shy, private kind of guy. He'd grown up in Sapphire Falls. Being shy and private was pretty much a losing battle around here anyway, and the sooner a guy accepted that, the less stress he had in his life. It also worked for his general nature. He shared. Sometimes overly. But he wasn't embarrassed by his feelings, his thoughts, his dreams, and he was very open about them all.

"Yeah, I know," Derek said, turning back to the cleaning he was doing behind the bar. "It's just that Tess is different than your usual girls. And you've been gone for a while. I just wanted to be sure you realized that."

Bryan felt a stupid surge of jealousy. Was Derek insinuating he knew Tess better than Bryan did? Why did Derek feel protective of her? "I've known Tess all my life. And on some level I've loved her as long as I've known her. She's loved me too."

Derek nodded as he wiped down a bottle of Jack. "Oh, I know. Everyone knows that Tess has been waiting for you. That's why it's been funny having you warn guys off."

"Funny how?" Bryan asked.

"The only guys who would actually ask her out are from out of town. Everyone around here knows they wouldn't get anywhere with her." Derek replaced the Jack on the middle shelf in front of the mirror that covered the wall behind the bar. He pulled a bottle of Jose Cuervo down next.

"Meaning she would say no?" Bryan asked, wanting that clarification for some reason.

"Meaning they wouldn't get anything more than a good-night kiss," Derek said, wiping the shelf and setting Jose back up there.

Something prickled along the back of his neck. An awareness, or a realization, or something. "You mean on the first date?" Bryan asked.

Derek finally turned to face him. "Ever," he said. Then he peered closer at Bryan. "Do you not know?"

"Not know what?" Bryan asked, a prickling awareness dancing down his spine.

"Tessa's a virgin."

Bryan leaned his butt back against the cooler behind him. Shock, and maybe even a very teeny tiny bit of guilt went through him. But the absolute pleasure and *fuck yeah* feeling that followed immediately wiped anything out.

Tessa was a virgin. She'd never been with another guy.

"She's been saving herself for you," Derek said.

Again, a *teeny* tiny thread of guilt went through his mind. But the *damn right* obliterated it a millisecond later.

Tessa was *his*.

No matter what she was telling him—and herself—for whatever reason, she was his. She always had been.

"She told all these guys she was saving herself for me?" Bryan could admit he was reeling a bit. She was a *virgin*. It fit, he couldn't lie. But he'd always assumed she was just inexperienced and didn't go out much. He knew she didn't date a lot and the guys she had gone out with hadn't gotten serious or lasted long. But he wasn't sure Hailey knew Tess was a virgin. Surely that would have come up at some point when he had asked Hailey about her over the years Hailey had been coming to Denver to see Ty.

Derek chuckled. "I don't think she's put it quite that way," he said. "But everyone just kind of knows it."

"How?" Bryan's ego had taken a beating when he'd been hospitalized and needed people to help him with *everything* for a while there. But it was quickly reflating being around Tessa, the woman who'd put him on a pedestal so long ago. And now to find out that not only had she been waiting for him, in every way, but everyone knew it... Yeah, this was definitely healing a few ego bruises.

"Well, the girls know," Derek said, wiping at a nonexistent spot on the bar top suddenly.

"The girls? Her friends?"

Derek nodded.

Bryan knew she hung out with Kate Spencer and Delaney and Hope Bennett now, but all those women were newcomers to Sapphire Falls. He tried to remember who she'd been close to in high school. Her best friend growing up had been Kacey Sherwood, one of Phoebe's cousins, but Kacey's family had moved away before junior high. Tessa had been one of those girls that everyone liked, but he couldn't remember her being especially tight with anyone after Kacey.

"And one of her friends told you?" Bryan asked. No way. For one thing, Kate, Delaney and Hope all had husbands—the men who had stolen their hearts on their supposedly temporary visits to town. For another, they were all very nice women who would never share a friend's confidence.

Then again, he'd also seen her in the Come Again with Peyton Wells a few times. Peyton was almost eight years younger than Tess, but they worked together at the bakery. Peyton had been there for a couple of years, but Tess had started helping out after Caitlyn had left the shop, and town, to go with Eli. Peyton was a bit of a wild child and definitely came off as more mature...or maybe it was just streetwise. She'd settled down a little since her half-sister, Hope, had come to town, but she still had an edge. But Peyton was loyal and wouldn't spill a friend's secret.

Derek rolled his eyes. "I'm a bartender, Bry. People talk in bars."

"So you overheard this," Bryan said. That made sense.

"You know the kinds of things we overhear."

Even growing up in the small town where everyone knew everything about everyone else, Bryan was sometimes surprised by the private conversations people had inside the Come Again.

Liquor did that to people.

He nodded. "Yeah, I get it."

"So, anyway," Derek said, propping a hip against the back counter and folding his arms. "I just wanted to be sure you realize what was going on here with Tess. And make sure it doesn't mean more to her than it does to you."

With him being all protective of Tessa, *his* Tessa, Bryan realized that Derek was a pretty big guy. He had impressive biceps under the sleeves of his black T-shirt. He was probably six-two or three and in good shape. He was also three years younger than Bryan. Oh, and had a fully functioning spinal cord.

Bryan narrowed his eyes and nodded. "I completely realize what's going on with Tess. But thanks for looking out for her."

That seemed to be all Derek needed to hear. "Okay then." He pushed off the counter and returned to his cleaning activities.

Bryan thought it all over, and three minutes later, he realized he had no idea what the hell was going on with Tessa. She'd loved him for a quarter of a century—that sounded impressive when stated like that, and he thought maybe he'd use it the next time he talked to her. Now here he was, declaring that he wanted the relationship she'd been writing about in her diary all these years. She was a fricking *virgin* for God's sake. She'd been saving herself for *him*. But she was fighting him?

What?

And he was even more confused about the banging-on-his-desk stuff now. She was a virgin. What did she know about banging on *any* surface? And could he ogle her or not? Because he really wanted to. But there was surely some special care to be given a virgin.

Though Bryan was absolutely not the guy to know about that.

"Hey, Derek?"

"Yeah, boss?"

"You ever dated a virgin?"

There was a beat of silence and then Derek started laughing.

Bryan just waited for him to finish. "So that would be a no?" he asked mildly after Derek quieted down.

"Uh, that would be a not-on-purpose," Derek said. "My high school girlfriend was a virgin, of course. But I never got past third base there."

"So you've never been someone's first?" Bryan asked.

"Nope."

"Damn," Bryan muttered, racking his brain for a friend of

his who might have some experience with virgins. He came up very lacking.

"But," Derek said.

Bryan's head came up. "But?"

Derek shrugged. "Not to be crude, but it's kind of a blank slate then, right? I mean, she might not know what she likes and what she doesn't like, but that just means you should try it all out. Give her the whole buffet. Figure it out with her." He grinned. "I can think of worse ways to spend my time."

The whole buffet. Indeed. Bryan matched Derek's grin. "You know what? You're a fucking genius."

Derek nodded as if this was not news to him. "You're welcome."

Bryan headed for his office. This was so good in so many ways. He fucking loved that Tess was a virgin. No guy had touched her. She was *his*, so this was awesome. And...she didn't know what all was even *on* the buffet, so they could stick with Bryan's specialties and he didn't have to worry about her wanting the dishes he could no longer serve.

Oh yeah, this was great.

He couldn't think of anything hotter than teaching Tessa all about how to touch him, how to touch herself, how to move...

He most definitely was whistling again. And now he knew exactly why.

4

Tessa felt the familiar, very welcome burn in her quads and glutes as she finished her last mile. She got to the big oak tree on the edge of Tucker Bennett's property where she'd started her run eighty minutes ago. She'd done ten miles only two days ago, but she needed it today. Her adrenaline had been running high, and there was only one sure way to get rid of it—put on her shoes and go out.

As she walked the mile back to the road where she'd parked, cooling off and shaking out her limbs, Tess took a moment to marvel at the fact that she'd just run ten miles. Ten. Miles. There was a time not that long ago where the very idea of that would have made her laugh. She had never been a runner. She'd never really been an exerciser. Now she was going for a *run* to deal with emotions that would have sent her straight to the bakery a few years ago. Not that Adrianne's bakery wasn't amazing and not to say Tess never took advantage of her employee discount. But she liked that her first inclination when she got worked up was to use the energy more positively.

And just like that, her thoughts were back on Bryan.

She wasn't sure running was going to solve this particular problem.

Because the churning emotions simply produced more energy the minute her thoughts were back on him. Like a turbine making electricity from the winds that swept the Nebraska plains, thoughts of Bryan made all of her inner wheels turn and filled her with energy that felt difficult to contain.

She was going to need another outlet for it other than running. Her work wasn't going to do it, because as long as she was working on the festival, her thoughts would keep going back to this morning with Bryan and the older ladies. Her work with Delaney on the home renovation projects Delaney had going wouldn't do it. Tess would love to take a wall or two down, but they were past that point on everything they were doing right now. Her yoga classes she taught for Hope wouldn't do it. Yes, yoga was supposed to calm a person, but only if you could let go of all the thoughts and emotions stirring you up. Tessa was still learning a lot of that, and she suspected it would take years of intense practice to get to the point where she could override years of intense feelings for Bryan simply by breathing and stretching for an hour.

Maybe Hope had some herbs she could recommend. Hope seemed to have natural remedies for everything. Maybe there was a potion somewhere that could help with memory loss—as in causing it. Or help with heart problems—as in helping her get over the only man she'd ever loved.

She could *not* believe that she'd talked about him banging her on his desk. Banging. She'd said *banging* to Bryan.

Tess groaned as she remembered it. What was she doing? That was like poking a bear, and she knew it. She knew Bryan Murray better than anyone. And she knew that she'd essentially waved a red cape in front of the bull.

Bear, bull, whatever. He was going to see that as a challenge.

She shouldn't have said that, but she'd been lashing out at him because he'd been getting to her. By being sweet. He'd not only completely rolled with the situation she'd put him in with the lingerie show—and his ability to handle any situation with humor and heart had always gotten to her—but he'd been sweet with the older ladies and their self-esteem issues.

Sweet was supposed to be safe. It was supposed to help her *not* want him.

Dammit. That whole thing had totally backfired on her, and she'd let her frustration seep out. And she'd said the word banging.

And while she absolutely, for sure, wanted to go to Denver to take the next step in her running, and while she absolutely, for sure, did not want Bryan to romance her, she also absolutely, for sure, would not be able to resist him if there was banging involved.

Of course, Bryan taking it as a challenge wasn't the only reason she wished she hadn't said that. She was willing to admit she was maybe a little bit kind of nervous about the whole thing.

She read lots of romance novels. She knew that the women enjoyed sex. She knew her girlfriends who were sleeping with someone said it was amazing. But everything was banging, pounding, nailing. Words that didn't make it sound all that fun.

That was another reason that she'd always hoped it would be Bryan who would teach her everything she needed to know sexually. She trusted him. She knew he'd never hurt her. Not physically anyway.

So now she was torn. Sleeping with Bryan would make it impossible to ever get over him. She was already worried about if that would ever really happen anyway. But the idea of *not* sleeping with Bryan meant she would sleep with someone else. And that felt...wrong. And a little scary.

Hating everything, especially her stupid, romantic heart,

Tess pulled into her driveway and headed inside to quickly shower so she could get back up to the Community Center in time for the talent show rehearsal. She stubbornly kept thoughts of Bryan at bay as she soaped her foot...in spite of being in her shower and in spite of the fact that she braced her hand against the very wall she wanted him to put her up against.

She strode into the Community Center at quarter to six.

She had not been looking forward to this in the first place, and considering how she was stirred up from earlier with Bryan, she was feeling grumpy. But she plastered on a smile and greeted the participants who were already there.

There were twelve kids signed up to audition for the show, and she really could only take eight. If she let all twelve in, the show would last forever. It had been strongly encouraged —by people who had sat through a longer talent show in the past—that she make it only six acts. But she didn't want to turn anyone away, especially kids. She didn't like turning this into a competition. If someone loved something, they should just be able to do it for the joy of it, not because they wanted to be better than someone else. She'd really tried to work ten in, but she'd finally realized eight was the only realistic number with the time slot they had to work with. There were too many other things going on that would need to be rearranged.

Tess thought they could really take the pie-eating contest off the schedule altogether—no one needed to eat that much pie—or that they could run bingo at the same time as the show. That had been met with all kinds of protest though. A lot of the bingo players had grandkids in the show and wanted to see the performances. Tess had suggested, since bingo was being held just on the other side of the Community Center, that they could take a quick break when it was their grandchild's turn. But it had been pointed out that bingo got rowdy and they cranked up the old time country music and the boisterous shouts of *bingo* would be disruptive to the show.

Tess had rolled her eyes a lot during that meeting.

So now she had to eliminate four acts in this audition tonight. She frowned as she took her seat in the same chair Bryan had occupied during the fashion show rehearsal. Hell, he wanted to be involved and on her good side? She should make him do this thankless job.

"Okay, Kelsey," she called at six o'clock sharp. "You're first."

Kelsey Somers took the stage with her guitar. She was thirteen and had dreams of going to Nashville. Tess looked at her and knew she wouldn't be eliminating Kelsey. The girl had a dream. Far be it from Tess to tell her she couldn't sing in her hometown's talent show.

Kelsey was partway through her Carrie Underwood cover when someone pulled a chair up next to Tess. She glanced over, not shocked, but not pleased, to see Bryan.

"Sorry I'm a little late," he whispered, his eyes on Kelsey.

"How can you be late for something you're not supposed to be at in the first place?" she asked through gritted teeth.

God, he looked good. And she couldn't help that the word *banging* wouldn't stop repeating in her mind.

He leaned closer, putting his mouth near her ear. "You smell amazing."

His warm breath touched her neck and everything in her clenched. Hard.

Kelsey finished her song, and Tessa forced herself to look up at the girl. "Very nice. Thanks, Kelsey."

"So what do you need from me?" Bryan asked as the next performers, three little girls in sparkly tutus, took the stage.

He was sitting close enough that his shoulder touched hers. There was no need for him to sit that close, and she could point that out. But it probably also didn't *hurt* anything for his shoulder to be against hers for a few minutes. Of course, it made her incredibly aware of him and made her want to climb into his lap and kiss him. But she'd feel that way even if his shoulder *wasn't* touching hers. In spite of the lackluster kiss in his office. She knew Bryan had hot and sexy in him. He just wasn't using it on her. And the idea that she could get to him, get him to turn it on, was tempting.

Damn. She was in so much trouble.

"I don't need anything from you," she whispered back.

She felt his eyes on her but she refused to turn and look at him.

"Oh, Tessy," he said softly, using a nickname she hadn't heard from him in easily ten years. "I think we both know that's not true."

She gripped her pen tighter and glued her gaze to the stage where Sydney, Molly and Taryn Peterson were performing their dance routine. Even though all she really saw were purple ruffles and a lot of sequins.

Her mind wouldn't stop obsessing over the man next to her.

She wanted hot, amazing, blow-her-mind sex. She wanted the fantasies she'd been holding on to for all these years, the fantasies she'd played out in her mind so many times.

She also wanted to run. To be...free. She loved the feel of her blood pounding through her body, her lungs expanding and contracting, her muscles burning and tingling. But she also wanted to run through the mountains, along beaches, through fields and woods. She wanted to see the national parks. She wanted to run along the rim of the Grand Canyon. She wanted to breathe the air in Hawaii and in Italy and in Mexico and feel that air on her face while she ran.

Those were some fantasies she'd envisioned with just as much detail.

Okay, *almost* as much detail.

Tess had spent her life in Sapphire Falls. Not running— literally or metaphorically. She hadn't wanted to run. She hadn't wanted anything more than what she had. Except for Bryan. She'd basically been happy. Until she'd put on those running shoes the first time. It was like they were a portal to a new world. It sounded silly, but it *felt* true. She had suddenly *wanted* something, and it was something she could get for herself, something she was in control of. That was so much better than a crush on a guy who was out getting what *he* wanted. Which hadn't included her.

Three years ago, she'd planned to have the same life her parents had and her grandparents had and her aunts and uncles had—a local job, a house in Sapphire Falls, the same people and scenes and routines. It wasn't a bad life. In fact, it was really good and would have been enough. More than enough even. If it hadn't been for Bryan and his blog.

She'd started following to keep up on his rehab, but she'd gone in to the archives and found podcasts, YouTube videos, Instagram and Facebook posts about running and training and pushing and growing. He'd talked about everything from the health benefits to the personal challenges, how running had helped and changed him. Then he'd shown her the world—his photos, his travel journal. His enthusiasm for the trips had been obvious. And contagious. She'd started running because of him, and now she wanted to run around the world.

The girls finished their routine, and Tess and Bryan clapped appropriately.

Next up was Hunter Cranston. Doing stand-up comedy.

When Hunter finished, Bryan leaned over. "I don't think I understand what's happening."

She so wanted to turn her head. If she did, their lips would be only centimeters apart.

After that very *nice*, and nothing more, kiss the other night? Why was she thinking about being close to his lips?

Because she wanted him to use them on her. All over her.

"There are twelve acts auditioning," she said, looking straight ahead. "They can bring any talent they want to."

"Auditioning?" Bryan asked. "This isn't a rehearsal?"

She shook her head. He couldn't have put his hands up her shirt the other night? Or grabbed her ass? He couldn't have slid his hands into her hair...and pulled just a little?

Then she shook her head. No. She didn't want that. She wanted him to be sweet and romantic. It would be a lot easier to walk away from once Jake Elliot accepted her into his program.

"They're auditioning. There are twelve acts and we only have room for eight."

"But...that's ridiculous," he said as Mary Jo Robins took the stage and went to the microphone.

When she finished, Bryan leaned over again. "We have to let them all in."

Tessa did turn her head this time. She couldn't resist it any longer.

And sure enough, only centimeters separated them. Bryan had been trying to whisper, which was why he'd gotten so close, but when she faced him, he didn't pull back.

"We can't let them all in," she said softly, studying his mouth.

She'd certainly studied it before, but never this close up. He had an amazing mouth. Made for smiling and kissing. And lots of other stuff she wanted to know a lot more about.

"These kids are willing to stand up there and let it all hang out like this, we have to let them in," he said. "I can't tell any of them no."

She felt the same way. "There's not enough time to get everyone on stage."

"Sure there is. We double up."

That pulled her attention up to his eyes. "Double up?"

"The little girls who danced? They can dance along to Mary

Jo's song instead. And this piano solo coming up? She can play while this guy," he pointed at the page, "juggles."

Tess started to protest that it would never work but...it would totally work. Why not? "Okay, let's find four more acts that can be blended and we're good."

Bryan settled back in his chair, looking very proud of himself. "Bring 'em on."

Tessa was aware that four little kids were on the stage getting ready to perform a tumbling routine, but she couldn't look away from Bryan.

"Thank you," she said.

He gave her a smile. "What for?"

"For...being you. This morning with the ladies, you were totally *you*, and it ended up making them all feel good about themselves and smile. Now this—you want everyone to have their chance in the spotlight."

Bryan's expression grew serious and he sat forward, angling toward her slightly. "For being me? Wasn't that the thing that made you leave this morning?"

She swallowed and nodded. "You being you makes my life very complicated."

He looked at her for a long moment. "I want to talk more about that later."

Crap.

But, yeah, maybe they should. Maybe she should just tell him how everything had gotten turned upside down. Surely he'd be happy about her running and flattered that he'd had something to do with it. Of all people, Bryan should understand her desire to see the world. He'd talked about how important it was to see other places, to understand how big and diverse and beautiful the world was. Yeah, he would understand. And then he'd want her to go and he'd stop talking about being her boyfriend.

And she'd be able to sleep at night again.

"Okay," she agreed softly.

They watched the next six acts with only basic comments back and forth, but she was acutely aware of him the entire time, and her skin seemed to tingle with that awareness to the point she was feeling jumpy and wound tight.

While she was hyper-focused on Bryan, *he* seemed to be paying more attention to what was going on around them. Which meant their roles were right back to how they'd always been, Tessa realized, with far more humor than she'd ever found in the situation in the past. But thanks to Bryan, they easily found four more acts that could combine into two and everyone was going to have some spotlight time. Megan Newman could play her guitar while Cassie Carson, Stella's granddaughter, hula-hooped; and when Brittney Watson showed up and said her duet partner had to quit because she was getting her tonsils out, Dawson Miller had offered to fill in and the two acts had easily became one.

As act number eleven took the stage, though, Bryan leaned close again.

"Oh, and by the way, we should definitely talk about the virgin thing too."

His voice was low and gruff and seemed to rumble through her. She soaked all the sexiness in...for the three seconds it took her to realize what he'd actually said.

She swung to face him. "*What*?" But she forgot to whisper.

"The virgin thing," Bryan said quietly, his eyes on the audition, as if he were telling her he'd like chicken salad for lunch. "I have some thoughts."

"You have some *thoughts*?" Tessa asked, again much above the level of a whisper.

"Do I need to read louder?" Nicole Gordon asked from the stage. She was reading a monologue from an off-Broadway play Tess had never heard of.

Tessa turned to face forward in her chair, working to not

hyperventilate. He'd said *virgin thing*. He knew she was a virgin. Which meant someone in Sapphire Falls had told him that.

"No, you're perfect," Bryan told Nicole. "Go right ahead."

"I'm going to kill Ty Bennett," Tess said in not-quite a whisper but not as loudly as before.

"It wasn't Ty," Bryan said, still watching Nicole.

Nicole squinted down at Tess. "Is everything okay?"

"No," Tess said honestly. And just how *not* okay everything was hit her. Bryan was *here* in Sapphire Falls wanting to kiss her chastely and *date* her and give her some *thoughts* on her *virginity*. While she wanted to be in Colorado, running marathons in the mountains and being kissed like the man was starving for her and happily surrendering her virginity in hot against-the-wall sex.

In a very unlike-herself move, Tess stood swiftly and turned to face Bryan, not caring that Nicole was still auditioning.

"Dammit, Bryan, you can't ask me to date you and you can't have *thoughts* about my *virgin thing*."

Bryan seemed unable to respond, so Tess swung to Nicole. "You're in, Nicole. You're all in!" she called to everyone standing around waiting for the auditions to end. "It's going to be a great show. Thanks for coming."

And she turned and stomped out of the Community Center, her heart pounding, her face hot, her entire body charged up and needing an outlet and completely frustrated that it didn't seem running would do it.

So she went home and rummaged through her cupboards.

Of course, she'd started eating healthier as well, so she had no decent snack food. The best she could do was cupcake vodka.

Tess grabbed a glass and the bottle and headed for the couch. With helping Delaney with remodels, Hope with the yoga studio, Adrianne with the bakery and TJ with running

Sapphire Falls, it was rare for Tess to have time to sit and do nothing.

So she fully intended to do just that. With vodka. Though she did entertain the idea of heading to the bakery for some *real* cupcakes.

Screw good eating habits. Screw being healthy and losing those forty pounds and going down three pant sizes.

The weight loss had been a nice side effect of the running, but it hadn't been her motivation. She'd started running purely because Bryan had said such inspirational things about it. Peyton had wanted to do something healthier and had been questioning her ability to actually make a positive change in her life, and Tess had found herself quoting Bryan. Peyton had been convinced, and Tess had bought some shoes and jogged— okay, jogged and walked, mostly walked—with her friend for a mile. Tess hadn't missed a day since.

The healthier eating had come because of her increased distances and the need to properly fuel her body for the demand, and that, combined with the exercise, had caused a dramatic weight loss. She was still curvy and a size twelve. Hardly super-model size. But her body was toned and healthy, and she felt better about herself than she ever had. So she was wearing more skirts and dresses, more fitted shirts and jeans and more sleeveless tops.

And no matter how much she loved it, no matter how much she'd learned about herself, no matter that she'd gone out for *herself* every day after that first time, she could still trace this passion back to Bryan too.

Pathetic.

She poured a couple of fingers of vodka and took a sip. Hmm...not really like cupcakes. She tried to remember what her friends had mixed this with. They had to have mixed it. Of course, if they hadn't, that could explain why not much of it was gone.

Peyton would know—it was guaranteed Peyton had been here for cupcake vodka.

Tess texted her friend an SOS.

She had no intention of stopping running now. She couldn't. She honestly couldn't imagine *not* running. But she was not doing it for or because of Bryan. And she wasn't drinking because of him either. Dammit. If she wanted cupcake vodka, she'd have cupcake vodka.

She took another sip. The second taste was better than the first. Which was promising, because she needed to get her mind off of everything.

Glass to her lips, Tess flipped through the channels. Nothing was working for her. Typical. She finally had time to watch TV and nothing good was on. She tipped her cup again. Her sips were tiny, but she did feel a pleasant warmness starting.

She stopped at the travel channel out of habit. And because she saw a mountain.

Dammit.

Tess tipped her cup again. This was *not* the way to not think about Bryan.

She took in the sight of the mountains and valleys. She'd never been to the mountains. She'd never been anywhere with Bryan at all, yet she would always associate mountains with him. Even if she lived in Denver for years, trained there—even maybe fell in love with someone else.

Determined to *not* think about him, or how it seemed weird to even think about being in love with someone else, she focused on her goals and the things she could control—like finishing a bottle of vodka—Tessa poured another inch. Okay, so at this pace it would take a while to finish the nearly full bottle. Still, it was a goal. She stubbornly flipped to the food channel.

But only five minutes into the show about, ironically,

cupcakes, she was eyeing her computer. There was something she could do, something she could take control of.

She could submit her application to Jake Elliot's program in Denver.

She almost had the money. She'd finally have her savings account to the level she wanted when she got her next paycheck after the festival.

Tess took another sip and stared at her laptop on her dining room table. It was about five feet away. She could just get up, walk over there, turn it on and...change her life.

So why was she hesitating? Why was her butt still glued to the couch? What was she waiting for?

It was that thought that got her up. She was done *waiting* for anything.

Ten minutes later, she pressed Send. Her application had officially been turned in for Jake Elliot's coaching program.

She shut her laptop and tipped back the rest of the vodka in her glass just as she heard a knock at her door.

Tessa bounded to her feet. Maybe it was Peyton with something to mix with the vodka. Or maybe it was Kate or Hope. Or anyone who would share the bottle. Because finishing it by herself was feeling more and more likely and she knew she would regret it deeply in the morning.

Her visitor being one of the girls wasn't out of the realm of possibility. There had been a good number of people at the Community Center who had heard her tell Bryan not to have thoughts about her virginity. That would certainly spread around town fast enough that her girlfriends could have heard about it. She could use some girl talk.

But when she pulled the door open, it wasn't a female at all. It was Bryan Murray, looking sexy and gorgeous and pretty serious. For Bryan, anyway.

She should have seen this coming.

A fact that was confirmed a moment later when he said,

"You can't expect me to find out you've been saving yourself for me and then just let it go."

Something about the way he said "saving yourself for me" should have caused her to blush in embarrassment—he really had heard all about it—but instead, it caused her inner muscles to clench.

There was an almost possessive tone to his voice when he said it, and her stupid heart—or hormones—responded with an enthusiastic *I'm yours.*

"Tess, let me in."

There was still a screen door between them, and Tess had the fleeting revelation that if she pushed the door open, she was in huge, huge trouble.

She did it anyway.

Bryan grabbed the edge of the screen door the moment she pushed it open an inch. He pulled it open and stepped through quickly, almost as if he was afraid she'd change her mind.

He was using his crutch again, but there was nothing that took away from his big, strong, almost domineering presence.

When she started to step back, he grabbed her upper arm with his free hand and stopped her. He turned her so her back was against the open front door and crowded close.

Tessa's heart thudded. *Oh my God, yes* was the only thought she had.

"Have you been saving yourself for me, Tess?" he asked, that low, gruff voice rumbling through her again and setting all her nerve endings on fire.

She wet her lips, trying to decide how to address this. For some reason, she really thought confessing might *not* be the way to go. But her thoughts weren't exactly clear. There was something about feeling the heat from Bryan's body, inhaling the scent of him, and the way he was looking at her, that combined to make her feel very...stupid. Or it could have been the vodka.

"I don't really want to talk about my sex life," she said.

His pupils dilated, and he leaned in, putting a forearm against the door by her ear. "That's not a no."

She sighed. "Everyone knows how I felt about you," she finally said. "Even you."

"That is also not a no."

She closed her eyes. That was better. Easier. She could think *a little* clearer without looking into his eyes.

But she could still *feel* him.

"Do you have any idea how fuck—how *very* hot it is to think that you've been waiting for me like that?" he asked.

Tess felt heat suffuse her body. He was turned on by the idea that she'd been saving herself for him? That she was a virgin? Then she thought about *all* of his words. And the word he'd *almost* said.

She opened her eyes and frowned. "Did you almost say how *fucking* hot it is?" she asked.

He winced slightly. "Yeah, sorry. It's just that—"

"Dammit, Bryan!" She put her hands on his chest and pushed him back.

He wouldn't even *swear* in front of her? Really?

He stepped back, his crutch steadying him.

"What's wrong?" he asked, clearly surprised she'd pushed him.

Tess stepped away from the door and into the living room, where she had more room to move and more space between her and the hard body she'd wanted to get up against since her hormones had told her that being up against someone might be fun.

"You stopped yourself from saying fuck to me?" She crossed her arms.

"Yes. I'm sorry. I'm working on my language."

"Then you might as well just turn around and go home," she said.

He blinked at her. "What?"

"You're not going to be very good at dirty talk if you won't even say fuck to me. And that's definitely one of the words I would want to hear. Not to mention cock and pussy and clit and—"

He was practically on top of her a moment later. "Stop."

Damn, he could move fast even with a crutch.

She lifted her chin. He hadn't shaved today, and she suddenly, desperately wanted to feel those whiskers scraping over her skin. She put a hand against his cheek and rubbed over the sexy scruff. "Stop what?"

"You don't know what you're starting here." But he leaned in slightly.

Tess lifted an eyebrow. "I don't?"

"I know you don't. Virgin, remember?"

She rolled her eyes. "Yes, Bryan, I'm a virgin. That doesn't mean I don't know *anything*."

His voice dropped and he rubbed his jaw against her hand. "Do you know what it does to me to think that you've never been with anyone and that you want to be with me?"

Feeling sassy suddenly, Tess let her eyes drop to his crotch. There was definitely some rigidity there that told her a thing or two. "I have an idea."

He made a little growling noise in the back of his throat. Then he sucked in a breath through his nose. "I think we should talk about this. And how I'm making your life complicated. Because, honey, you're making a few things hard for me too."

Tess couldn't help it. She gave a little giggle at that.

A smile curled one corner of Bryan's mouth too. "Seriously," he said.

She wanted to keep playing. She wanted to tease and flirt and see what she could get Bryan to do or say. The way he was in her personal space, the deep timbre of his voice, the way he was looking at her, all made her hormones start jigging. But, yeah, the complicated thing. She needed to keep that in mind. And she should probably explain herself to him. Maybe he'd back off then.

Of course, at the moment, having Bryan move back even an inch made her feel desperate.

That was *not* a good state to be in.

Tess dropped her hand and took a breath, but Bryan grabbed her wrist. He lifted it back to his face and pressed her hand against his cheek. "I like you touching me."

Her heart squeezed and thirteen-year-old Tessa rejoiced deep inside her. "Maybe it's *you* who doesn't know what he's starting," she said softly.

5

B ryan frowned slightly. "What's that mean?"
"The girl inside me who's been in love with you all my life is thrilled right now," she admitted.

"Good," he said sincerely.

She shook her head. "But that girl is a romantic dreamer."

Bryan smiled at that. "And you're not a romantic dreamer?"

She sighed. "What you're starting is a conversation I'm not sure you really want to have," she told him honestly.

This time when she dropped her hand, he let her. But he didn't let up on the intense gaze he had pinned on her. "Okay, start talking."

"Maybe we should sit down."

Bryan hesitated, and Tess could practically feel what he was thinking. He wanted to pace. That was Bryan, always on the move, always with too much energy to be still for long.

She moved to the sofa and sank onto one end, pulling a throw pillow into her lap and hugging it tightly.

But Bryan surprised her. He stayed standing—and paced.

There was a crutch, but honestly, that didn't slow him a bit.

And it took none of the tightly wound vitality away from the picture he presented.

She felt her body heat just from watching him move. As it had so often in her life. She'd become a baseball, basketball and football fan simply because Bryan played and she'd loved watching him. He was one of the best players on all the teams, no question, and it had seemed, even from a very young age— and to a very biased observer—that he was just made to *move*. It didn't matter if he was jumping or twisting, shooting, throwing or swinging a bat, it was a beautiful sight that demonstrated all of the amazing things the human body was capable of.

But where he'd really shone was on the track. Bryan had run with a natural, powerful grace that was matched only by Ty Bennett's. But Ty didn't play other sports. He ran track, but during the off season he trained for triathlons by adding swimming and biking to his regimen. And Ty had never seemed to *enjoy* it all like Bryan did. Ty was all about being the best, about winning. Bryan seemed to do it just because he liked it and it felt good.

And now, even with a crutch under one arm, all of that natural athleticism was fully apparent.

Tess swallowed hard and tried to remember why she didn't want to have sex with him.

Something about never recovering from it. Never leaving town. Something like that. But for a moment, she didn't mind the idea of staying right here and looking at Bryan forever.

Okay. Right. *That* was the problem.

Her life could not revolve around Bryan. She needed to be independent, stop waiting, make things happen.

"Tell me what's going on, Tess," Bryan said, facing her from two feet in front of the sofa, only the short coffee table between them.

She pulled in a breath and nodded. "Okay. I'm not interested in a relationship with you."

"Anymore," he added.

So they were going to really rub in the fact that she'd been his number one admirer...forever. No. Not forever. She hadn't known him until she was five. And she'd gotten over him two and a half years ago. "Yes, okay, anymore."

"Which seems—and you said that you were okay with me using the word fuck, right?"

She gave him a *seriously* look, but nodded.

"Which seems pretty fucking crazy, everything considered," he said.

"What is everything you're considering?" Tess asked. "Besides the huge ego that won't let you believe someone could get over you, of course."

He narrowed his eyes. "*Considering* that you've wanted a relationship with me as long as we've known each other, and now I'm here, living in the same town, and very much interested."

She nodded. "Okay, well, the living-in-the-same-town thing would be okay if it wasn't Sapphire Falls."

He leaned on his crutch with a frown. "Why is that?"

"Because I don't plan to be here for long."

Bryan seemed to freeze at that. "I'm sorry?"

"I'm saving my money to leave. I love Sapphire Falls, but there's a big wide world out there." She paused. "There's no better way to appreciate where you are than to see all the other places you could be."

That was a quote. From Bryan. From his blog.

But if he recognized it, he didn't give any indication. "Where is it that you want to go?" he asked.

"Denver." It wasn't like it was a *secret*. Okay, it was kind of a secret. She hadn't told anyone because she didn't know how long it would take for her to save the money, and she hadn't known if she would get accepted into Jake's program, and she didn't really have a plan B. She also didn't want to talk about how serious the running had become. It wouldn't make sense to most people.

But it would to Bryan, a voice in her head said.

Yes, it would. And it broke her heart again that she couldn't share it all with him.

"Denver," he repeated as if sure he'd heard her wrong.

She chewed her bottom lip while he processed that.

"You're saving up money to move to *Denver*," he asked, his voice rising slightly.

"Yeah."

"Denver," he said again. "As in the city I just came *back* from?"

"Yes."

"Is that a coincidence, Tess?" he asked, his voice firm. "Tell me that you threw a *fucking* dart at a map and came up with Denver."

Well, at least he was over the swearing-in-front-of-her thing.

It wasn't exactly a *coincidence*. Jake Elliot lived in Denver, and she knew about Jake because of Bryan. "I have to admit that I became obsessed with the mountains because of you. I've wanted to go for a long time." There, that was true. And it didn't tell him things he didn't need to know.

No one needed to know about her running. With her not-so-secret crush on Bryan, everyone would assume it was because of him. She did *not* want that. Because she didn't have time to explain the complicated reality of how it kind of was because of him, but mostly wasn't. And no one would believe that anyway. Least of all Bryan himself. She'd humiliated herself more than enough in front of and because of him.

She was proud of what she'd accomplished with her running. And she didn't want people to think it was about anything other than *her* hard work. She didn't need praise or accolades. *She* knew what it was about. That's all that mattered.

Bryan stared at her for several heartbeats. "You've got to be fucking kidding me," he finally said. He moved swiftly, coming forward and sitting down on the coffee table right in front of her. "You were going to Denver for me, right, Tess?" he asked gruffly. "You were done waiting and you were going to make a move since I wasn't?"

She started to answer, but he wasn't done.

"That's amazing." He reached out and cupped her face. "You're amazing. You've loved me all these years. You've made me feel like a rock star even when I was feeling like a joke. And then when I woke up in the hospital, and I realized my life was about to change forever, the one bright spot was you. I knew I was coming home, and knowing you were here made it something to look forward to. I didn't worry about what I was giving up. Only what I was moving toward."

Holy...*crap*. Tess stared at him. What was *that*? What was she supposed to say to all of that? And of course, he was assuming it was all about him. That was partly her fault, she supposed. But she'd been over him for more than two years. She hadn't given him any indication that she was still all wrapped up in him, dreaming about him, *waiting for him* since he'd been back. For *over a year*, without saying a word about wanting her.

"Are *you* fucking kidding *me*?" she asked him.

That was clearly not the reaction he'd been expecting. "What?"

"You've been home for a *year* and *seven months*, Bryan. And you're telling me this *now*?"

It wouldn't have mattered. She would have still wanted to go to Denver to train even if he'd said this a year ago. But what the *hell* had taken him so long?

"I wasn't...ready. I was still doing rehab and trying to get settled, to show you I was serious about staying. Then I got hurt again."

He had kept her *waiting* because he was trying to prove to her that he was serious about *staying*? Tess couldn't believe this. Or how much she wanted more vodka.

"That's stupid," she told him.

"No. Listen, we're talking about forever here. I knew you weren't a girl to mess around with. But now I'm ready. No messing around. For good. For real."

She looked into the green eyes that she had lived to see in the hallways at school every day of her junior high and high school career. Dammit.

"I'm going to Denver, Bryan," she told him. "I...have to."

"Why? What's in Denver now?"

Because he wasn't there. Oh, she knew exactly what he meant. And a piece of her heart smiled. That was Bryan. Things worked out for him. Looking at him in a wheelchair after a bad accident in the mountains might not seem that way to an outsider. But to anyone who knew Bryan even a little knew that he was fine. He looked at everything with optimism and the knowledge that he could learn and grow from anything. He was amazing that way.

But his eternal optimism also lent itself to thinking that everything would always work out and he'd always get his way in the end.

It was probably incredibly hard for him to imagine a world where Tessa didn't want to do whatever she could to be with him. She'd done what she could to be a part of his life for almost as long as they'd known each other.

But she'd very specifically *not* mooned all over him since he'd come home this time. She'd been careful to treat him like she did all of the other guys in Sapphire Falls.

"I want to travel, Bryan. I want to try new things, meet new people, have some amazing experiences." She didn't want to mention his travel posts. He'd given her a taste of the world, the hint she wanted to travel, but he wasn't the reason she was going now. "You should know what that's like. You've been to so many great places. Surely you can understand why I want that too."

"Really? You've always seemed so settled and happy here." He looked genuinely perplexed.

"I have been happy here," she felt compelled to say. "But there's so much more out there."

"Why have you never gone?"

She looked him directly in the eye. Okay, new tactic. Maybe if he knew just exactly how wrapped up she'd been in him, he'd agree she needed a life. Like right now.

"I was waiting for *you* to realize all of this crap about how amazing I am, and for you to want to take me with you." She had been. Up until two and half years ago when she'd realized she could make her own dreams come true.

"But—" He huffed out a breath. "I realized how amazing you are a long time ago. I was waiting until I was ready to come home to do anything about it."

Well, so he'd been waiting a little too. That was nice.

Focus, Tess. You're not a pitiful teenager who grabs on to every little smile or hears what she wants to in what he says. You're a grown woman, with a plan and a life, and Bryan Murray was just a guy. A guy who was too late.

She sighed. This was all a lot harder to tell herself when he was right here, so big and hard and strong and warm. And when she'd had some vodka.

She really was a lightweight.

He hadn't *waited* for her. He'd seen the world, had tons of women, lived his life fully and well. She narrowed her eyes at that thought. She deserved all of that. Traveling *and* tons of men.

She cleared her throat. Everything she knew about sex

came from books. She was going to have to try a new genre if there were going to be *tons* of them.

"But you do understand me wanting to travel," she managed to say.

He looked pained for a moment. Then he nodded. "Yeah, of course I get it."

Tess pressed her lips together. Maybe he was going to leave her alone now. That was what she wanted. Then why did she feel a niggle of disappointment at hearing him agree with her?

He dropped his gaze to the floor between his feet. "I'm sorry I can't show you the world, Tess."

Aw, dammit. She felt a prickle of tears at the back of her eyes. She was sorry too. She was eager to see the Grand Canyon and the Rocky Mountains and the Pacific Ocean and the black sand in Hawaii. But there was a part of her that knew it would have been even better with him. "You didn't even know I wanted to see the world."

He lifted his head. "No, I didn't." He gave a short laugh. "I've been completely focused on the idea that you *didn't* want to leave Sapphire Falls."

She wanted to reach out to him so badly. "We're just at two different places," she said, her own voice sounding a little gruff.

"I would have loved showing you some of the awesome places I've been," he said.

Her heart cracked a little and she just nodded, because she wasn't sure her voice would work. It was one thing for her to have realized on her own that Bryan wouldn't be with her, but it felt way worse to hear him say it.

"You don't want to travel anymore?" she asked.

It had occurred to her, of course, that he could still travel. It wasn't like he was bedridden. But he'd been so intent on settling in Sapphire Falls. He hadn't just moved back. He'd bought a house, bought a business, thrown himself in to town activities and, most of all, he talked all the time about how great it was to be back, and how this had always been his plan and how he was happy he'd seen and done so much, and that the accident had been the universe's way of telling him it was time to settle down.

That didn't mean she'd been hanging on his every word. He owned the only bar in town and was there a lot. And Bryan talked openly, candidly and loudly about his life, his feelings, his thoughts...everything.

"I could, I guess," he said. "But I've already taken all the trips on my bucket list and seen those places the best way. I've seen the Italian countryside from the back of a bike and I've run along back roads in Yellowstone. I've hiked in Ireland and climbed in the Grand Canyon. I think I'm ruined for any typical touristy trip."

She believed him. She'd felt like she was there with him, reading his words about his travels. She wanted to do it the same way he had. No question.

The money she was saving was not just to move to Denver and pay a coach, it was so she could enter these races and travel to these places and really experience them. She wanted to replicate the way Bryan had traveled. On the rough days running the roads around Sapphire Falls, she would picture Bryan's photographs and remember his words and be able to imagine she was running outside of Paris or along the beach in Honolulu.

Now she wanted to see it for herself.

"I'm sorry you've had to give that up," she said sincerely.

"I'm not," he said. "I did all of that. I'm ready for a new adventure."

She scoffed at that. "In Sapphire Falls?"

He nodded. "Yeah."

Tess realized, as the back of her neck tingled, that he meant *her*. Oh boy. "Settling down is an adventure?"

"You say settling down like it's a bad thing," he chided. "Staying in one place can be a lot of fun too."

Why did her mind go instantly to her *bed* as a place that it could be fun to stay? Oh, yeah—Bryan. "I wouldn't say it's *adventurous* though."

"Oh, honey, an adventure is really just something you haven't done before."

She was pretty sure he was referring to sex. "Well, for me, that list is long." That was true for adventures and for sex.

"Yeah, that's the best thing I've heard in a long time."

The way he said it, and the way her nipples and other parts responded to it, she knew he definitely was referring to sex. She immediately blushed.

He moved, sliding onto the couch next to her. He turned toward her and rested his arm on the back of the couch, his fingertips only a millimeter from her neck. Tess had the urge to do a not-so-subtle cat stretch up against those fingers.

"No need to be embarrassed, Tess," he told her. "I might not be able to show you the wonders of the world, but there are a lot of wonders I *can* show you."

She swallowed hard. Yep, that had to be about sex. Her mind flashed to the against-the-wall stuff that she'd been imagining. It was her favorite thing in the books. But suddenly, with Bryan, her couch seemed just fine.

"But I'm leaving," she said. She barely recognized the husky voice as her own.

"All the more reason to get to this."

She wet her lips and loved the way Bryan's eyes flared with heat. "You wouldn't use sex as a way to get me to stay would you?" she asked.

He leaned in and wrapped a big hand around the back of her neck. "Oh, I didn't promise I wouldn't try to get you to stay."

His hot breath was on her mouth, and she instinctively

turned toward it. "You understand that I want to see the world though? Do new things."

"Tess, you can see the world and do new things. Take trips. Go places. Experience it. And then come back to me."

Dammit. She didn't want to be romanced with sweet words and soft touches. But wow, how did a girl not melt *a little* at that?

Still, she wasn't talking about vacations or long weekends on the beach or shopping in Paris or sightseeing in Washington D.C. She was talking about really *being* in other places. Taking the back roads, finding the out-of-the-way places, experiencing the cultures and the food and the people. And running. Training in the flat plains of Nebraska was not the same as training in the mountains.

Bryan would get that. She knew he would. She doubted if Bryan had ever been on a tour bus of any kind ever. He didn't want to see the things he could look up online or read about in other people's books. He'd made his own experiences.

So, yeah, he'd understand. If she could bring herself to admit that she'd read and listened to every word he'd ever said on the subject.

That wasn't going to happen today.

"But for now, I'm going to concentrate on you doing new things right here," he said.

He ran his thumb up and down the side of her neck, and he could have just as easily been touching her breasts if her reaction was any indication. She moaned softly and arched toward him.

"You really like this virgin thing, don't you?" she asked.

"You have *no* idea."

"Why? What's that about?"

"Knowing that no one else has ever..." He cleared his throat. "Tess, I can't even tell you how much I love knowing that no one else has ever touched you the way I'm going to touch you."

She'd never even felt some of the parts of her body that tightened when he said that.

"You sound pretty sure you're going to be touching me."

"Oh, I'm *very* sure about that."

She cocked an eyebrow, even though it felt like every cell in her body was straining to be closer to him.

"Come on, Tess," he said with a slow, sexy grin. "This has been building up since I stole you from Ty."

"We were five," she said with a choked little laugh. "And I don't think Ty wanted me for his girlfriend."

"Well, you don't know Ty as well as I do," he said, running his thumb up and down her neck again.

The rasp of the rougher skin of his thumb against her skin made goose bumps erupt and skitter down her arm.

"You didn't know Ty then," she said, trying to keep her mind on his words. "You two met that day for the first time."

All of her reasons for not wanting to have Bryan touch her *all over* had disappeared from her brain, so she thought she should at least try to carry on a conversation.

"Guys know some things instinctively," he said. "Like when another guy is moving in on the girl that's supposed to be *his*."

His.

God, for so long she'd wanted to be his. In every way.

But that had been back when she'd been a sad little stalker girl.

She was over that. She was moving to Denver even though Bryan had moved home. That wasn't the action of a stalker girl at all. That was the opposite of sad and stalkery, in fact.

"So what do you say, Tess?" Bryan asked, snapping her back to the moment. "You up for an adventure with me in the here and now?"

He leaned in, putting his lips against her neck, and Tessa felt the heat shoot through her to her toes.

"I've thought about this for a long time," she told him.

She felt him smile against her neck. "I know."

Again, she almost laughed. That was such a Bryan thing to say. But she suddenly felt the flutter of butterflies unlike any she'd felt before. Not good ones. Bad ones. Very bad.

She couldn't do this. Not like this. He was going to be sweet. He was going to seduce her romantically. He was going to go slow and take care of her. He was going to be concerned with her being a virgin and the idea that he wanted her to be the mother of his children. He was going to kiss her like he had in his office the other night instead of *ravishing* her.

Dammit. She wanted some ravishing.

Slow and romantic seductions were *not* what she'd been imagining while she read her romance novels and listened to the guys joke about Bryan's exploits. Of course, none of them had known Tess was listening. Heaven forbid they say something scandalous in front of sweet Tess.

Biologically or physically or whatever, she might be a virgin. But she had a dirty mind. And she wanted to use it.

But Bryan could barely say the word fuck around her. And frankly, she couldn't take that. Not from the star of her naughty dreams.

She wanted Bryan to give her the hot, world-rocking fantasy she'd been...well, fantasizing about all this time. If he didn't, she was going to be devastated. Truly. It would ruin her crush forever. And that crush was as much a part of her as her love for peanut butter chocolate chip cookies and Miranda Lambert.

She couldn't let Bryan Murray *make love* to her.

"Bryan?"

"Yeah?"

He softly kissed her neck and trailed his lips to her collarbone.

Okay, soft kisses weren't really where she wanted to go, but that wasn't so bad.

"I can't do this like this."

He stopped, his lips still on her skin but no longer moving.

Slowly, he lifted his head and looked into her eyes. "You don't have to be nervous, Tess. I'll take care of you."

She laughed at that, but it wasn't funny. It wasn't funny at all. Of course he'd take care of her. That was the problem.

"I know." She pushed away from him and scrambled to her feet. It was warm and comfortable in Bryan's arms. Having his lips against *any* of her was hardly torturous. But this wasn't what she wanted. Warm and comfortable wasn't what she wanted.

She wanted *hot* and...not comfortable. Tess frowned. That wasn't quite right.

She wanted...out of her comfort zone. Yes. That sounded better.

And it was time for her to get what she wanted. To stop waiting around and living vicariously through someone else. Bryan had done the traveling she wanted to do. Bryan had had the hot sex she wanted to have. She wanted things for herself. Real things. No more fantasies. She wanted to experience what she could and have her own memories—hot shower sex, hiking in the mountains, hot dining-room-table sex, running in Rome, eating at a roadside pub in Ireland, hot we-could-get-caught-but-don't-care sex, photos by a waterfall in Hawaii.

But she was a virgin in Sapphire Falls at the moment, and it still felt right to think that Bryan Murray would be her first. In this town. She wanted to be a grab-the-moment girl. This was a moment definitely worth grabbing.

Bryan was watching her with some concern. "You okay?"

"Yes." She said it with conviction and was proud of it.

"You sure?"

"I want you."

That made him straighten. But he didn't say anything. After a moment, he shifted, leaning back on the couch and propping his elbows on top of the cushion behind him, watching her with a heat Tess swore she could feel across the few feet that separated them.

"You can have me, honey."

He was the picture of patience and pure *maleness*.

Was that a word? Tess wasn't sure suddenly. Hell, she wasn't sure *word* was a word at this point. But it did not matter. Maleness was a word now. And it was sitting on her couch.

She was definitely doing this.

"Bryan."

"Yes, Tessa?"

"I'm not getting naked until you promise to say fuck at least once. And I'm definitely going to need you to suck on my nipples."

Heat flared in his eyes.

"Tess?"

She wet her lips. "Yeah?"

"Come here."

With that, she climbed into his lap.

His hands went to her hips, and the moment he touched her, the bravado left her.

"Is this okay?" she asked, straddling his thighs and resting her hands on his shoulders.

He gave her a smile that was somehow tender and hot at the same time. "Never been more okay, ever."

And so maybe he didn't need to use the word fuck. His words seemed to work for her anyway.

"You with me, honey?" he asked.

She was staring at his mouth and couldn't seem to stop. And damn, that honey thing was good too. The closest he'd ever gotten to a nickname or endearment had been Tessy before this. But honey was good. She liked honey.

She nodded. "I'm with you."

Because, no matter what else she wished for, she would always be *with* Bryan.

"Good." He gave her a little nod. "Then come here."

"I'm already here." She was straddling his lap, but she was holding herself up off of him.

"Oh, no," he said with a half-smile. "You can be a lot more *here* than that."

She looked at his fly. She'd been trying not to look at it. Or stare at it. Or drool over it. But now she couldn't help it. She looked at his fly, then back up to his face.

"Yep," he said, his smile full now. "Come here."

She took a deep breath and inched closer to his torso.

"Relax, honey," he told her gruffly.

"I'm fine."

He chuckled. "You're holding yourself so tight you can barely breathe."

"No, I'm—"

"Relax, Tess." He squeezed her hips. "It's me. This is going to be good. I promise."

He was right. Everything in her was tight and nearly vibrating. But she wasn't *worried* exactly. "I'm not tense because I'm scared," she assured him. "This isn't a virgin thing."

He chuckled. "Okay. Good to know. So what's the problem?"

She looked into his eyes and saw the humor and affection that she'd seen so often over the years. Humor and affection wasn't exactly what she wanted him to feel, but she'd seen more than that earlier. A heat she never would have guessed she could make him feel. That gave her the boost of self-confidence she needed.

"I can't believe that my ass is actually going to touch a part of you."

She'd surprised him. She could tell by the pause and then the short bark of laughter. "Oh, honey, there is going to be so much of you touching so much of me."

The rest of the tension left her body as she felt her muscles melt. They *all* wanted him touching them. All at once. Now.

She sat down on his lap without further ado.

"That's right," he said gruffly. "Now put your hands on me."

She did. Not a moment's hesitation that time. She ran her hands up his chest, over his shoulders and down his arms. The thick muscles were hard under her touch and so warm. Even through the cotton of his shirt, she could feel how warm his skin was.

"Now kiss me."

Tess hesitated. The kissing thing. This was where she'd gotten tripped up last time. The kissing had been too *nice* and sweet the other night. She wanted to see his chest. She wasn't sure she wanted to kiss him.

And wasn't that the stupidest thing?

"Can you take your shirt off?" she asked, studying the gorgeous bulge of his biceps under the edge of the sleeve.

Bryan cleared his throat. "*You* can take my shirt off," he told her.

She looked up. He wasn't smiling now. Huh. But she really did want to see his chest. She slipped her hands under the bottom of the shirt and slid it up, revealing his hard abs, his ribs, the soft dusting of hair over his well-defined pecs and then up over his head. He moved his arms only enough to let her get the shirt off, then he put his elbows right back on the couch behind him as if fully comfortable being naked in front of her.

He was magnificent. Not that Tess had seen a lot of naked males, but she'd certainly seen shirtless ones. One of the best things about living in Sapphire Falls was that there were lots of farm boys here, and farm boys went shirtless a lot.

She'd even seen Bryan shirtless before. Swimming, playing basketball down at the park, biking, running. But wow, having him *right here. Under her.* Within touching distance...

Hey, he was within touching distance.

Immediately, Tess flatted her palms on his chest again, running her hand over his hot skin and hard muscles. Muscles that tensed under her touch. She noticed that he gripped his hands into fists and tensed his jaw, but otherwise didn't move. He let her explore—chest, shoulders, arms, abs.

She looked up at him as she neared his fly.

As if reading her mind, he said, "Go ahead, honey. It's all yours."

It was like Christmas, her birthday and the first day of summer vacation all rolled into one. She ran her hand down the front of his jeans, over the steel-like flesh behind it. Bryan sucked in a soft breath while Tess blew one out.

Wow. She liked that.

As she traced his shape behind the denim, her thoughts went to all the hot romance novels she'd read. The ones she liked best used the word cock. And they talked about the guys' cocks being big. She had nothing to compare to in real life, but Bryan felt absolutely perfect to her.

"Tess," he said huskily. "You're killing me, honey."

She looked up. "Sorry." She kept running her hand up and down his length though.

He gave her that sexy half-smile again. "Killing me in a good way. Kiss me."

Dammit. There was that kissing thing again. Okay, well, she wanted it to be different than it had been in his office. Maybe she needed to show him that. She'd read enough romance to know something about hot kisses.

She kept her hand against his cock but leaned in and ran her other hand behind his head and into his hair. She touched her lips to his and ran her tongue along his lower lip.

She felt the low growl rumble through his chest where it was pressed against hers. A thrill shot through her and she opened her mouth.

But Bryan didn't follow her lead. He kept his lips closed even as he tipped his head slightly to press their mouths together more fully. Tess didn't *hate* the kiss, but she wanted more. She sensed he was holding back, and she knew exactly why.

She pulled back. "If I put my hand *in* your pants, can I get some tongue?" she asked.

Bryan's eyes widened. "What?"

"What do I have to do to get you worked up enough to *kiss* me?" she asked. She reached for the hem of her tank top, for the first time realizing that she was dressed in only a tank, bra, cotton shorts and panties. She ripped her shirt off. "Does that help?"

Bryan's hands were clenched tighter now as he took in the sight. "Tess—"

"Or do you need this too?" She pushed off his lap and stripped out of her shorts. It wasn't until they hit the floor next to the coffee table that she realized she was now almost naked in front of Bryan Murray.

She was never almost naked in front of *anyone*, not to mention doing it in front of her biggest crush of all time. She worked on *not* sucking her stomach in. That was something she'd been trying to be less self-conscious about. She wasn't fat. She was curvy. She took care of her body but, yeah, she still had a little tummy. But that was okay. She needed to love herself as she was.

But dang, in full light with Bryan looking her over slowly from head to toe, it was really hard not to suck in.

Hell, it was hard not to run screaming from the room.

"Jesus, Tess." He breathed out.

She was going to just tell herself that was a good *Jesus, Tess.* She really had no idea. Maybe she'd just surprised him.

She glanced down at her light blue silk bra and plain white panties. She hadn't been expecting company. Especially company that would be seeing her underwear.

"Now will you *really* kiss me?" she asked, hoping to distract him from the mismatched, distinctively unsexy bra and panty set—that wasn't even a set.

Maybe she should take them off too so they wouldn't remind him that she didn't know that much about being sexy. Of course, with them off, her large breasts wouldn't be pushed up and her tummy wouldn't be covered—by anything.

She wasn't sure she could actually suck hard enough to make *that* okay.

Finally, Bryan pulled his gaze to her face. "What does that mean?" he asked.

"The really-kissing-me thing?" she asked, propping a hand on her hip, frustrated anew and less concerned about her panties.

"Yeah."

"I don't want this sweet, lips-only stuff. You kiss like you're fourteen and don't know what you're doing."

Bryan's eyebrows shot up. "I *what*?"

She nodded. "You kissed me on the lips once, and I know that's not how a guy kisses a girl he wants to have sex with. I want hot, wet and hungry."

His eyebrows went even higher. "Hot, wet and hungry?"

"Yes. Dammit. Like the Ferris wheel five years ago."

He shook his head. "I am *trying* to kiss you..."

"Nicely," she supplied. "Sweetly. Romantically."

He nodded. "Yeah."

"Well, you kind of suck at nice, sweet and romantic," she told him bluntly. "But," she added as he looked offended, "I'll bet you do hot, wet and hungry *really* well."

Bryan seemed to be thinking that over while studying her face. Then his gaze dropped and went over the rest of her. Thoroughly. Slowly.

And *there* was the hunger part.

"Come here," he finally said.

6

O*h, please, please, please*, Tess thought as she happily
moved forward and climbed back into his lap. She sat
waiting, not sure what she should do.

"You want hot, wet and hungry, huh?" he asked. He moved
his arms, dropping his hands onto her thighs and running
them up and down.

Thank God she'd shaved that morning.

Really—did women who were having regular sex have to
shave *every day*? And remember to match up their panties and
bras? This might be a lot of work.

Then he ran his hands around to her butt, and she realized
that she had never been so happy that she'd started running as
she was in that moment.

Tess knew her butt was a lot tighter than it had been before
the running. It was still a little wider than she liked, and there
was no question that she had hips, but she was surprisingly fine
with having Bryan appreciate the swells under his hands. He
seemed to like them. He kneaded her flesh and she felt her
body getting hotter.

He slid his hands up her back, running them up and down either side of her spine. She arched slightly, resisting the urge to purr.

"Take your bra off."

She did hesitate for one breath. She had large breasts. She needed heavy-duty sports bras for running. She'd had to order them online. She had gone down a bra size or two since she'd started losing weight, but she was by no means perky up there. *But guys like breasts*, she reminded herself. Maybe Bryan was a breast guy.

Tess reached back, undid the hooks and let the bra slide down her arms.

Bryan sucked in a deep breath as she tossed the bra to the side, leaving her naked but for her panties.

She was *naked* except for her panties on *Bryan's* lap.

This couldn't be real.

But when he brought his hands around to cup her breasts, brushing his thumbs over the stiff tips, it definitely *felt* real.

"Damn, Tess, you're beautiful."

She liked that a lot. And it made her nipples stiffen even further.

"Harder," she almost whispered.

Bryan's eyes became a deep green she'd never seen before. But he said, "Let's take it easy, honey."

Dammit. She didn't want easy. Her hands flew up to cover his. "Please."

"Tess—"

"*Please*." She knocked one of his hands out of the way and took her nipple between her thumb and finger, tugging rather than brushing over it. Her pelvic muscles tightened and she gave a soft moan.

"Holy shit," Bryan muttered. But he did mimic her action that time, pinching her right nipple.

ERIN NICHOLAS

She moaned louder. "Yes." It was so much better when he did it.

He leaned in and cupped the breast she was fondling, plumping it and bringing the nipple to his mouth. Tessa's head fell back as he licked and then sucked gently.

"*Harder*," she told him again.

He didn't hesitate or argue that time. He sucked harder, and Tess found herself pressing down in his lap in an attempt to relieve the pressure building between her legs.

He played with her, using his fingers, tongue and mouth for a few minutes. When he leaned back, his eyes were dark and his breathing uneven.

Tess wasn't sure she'd ever breathe normally again. Because even when this was over she was going to replay it constantly.

She ran her hand over the hard ridge of his erection, and he cursed. He grabbed her hand. "Can't take that, honey."

She frowned. "That's not good."

"It's so good. But I need some control here."

"No, you don't," she said quickly. She wanted him out of control. She wanted things hot and fast and wild. Maybe she could push him to that point. "Just go for it. Do whatever you want. Lose control like crazy."

He chuckled softly but shook his head. "No way. This is your first time. That's not how it's going to go down."

She huffed out a breath, and he laughed louder.

"Trust me, Tess. We'll get to everything. I promise."

"Tonight?" She suddenly had a suspicion that was *not* what he meant.

And sure enough, he shook his head. "Not tonight. But we're going to have some fun."

"So you *don't* want to take my virginity?"

He sucked in a sharp breath. There really was something about that word, or the concept of her virginity, that got to him.

"Tess, there is no way in *hell* I'm *not* going to be that guy," he

106

told her so sincerely she felt her toes curl. "But we are *not* going to rush into that."

Well, crap. He was going to seduce her. He was going to make it special. Damn him.

"Oh, wait—do you need one of those pump things or pills or something?" she asked as the thought occurred...without *really* thinking. She'd googled sex and spinal cord injuries about a year and a half ago. Before she realized that Bryan being back in Sapphire Falls meant *nothing* for her sex life.

But in her defense, he'd muddled her brain with horniness.

He pulled back quickly, taking his amazing mouth farther away from her breasts. That was too bad. "What?"

"I read that with spinal cord injuries, sometimes guys need help with pumps or pills to get an erection," she said, blushing to the tips of her toes. But the guy had had her nipple in his mouth. Surely they could talk frankly about this stuff. They kind of needed to, didn't they? This was one part of this whole thing that had her a little intimidated. She didn't have experience with guys with regular erections. and she sure didn't know about how to help it along in a situation like Bryan's.

He coughed. "I, uh—"

"You don't have to be embarrassed," she said quickly.

"I'm not embarrassed," he said. He shoved a hand through his hair.

A hand that had just been making her nipples feel really good.

Dammit, she needed to stop talking.

"I haven't needed help for a while," he said. "There was a short period when I needed pills to sustain long enough. But that's been good for..." He coughed again. "It doesn't seem to be a problem."

"Oh." She shrugged. "Okay. I probably wouldn't know the difference anyway."

He gave a short laugh. "I think you'd notice if I could only make it halfway through."

She tipped her head. "Would I?"

"Uh, yeah." He put a hand on the back of her neck and pulled her forward. "But I think we're going to be okay."

"Well, if you need...anything..."

"Tess, can we stop talking about my potential erectile dysfunction?"

"Sure. I mean, you could start talking dirty about what you want to do with me," she said hopefully.

He shook his head as he looked at her, almost like he couldn't believe she was saying this stuff. "I don't know if I can talk dirty to you, Tess."

At that her shoulders slumped. "That is *not* good."

"You want dirty talk, huh?"

"I do," she told him enthusiastically. "I mean, I think I do. I love reading it."

He ran his hand up and down her bare back. "Why don't you tell me about some of this dirty talk?"

Oh, he wasn't sure they were on the same dirty-talk page. Got it.

"Fuck me. Hard. Deep. I'm so wet for you I can hardly stand it. I need you, Bryan. Please. Make me come."

Bryan went completely still, his eyes flaring hot, his breathing choppy.

That wasn't a direct quote from anything, but it was in the same ballpark.

It seemed that maybe she'd done okay with it.

"Tess?"

"Yeah?"

"Take your panties off."

Yep, this was definitely going in the right direction. She pushed back off his lap and shimmied her panties to the floor.

"Now get back up here."

She slid back onto his lap and his hands went directly to her breasts. This time she didn't have to ask him to tug or suck harder. He did, almost as if he was having a hard time holding back. Which was awesome. He skimmed his hands over her back, then down to her waist. He caressed the curve of her hips, slid up and down her thighs and had her squirming in minutes. Tess simply put her hands on his shoulders and held on. He seemed fine with that.

"You're gorgeous," he told her. "I love your body. You're so soft. Your skin is so soft. You smell amazing." He just kept up with the sexy sweet talk as he touched her, kissed her body, pressed her down against his body.

But he didn't say one dirty word. And he didn't take off any of his clothes.

"Bryan, need more," she said.

"I know, honey. I know."

"Take your pants off."

He didn't chuckle. He didn't smile. He shook his head. "Not tonight."

She stared at him. "*What*? I thought you wanted to have sex!"

"Oh, Tess, I'm not sure I've ever wanted anything as much. But not tonight."

"So I'm just...you're not going to...you're just going to get me all wound up and leave?"

He shook his head. "I'm not going to *just* do anything." He ran a big, hot hand over her stomach.

Tess sucked in a breath.

"I'm going to make you come. But this is our warm up. This is just a taste of what's ahead of us."

"But, I..." She lost every single thought in her head, including the ability to even form words, when he ran his hand lower and cupped her, sliding his middle finger over her clit.

The touch was a strange combination of relief and torture.

It was as if all the other touches had led up to that one, and at the same time, she needed so much more.

He ran his finger over her clit again and again, pressing slightly each time. He watched her face as if he'd never seen anything more fascinating. "That's it, honey," he praised as she moaned and moved against his hand. Then he slid lower and eased the tip of a finger into her. She gasped.

"God, you're so tight," he groaned. "This is going to be amazing."

Her fingers dug into his shoulders. "*Bryan.*"

"That's right. It's me. It's all me. And I'm going to make you feel so good."

"I already do."

"This is just a little bit. There's so much more."

Instinctively, she moved against his hand again and more of his finger slid into her.

"Tess," he said tightly. "Easy, honey."

She shook her head wildly. "More."

"We'll get there, but—"

She grabbed his wrist and pressed his finger deeper as she moved, the whole digit thrusting into her. "*Yes.*"

"God, you're killing me," he muttered.

She got the impression he wasn't really talking to her. Which worked, considering she had a lot of great stuff to concentrate on other than trivial things like words and sentences.

Tess moved against his hand, the pressure of his finger so delicious she thought she could stay right there like that forever. Then he slid it out and back in. She let her head fall back. No, *that* was where she could stay.

Then he moved it faster, and *that* was amazing.

"Okay. Let's do this," he said. He circled his thumb over her clit while pumping his finger into her and leaning in to capture a nipple in his lips. Her hand flew to his head and she gripped his hair as sensations rolled over her. "Bryan!"

"Go with it," he coaxed. "Let go."

Her body felt like it was tightening more and more, like a rubber band being stretched farther and farther. Until, finally, it snapped. She seemed to come apart inside, pleasure coursing through her like she'd never imagined. She wanted it to go on and on, and it did for a few minutes, ripples and waves washing over her. But over time, it gentled and faded.

Bryan held her after she slumped against his chest, stroking her back. She could still feel the hard ridge of his cock under her, and in spite of her orgasm of only moments before, she wanted it again. With *that*.

"It never feels like that when I do it," she said against his neck.

His laugh vibrated through her. "I think I'm glad. But I wouldn't mind seeing how you do it."

She pushed back. Okay, that was a little naughty. At least for Bryan with her. "Really?"

He stroked a hand over her head and chuckled, though it sounded tight. "Um, yeah."

"Okay."

He shook his head, as if in wonder. Was it her enthusiasm?

"Do you use your fingers or a vibrator?" he asked roughly.

"I don't have a vibrator." She'd *almost* bought one so many times, but she'd never gotten up the nerve.

And she realized that she was right back to being a big dork.

She thought she'd gotten over that a little. But here she was, thirty years old, no sex life, no boyfriend, a twenty-some-year-long crush, without even a vibrator. She didn't have a career— she just had a bunch of jobs—she'd never really been anywhere, she'd never really done anything noteworthy.

Tess felt her face getting hot. She started to push back from him, but Bryan tightened his arms around her.

"Hey, what's going on?"

"Nothing. I just realized...how...embarrassing this all is," she finished miserably.

"There is *nothing* to be embarrassed about," he said, brushing her hair back from her face again. "Tess, you're amazing."

She rolled her eyes. "You mean I'm *sweet*."

Bryan sighed. "You have no idea how much more sweetness most of us need, honey."

She pushed on his chest again, and he loosened his hold. "Either you get less dressed or I'm going to get more dressed," she told him.

Hot, dirty sex would change up her M.O. She was a thirty-year-old virgin with a stupid crush and no great stories to tell. She *had* to change *something*. She couldn't get to Denver yet. She couldn't leave Sapphire Falls *yet*. But she could change the sad-little-virgin thing.

"Not tonight," Bryan said. Though he didn't seem especially enthusiastic about it.

"Fine." She reached for her clothes and pulled them on without her bra or panties. "I'll buy a vibrator tomorrow." And she would. Absolutely. It was time.

She started to turn away, but Bryan leaned and grabbed her wrist before she could. "Tess."

She looked at him with a sigh.

"This is going to happen. With us. And it's going to be amazing. But it's going to happen the right way."

She shrugged. "Maybe it shouldn't. Maybe I need to get over yo—"

"No." He got to his feet swiftly. "Neither of us is getting over anything. This is going to happen."

She was supposed to already be over him. Her shoulders

slumped as she finally admitted the truth. She was never going to be over him.

"Let me take you out tomorrow night," he said.

"You mean on a romantic date?"

He smiled. "Yeah."

"Candles? Dinner? Dancing?"

"Yes." He seemed very happy about the idea. "Whatever you want."

She felt the regret filling her chest. How could someone feel *regret* about anything after having an orgasm?

"But see, that's not true," she told him. "If this was going the way I wanted it to, we'd *both* be naked and sweaty and spent right now."

"We'll get there." He sounded like he was gritting his teeth.

Bryan Murray had been calling the shots—or rather *not* calling the shots—between them from day one. He'd gotten his way for far too long. It was her turn.

"Really? About the time you get comfortable saying 'bend over, Tess. I want to fuck you from behind'?"

His nostrils flared and his eyes narrowed. "Why can't things be sweet and romantic, Tess? What's wrong with that?"

"What's wrong with wanting hot, dirty sex?" she shot back.

"I've done the hot, dirty sex thing!" he exclaimed. "Now *I* want more than that."

Tess felt her throat thicken with emotion. "I guess we just want different things."

"No." He shook his head adamantly. "There is so much more I want to give you than orgasms. Sex is...sex. But a long-term, serious relationship—dating and making love and making a home and building a family—that's an adventure neither of us has been on. Let's do that together."

She stared at him. There was no way he'd just said that.

"Did you just offer to get me pregnant as a substitution for me traveling the world?"

He blanched. "Well, not—not like that." He huffed out a breath. "I thought you wanted all of that too. I thought that's what you were here waiting for."

She felt her mouth drop open. Whoa. A million thoughts spun through her head. Then she snapped it shut. "You think you want me because *I* want to marry *you*," she said. "You're looking for a new adventure—this family-and-settling-down thing—and you've had to give up your career of inspiring people to make their dreams come true. So, of course, your mind went to me. Because I'm Tess. I've always been here, the same girl, wanting the same things forever. This way, you can settle down and make someone's life-long dream come true."

She should be mad. She was a little...shocked. But it made sense. This was Bryan. He cared about her. It might not be passionate, crazy love, but he did care. And making her happy, after all this time, would be appealing to him.

Tess felt her heart softening. And cracking slightly. She wasn't staying here anyway, but even if she was, she didn't want to be his good deed.

She put her hand against his cheek. "You'll find someone who wants all of that with you." Her heart thumped as something else occurred to her. He'd had hook-ups, but he hadn't had a relationship since the accident. Was he afraid he wouldn't find someone serious? Because of the accident? "Your accident won't matter to the right girl, Bryan."

He frowned, looking confused and hurt at the same time. "My accident doesn't matter to *you*."

It didn't. This was Bryan. "No. But you can't cling to me just because of that."

God, she couldn't handle thinking that he really thought no one else would love him the way she did. Had. Okay, did.

"I'm *clinging* to you?"

"I am sweet," she said. She knew three women in Sapphire Falls who would marry him tomorrow, give him ten kids and grow old with him. But he wanted Tess because she was a sure thing and because he thought he was saving her from her sad spinsterhood. "I'm sweet enough to tell you goodnight before this gets even more complicated." If he took her virginity, he'd never feel like he could leave her alone.

She walked to the door, still feeling tingles between her legs as her shorts rubbed over the sensitive skin that Bryan had stirred to life.

Dammit.

She opened the door.

Bryan came to her, his expression nearly impossible to read.

Tess swallowed hard and made herself not look away. She was throwing Bryan Murray out of her house. After he'd given her an orgasm. Her first orgasm ever with someone else. A sob caught in her chest. She really needed him to go.

He stopped in front of her. "Tess—"

"If you care about me at all, please go before I start crying."

He hesitated. She could see the battle on his face. He didn't want to leave her. He hated that she was on the verge of tears. He *did* care.

He looked at her for a moment, then cupped the back of her head and pulled her in to his chest. "I definitely want you to *care* about me and what happened and what I can and can't do. Because if you didn't care about me, my world would be a very different place." He kissed her forehead. "This isn't over."

Then he left.

But she didn't cry. She wasn't sad. She was angry. So, no, she wasn't going to cry. She was going to make her dreams of travel and marathons and high-level, specialized training come true. And she was going to buy a vibrator.

But first she was going to have chocolate.

She completely bypassed the sugar-free pudding cups in the kitchen—there wasn't enough chocolate pudding, even the good stuff, in the world for this. She headed straight for the bag of chocolate kisses with almonds that she stashed in the back of her freezer for just such an emergency.

And thirty minutes and several little gold wrappers later, she had to admit that she'd been duped. All these years, she'd believed what she'd heard about chocolate producing the same endorphin high as an orgasm.

What a bunch of crap.

7

Tess was late getting to the fashion show rehearsal the next day, and all Bryan could think about was what if she'd left town late last night?

For Denver.

She fucking wanted to go to Denver.

And that had been only one of the many surprises from her last night.

She'd kicked him out of her house. After reassuring him that someone would love him someday. Tess Sheridan had turned him down for forever.

That was *not* how he'd expected last night to go.

He'd alternated between thinking all of that over and remembering her naked on his lap, coming apart for him.

He hadn't slept much.

And he *needed* to see her.

She had been right on with the things she'd said, he'd finally admitted. He'd been counting on Tess because he thought she was the epitome of the small-town girl who wanted a small-town, sweet, simple life. And, okay, because she'd loved him forever.

But was he only in this because she was easy? Because focusing on making a real relationship work and building a life in Sapphire Falls was better than focusing on his injury and the things he'd given up? Because he wanted to feel like someone's hero and he wanted to make Tess happy?

No.

Well, *yes*. He wanted to make her happy. But he wasn't rewarding her for waiting around for him. He wanted her. He wanted a relationship with her.

Had he quickly shifted his focus away from his losses to new things ahead? Yes. That was what he did. He coached people with that attitude and he applied it to himself. That didn't mean he was in denial.

He had a partial spinal cord injury—nothing could change that. He'd rehabbed back to his maximum potential, but he'd never be back to one hundred percent—nothing could change that either. What good did it do to focus on that and wallow?

So he'd turned his attention to positive things, uplifting things, things that made him happy and hopeful.

Like Tess.

But he had to admit that seeing her now, not just sassy but able to say no to him, made him think of her differently. It was damned attractive. He liked a challenge and thinking that Tess might need to be actually won over made his heart beat faster. He'd wanted her in his life when she'd been sweet. Now he wanted her...bent over his desk.

Which sent him right into wondering if she was late because she was shopping for a vibrator, as she'd threatened.

She would have had to go to York, probably, but he wasn't sure York even had a shop that sold sex toys. It was hardly a big, fast-paced city. It was about six times the size of Sapphire Falls, but even so, it wasn't impossible that you could run into your first-grade teacher or your pastor on the downtown streets.

Coming out of a sex shop. With a vibrator in your bag. So, no, York might not have a sex shop.

Of course, Tess could have bought a vibrator online. But Bryan wasn't sure she knew that. Surely she did though, right? Didn't everyone know that? She wasn't a kid, she was just a little inexperienced.

Except for those romance novels. He liked the dirty talk that had come from them. He might need to get a hold of one of those so he could figure out what she knew exactly. Or thought she knew anyway.

And clearly, he'd been giving this whole thing a lot of thought.

Bryan tried to relax in his chair as he watched the ladies putting on the jewelry and hats that went with the summer wear they would be modeling.

Cora's hat was nice, if huge. Bright yellow with pink flowers and a pink ribbon trailing from the brim seemed a bit much to him, but what did he know? Stella was wearing a purple shawl with her blue dress. Ruby had green and orange on. Overall, it was very colorful.

And he didn't give one damn about it.

He wanted to see Tess. He *needed* to see Tess.

He'd left her last night. That was not something he did. He stuck. He worked through things until they were fixed. He was the pro at pep talks and giving people perspective and coaching them through. But this wasn't a big race, this wasn't a tough training week, this wasn't a loss that someone was trying to come back from.

This was a woman.

And she'd given him some stuff he'd needed to think about. She'd clearly believed the things she'd said. So much so, that for a little bit, he'd believed them too. But as he'd pondered if her sweetness had made her easy for him, and if that was the whole attraction for him, it was the passion and confidence he'd seen in her while she'd been telling him that he didn't need her that had made him certain Tessa was the girl for him. He'd been assuming a lot. And he was kind of enjoying being surprised. And he liked thinking that Tess would tell him no when he needed to hear no. Or that he was being an assuming ass.

He was a good guy, but he was under no illusions that he wouldn't definitely need someone to tell him he was being an ass again at some point in his life. He'd had his doubts about Tess being that person. He'd figured he would have to rely on Hailey and Ty for that. Maybe his sister. Maybe. But Caitlyn hung out in sweet-girl land a lot of the time too. Ty had been his shape-up-you're-being-a-dick advisor for years. Bryan had assumed Ty would keep the title and that Hailey would be a fantastic backup.

But Tess was clearly not overwhelmed by him or going to fall at his feet. She wouldn't put up with him being an ass. That was wonderful. If Tess could be comfortable calling him on any behavior that got out of hand, it meant that he didn't have to be so careful. He didn't have to walk on eggshells around her or treat her delicately. He wouldn't be a jerk on purpose, of course, but he could relax a little bit, be more natural, be himself.

He was still stunned that he was off-balance over Tessa. The woman he thought he knew all about.

He wanted to make love to this woman, not just have sex with her, and that was, as it turned out, the whole problem.

He'd spent many sleepless hours last night pondering that. After all, Tessa Sheridan had said words like hot, sweaty, sex, fuck and deep. She'd kept asking for more. When he hadn't given it, she'd *taken more*—playing with her own nipples, pushing his finger deeper. She knew what she wanted. She just hadn't had it. Yet.

She was a gorgeous, curvy, blonde contradiction. Sweet but sassy, innocent but demanding, the glue that kept

Sapphire Falls together but ready to move to the mountains and see the world. In love with him but preparing to leave him behind.

How was he supposed to *not* think about that?

Bryan had spent almost as many hours wondering if treating Tess sweetly was the wrong move as he had spent aroused and frustrated remembering having her in his lap, her beautiful bare body under his hands and mouth, making her moan and squirm and finally come apart.

The bottom line was he needed to see her. And his heart was going to stop if she walked in with a bag from a sex shop.

But surely she wouldn't bring the bag *here*, he thought, watching Dottie and Susan compare their sandals.

"Tess!" someone greeted just then.

Bryan turned on his chair so fast he almost slipped off and fell on his ass. Tess came into the room with a ball cap on her head, her hair pulled through the back, cut-off denim shorts, fitted white tee covered by an open button-down light pink shirt, flip-flops, and huge dark sunglasses.

"Hi everyone," she said.

But there was a definite lack of *Tess* in her tone. It wasn't bubbly and sunny and upbeat. She sounded tired.

Bryan turned back toward the stage with a smirk. He didn't want her feeling bad. Exactly. But he didn't mind knowing she'd lost some sleep last night too.

Especially if it was because she'd stayed up all night practicing giving herself orgasms. And thinking of him.

Bryan's body tightened immediately, and he had to clear his throat as she took the chair next to him.

"Morning."

"Hey," she said, not meeting his eyes.

"You're late."

"Yeah, I was finishing up at work."

"Work?"

She nodded. "Okay, girls, let's do this!" she called to the women onstage.

"I thought *this* was work," Bryan said.

She leaned over and set something on the floor. Bryan heard the rustle of plastic and he gritted his teeth. He could not look down. It was a bag of some kind, and in his mind it was full of vibrators and a chocolate body pen.

"This is work too," she agreed. "Okay, Dottie! You're first."

"This is work *too*?" he asked.

"Read your script, Bryan."

"Am I supposed to come on now?" Dottie yelled from the stage. "Or do I wait for him to read?"

"You wait for him," Tess told her. "Bryan, read."

"But I—"

"I can't hear you!" Dottie shouted.

Bryan gave a little growl, but he turned to the script and started reading.

They got about halfway through before Linda decided that she couldn't do her turn the way she wanted to at the front of the stage in the shoes she was wearing. A pow-wow commenced with all of the women passing their shoes around and trying them with the different outfits. And it didn't seem to matter if they matched or not. The stage was an explosion of color, and Bryan thought it really looked like they were going for the most *mis*matched concoctions they could come up with.

As they debated heel height and strap placement, Bryan turned to Tess.

"You okay?"

She'd pushed her sunglasses to the top of her head to perch on the brim of her cap. She wore no makeup and definitely looked tired, but she looked completely beautiful.

He remembered everything about the night before in one brief, hot, shining moment. The shape of her breasts, the silkiness of her skin, the taste of that skin, how tight and wet she'd been for him. And maybe most of all, the way she'd responded to him. And if his ego hadn't been enormous where Tess was concerned before, now he felt like the king of the world. Other than the thing about her kicking him out.

"I'm fine," she said.

As if commenting on her breakfast. Breakfast was fine. It was rarely amazing or life-changing. And she definitely didn't sound as if she felt amazing or as if her life had changed now.

Tess kept her eyes on the stage as Bryan watched her, biting back the first words that came to mind. Words like "bullshit" and "I can make you very okay".

He couldn't. Not yet. This would be her first time. He was going to be her first...and her last. No matter what she'd said or what she thought about him finding someone else.

Their first time called for something special.

"You sleep okay last night?" he asked instead of telling her about his romantic plan. But he couldn't leave it totally alone. He realized he really wanted her to have had as restless a night as he'd had.

She shrugged. "Sure." As if it was strange to think otherwise.

Sure.

Sure? Not only did he want her to have lost *a little* sleep over him, but he wanted her to acknowledge why he was asking. She had to have thought about what had happened on her couch. She had to have. She was a virgin. How many naked make-out sessions had she had?

"Last night was awesome, Tess."

That got her to look at him.

"Really? We're going to talk about that here? Now?"

He glanced at the stage and back at her. "It's all that's on my mind. Yours too, I'm guessing."

Tessa's eyes narrowed. "As a matter of fact, I've had a lot on my mind."

"About last night?"

"No, Bryan, not about last night."

He frowned.

"I've got an entire festival to organize. I have a kitchen remodel to finish in the next couple of weeks. I have yoga classes to teach." She swallowed and finished with, "And I sent an email last night that's been on my mind. So I'm sorry I haven't been mooning over you since last night, but I have a lot going on—an entire life actually—that isn't about you."

Before he could respond to that, she stood from her chair. "Girls?" she called. "I gotta get going. But you all look marvelous, and Bryan is going to stay and make sure everything is organized and ready to go."

Bryan sat forward in his chair. "What are you doing?"

She looked down at him. "Thought you wanted to help me. You finishing this up would be *very* helpful."

Damn. She had him. How could he say no? But if he said yes, she was hightailing her pretty little ass out of here, and God knew when he'd see her. "Go out with me tonight."

"I can't." She bent and picked up the bag she'd brought in with her. "I have other plans tonight."

"Tess—"

"Bryan, in third grade, when you asked me to babysit your dog's new puppies while you and your family went to that all-weekend baseball tournament, I did it. And in seventh grade, when you called me up and asked me to come listen to your band practice and then had me putting stickers on CD cases for four hours, I did it. And in tenth grade, when you came over at midnight and asked if I would say that Heather Vilson was spending the night with me so her parents wouldn't know you two were camping out at the river, I said sure. Because I didn't have anything else to do because my world revolved around you. And that's totally on me. I could have said no, but I never did. You have no reason *not* to think that I would always be at your beck and call. But I've got a few other things on my plate now. I'm sorry."

Then she turned and walked out.

Bryan sat staring after her. Damn, that little bit of temper made him hot. All of these new sides of Tess made him hot. She was perfect for him. She could turn him on while putting him in his place. Perfect. Even though she no longer thought he was the center of her universe. That was going to take some getting used to.

A long, low whistle caught his attention, and he turned to find all of the women in the fashion show lining the front edge of the stage.

"She told you," Stella commented.

He sighed and sat back in the chair. He regarded the women watching him. These women had been in Sapphire Falls most, if not all, of their lives. So had Tess. Tess hadn't even gone away to college. So he would bet these women knew things about Tess that he needed to know.

"She sure did," he agreed with Stella. "I guess I probably deserved that. I thought she'd wait around for me."

"Oh, she waited around for you," Dottie said with a laugh. "All Tessa's been doing is waiting."

Bryan decided to play this cool. But he really wanted to know how much these women knew. And how much they would tell him. "She doesn't seem so happy to have me now that I'm here."

"That's because you're *here*," Stella said. "She's been waiting for you to come and take her away."

Bryan sat forward in his chair. "Go on."

Ruth nodded. "She was in love with you growing up, but she *really* fell for you after you left."

"She liked me more after I was gone? That doesn't sound so good."

Ruth chuckled. "Apparently, being a world traveler is very sexy to Tess."

Bryan frowned. "But I've been waiting until I was ready to come home and settle down to be with her."

"We know, darlin'," Dottie said. "It's been frustrating as heck to watch her pining for you, and seeing you coming and going but never taking her along."

They'd talked about all of this yesterday—her wanting to go to Denver, her wanting to see the world, her planning to *move* to Denver. Bryan understood her wanting to travel and see places she'd never been, but now that he was *here*, why was she so intent on Denver?

"I'm trying to romance her now," he admitted to the nine older women.

"Ever heard the term 'too little, too late'?" Stella asked him. "She's got her plans, and I don't see flowery words and chocolates changing them."

"She can get her own chocolates," Ruby added. "And she doesn't go for flowery words."

"In regard to your advice, ever heard the term 'too little, too late'?" Bryan asked drily.

The women just laughed.

"So I should leave her alone?" he asked. No way in hell was he going to leave her alone. "Or do you have *useful* advice?"

None of them seemed to take offense at that.

"My advice would be to do something no one else has," Dottie said. "Give her something she can't get in Denver, or anywhere else."

Bryan's brain went immediately to a few things that no one else had done for Tess. And they all involved her being very naked. He wasn't sure Dottie meant her advice quite that way, but he couldn't shake it.

He was the first guy to have her heart, even if he didn't have it as fully now. And he was the first guy to give her an orgasm.

He'd been her first kiss. He'd danced with her at homecoming when he'd seen her in the corner. She'd planned the entire party, of course, but didn't have a date and was off by herself. That had struck him as really wrong. So he'd pulled her onto the dance floor in spite of her protests that she was on her way home.

She'd stayed for the rest of the dance with him, pissing off *his* date completely, and told him afterward it had been the best night ever.

He needed to do that again. Convince her to stay and dance with him. So to speak.

He was the guy she'd been saving herself for and waiting on.

That was something she couldn't get anywhere else.

"Has she dated a lot?" he asked the women. Hell, he could probably get more gossip from these ladies than the people at the Come Again.

"She's dated *some*," Cora said. "But no one serious."

"What have the guys been like?" he asked.

"Like you, I guess," Dottie said, studying him. "Local boys. Farm boys. But nice guys. Sweet and romantic."

Ah.

There it was again. Sweet and romantic. So that wasn't Tessa's style.

The damnedest thing was he *wanted* it to be Tessa's style. Because he wanted to be that way for her.

"I've never been all that romantic with the other women I've been with," he confessed to the older ladies who had also known *him* all his life. "I was kind of thinking it'd be nice to be different with Tess."

"Well, there's your damned problem right there," Stella said. "She's been in love with *you*—the naughty you—all this time."

Bryan raised an eyebrow at the *naughty* comment.

Stella scoffed at his surprise. "Everyone knows all about you, Mr. Murray," she said. "We all know that sweet and romantic isn't your thing, and if she's wanted you all this time, as you were, then it's clearly not Tessa's thing either."

Bryan shook his head. He had to admit that discovering Tessa was a virgin had been a surprise...but a hot one. Discovering that she liked the idea of naughty too? Yeah. He had been trying *not* to like that, but he did.

"Tess reads a lot of romance novels," he said, hoping he wasn't giving anything away.

"We know," Stella said.

Something about the way she said that made Bryan wonder. "Do you?"

"Sure, she's in the club."

"The *club*?" There was only one kind of club that Bryan put together with the word *sex*. There were a few of those types in Denver. He'd only been a couple of times. He wasn't big into watching other people. But if *that* was Tess's flavor...

"Our romance book club," Cora said.

Ah. Right. *Book* club. He supposed that made more sense. "There's a romance book club in Sapphire Falls?"

"Of course." Dottie laughed. "And we all love when it's Tessa's turn to pick."

"She picks good stories?" Bryan asked, already suspecting where this was going.

"She picks *hot* stories," Stella said. "You know—"

"I should read a couple," Bryan said, before she could.

"Definitely," Stella agreed.

"Oh, here." Cora moved surprisingly quickly with her walker when she was inspired.

The older woman headed for her purse off stage. She brought it back out with her and rummaged inside. Finally, she pulled a small paperback book from the depths. "You can start with this one."

"Don't you need it?" he asked, getting to his feet and approaching cautiously. Not because of his leg, but because he wasn't sure he was ready for this.

He wanted to know what Tessa found hot.

He wasn't sure he wanted to know what Cora, or Stella, or Dottie, or any of the others found hot.

"I have it on my iPad," Cora said with a wave of her hand. "I downloaded it so I could increase the font size after trying to read this damned thing for two days."

Bryan blinked at the cover of the book. It was dark blue with a bare-chested man kissing the hell out of a girl in only her underwear. The title was *Wilder than Love*.

Seriously?

"Tess picked this one out?" he asked.

"No," Cora said. "That one's Kathy Bennett's. But Tessa's already finished it. Said she loved it."

Bryan groaned. Now he had to think about Kathy, Ty's mom and Bryan's second mother, reading this stuff? "Maybe I should pick one you all haven't read."

"Why is that?" Stella asked. "Chicken?"

"Because I love going to Kathy's for Thanksgiving dinner," Bryan said. "And I love eating at the diner, and I love saying hello to you ladies on the streets, and I'm enjoying being emcee for this fashion show, and now I'm going to have to think of all you dirty girls in a whole new light."

They all grinned, unabashedly.

"Here's something you need to realize, Mr. Murray," Stella said. "People have been having hot sex in this town far longer than you've even been alive. Hell, longer than *Cora's* been alive. So you just need to deal with it."

"And think about this," Dottie added "If you *don't* read that book—and take some notes—the next time I see *you* in the diner, I'm going to be thinking how sad it is that you've been deprived of it."

"And we're going to be helping Tessa pack up and move out of here," Cora added.

Bryan sighed and looked down at the book again. Could he do it?

Did he really have a choice?

———

S ix hours later, Bryan pounded on Ty's front door.
His friend answered a minute later. "Hey, Bry—"

"I need to talk to you."

Ty frowned. "Okay, come on in. Everyone's here though. You okay?"

He was not okay. There were just some things that couldn't be erased once they were in a guy's head. And since he couldn't forget what he'd read, he intended to share it with his best friend.

"Everyone?" Bryan asked and pushed his wheelchair up the small ramp Ty had built over the threshold of his front door and into the foyer of Ty and Hailey's house. It was simply easier to move fast, as was required when feeling riled up and indignant, in his chair versus his crutch.

Fortunately, Ty's house happened to be next door to the house Bryan was now living in. It was the house that Ty had bought when he'd first come back to Sapphire Falls, because it was next door to Hailey's. Bryan had bought it from him and then Ty had turned half of it into a boarding house for the high-level athletes who came to town for intensive triathlon training sessions with Ty and rented it from Bryan.

Bryan had no problem living with the athletes. He'd been around athletes in training almost constantly since leaving Sapphire Falls with Ty. He'd even agreed to be the on-site athletic trainer, nutritionist and psychologist. He'd gotten his degree in athletic training and nutrition at the University of

Colorado Denver and then his masters in sports and performance psychology from Denver University, and had worked with athletes at various levels over the past few years.

"TJ, Travis and Tucker," Ty said, naming his three older brothers.

"Good." They needed to know about this. "Are the girls here?" Bryan asked, starting for the living room. If the guys' wives were here, Bryan wanted to talk to them too. They had to have known about the book club.

"Yeah," Ty said, following him. "What's going on?"

Bryan rolled to the middle of the living room where Hailey and Ty, Tucker and Delaney, TJ and Hope, and Travis and Lauren were gathered.

"I have something to tell you all," he informed them. "This won't be easy to hear."

"What's wrong?" TJ asked immediately, shifting from where he'd been lounging with his arm around his wife to sitting forward on the couch cushion.

Bryan held up *Wilder than Love*. "Your mother is part of a romance book club. And this was *her* pick for the club recently."

Ty looked from the book to Bryan and back again. "What are you talking about?"

"Your mother read this book and then recommended it to a bunch of her friends. Who read it. And then sat around and talked about it."

Ty took the book from him, frowning harder. "No way."

"Seriously. And I would like you to open up to page five."

Ty gave him a suspicious look but flipped the book open. "Okay."

"Start at the second paragraph. Read it out loud."

"She had always dreamed of being take—" He stopped and looked up. "Seriously?"

"Keep reading," Bryan said grimly.

Ty was his best friend. He shared almost everything with him. He was most definitely going to share one of the most painful moments of his life.

"She had always dreamed of being taken like this. Outdoors, in the wilderness. From behind. Hard. Savage. By Arog and his pack." Ty frowned. "What the hell? His *pack?*"

"Oh, yeah. He's a werewolf," Bryan said.

He glanced around the room. All of the guys wore expressions that were a combination of horror and confusion. But the girls...didn't.

Bryan narrowed his eyes as he watched Lauren, Hailey, Hope and Delaney. They were exchanging looks. They were also fighting smiles. And two of them were blushing.

"A *werewolf?* Come on," Ty said.

Bryan shrugged. "Well, more like just a wolf. He changes into a wolf. And he shares the woman with his pack."

Ty grimaced and thrust the book back at him. "What the hell are you doing?"

"Outing your mother." Bryan crossed his arms and looked at the women in the room. "And the other women in the club."

Travis shifted on his chair, looking incredibly uncomfortable.

Good.

"Who told you all of that?" Travis asked.

"Cora Munson. But it was confirmed by Dottie, Stella, Linda...hell, all of them!"

"And you have the book because...?" Tucker asked.

"Cora gave it to me. Said Tess loved it and I should read it to get insight into what she likes."

That was apparently the final straw. Lauren and Hailey burst out laughing.

Bryan just waited for them to gather themselves.

"What's up, City?" Travis asked his wife. "You know something about this?"

Lauren nodded. "Of course. We all do."

"You all do what?" Ty asked Hailey, hands on his hips.

"We all know about the book club. It's kind of an underground thing," Hailey said. "But only because it makes the gals feel like they're getting away with something to keep it a secret." "The gals?" Ty asked.

"Cora, Stella, Dottie, Linda," Hailey said, confirming the names Bryan had listed. "Viv, Margie Ferguson, Bernadette Cayne, Tina Marie Moran, Debbie Moran, Jolene Parker, Phoebe, Tess." She looked to Lauren. "Us. Sometimes."

They both started laughing again.

Tucker turned to Delaney. "Have you been there?"

She blushed and grinned. "Maybe once."

Bryan watched as TJ sat back and put his arm around Hope again.

"You're not going to ask Hope?" Bryan wanted to know.

TJ pulled her up against his side. "Those books have nothin' on Hope."

His wife blushed but snuggled close. "Damn straight." She looked up at Bryan. "But of course I've been there."

Bryan looked at the other men. "Am I the only one disturbed?"

Lauren scoffed. "Seriously? You're *disturbed* by the women in town reading naughty romance novels?"

"I'm disturbed by the idea that women want to be passed around by a pack of *wolves* to get off," Bryan said.

"How's the book end?" TJ asked mildly.

"She ends up with the alpha," Bryan said. "He tells all the other guys, wolves, whatever, to leave her alone."

"So you finished it," TJ said.

"Well..." Bryan narrowed his eyes. "Yeah. I was trying to figure out what Tess liked about it."

"The hot sex?" Hope asked.

That's what he was afraid of. He knew that Tess didn't have

fantasies about wolves. At least, he was pretty sure of that. But...

"With *multiple* guys? At the same time? While they all watch?" he demanded.

"Oh, she—"

"What if she did?" Lauren asked, cutting Hailey off. "What would you do if that was what she wanted?"

Son of a bitch. Wasn't that the question of the hour? The book was supposed to have given him insight into his little virgin's fantasies. But he would never have guessed that Tess wanted some of the stuff that the book had in it. He would never have guessed that Tess even knew about some of that stuff.

Then again, he never would have guessed she'd say some of the stuff she had to him—and he didn't just mean the dirty talk. He was equally surprised by the times she'd essentially told him she wasn't interested in him anymore.

"Well, I'd do it if that's what would make her happy," he said. He was losing her. He felt it. Actually, he was starting to wonder if he'd ever had her. And if he had, why he'd been such a dumbass, assuming he always would without giving it any effort.

He looked at the other guys. Travis nodded as if he understood, Tucker looked like Bryan was nuts, TJ was definitely *not* agreeing with that decision, based on his expression, and Ty looked like he had a headache.

Which made Bryan roll his eyes. Ty had been wrapped around Hailey's little finger since he was fourteen, but he'd had his share of other women in the years it had taken him and Hailey to figure their stuff out. And multiple partners wasn't a completely foreign concept to either Ty or Bryan. But neither of them had ever been into sharing with other guys.

"But it would be a problem," Bryan went on. "Because I'd have to kill any other guy who so much as saw her naked, not to mention actually touching her while she was naked. Not to mention all of the other stuff they all did to the girl in the book. And killing *five* other men would probably end up being a problem."

Lauren gave him a big smile and sat back. "Okay, now you can tell him," she said to Hailey.

Bryan looked at his best friend's wife. "Tell me what?"

"Tess didn't read that book," Hailey said. "She passed on that one."

Bryan looked at her, processing that. "Excuse me?"

"Tess didn't want to read about multiple partners. She'll read a ménage once in a while, but she really prefers the ones with just one guy and girl."

"Then why did Cora say she did?"

"Cora was messing with you," Lauren told him. "Which is hilarious. I hope she doesn't hurt herself patting herself on the back."

Bryan narrowed his eyes. "And *all* of those sweet little old ladies were in on it?" he asked. First the lingerie and now this. He was going to have to come up with some great payback for the next fashion show rehearsal.

Hailey snorted. "I'm not sure how many sweet little old ladies we have in Sapphire Falls, but I can assure you that the women you named off are not in *that* club."

"They're in the *Blue Brigade*," Bryan said. "They go around town fucking spreading sunshine and shit."

Hailey and Lauren both laughed at that.

"It's a great cover, isn't it?" Hailey asked with a wink.

"Don't worry," Lauren told him. "I was totally sucked in by them too when I first met them."

"Okay," Bryan said, back on the topic at hand. "So Tess is definitely not into having a pack of wolves ravage her."

"Definitely not," Lauren agreed.

Bryan slumped slightly, relief washing over him. "Thank God. She likes the sweet stories."

Hailey lifted an eyebrow. "We didn't say that."

"What?"

"That the ones Tess likes are sweet," Hailey told him.

Lauren shook her head. "Nope. Not at all."

Bryan felt his stomach knot again. "What's that mean?"

He'd messed around with silk ties, handcuffs, spanking and nipple clamps over the years, but he really preferred being able to make a woman beg *without* all of that. Like the other night at Tess's house. He had been the only thing giving her pleasure, and that had been everything he needed. Though the idea of her with a vibrator was hot.

"Your girl loves the really hot stuff. Just a guy and a girl, not a lot of extras, but plenty of heat," Hailey said.

"Not a lot of extras?" Bryan asked. And was he really having this conversation in the middle of his best friend's living room with eight other people? None of who were the girl in question.

He did really like Tess being referred to as his girl though.

"She likes the big, bossy dirty talkers," Lauren confirmed.

"Well, who doesn't?" Hope asked.

TJ leaned in and said something in her ear that made her blush.

Big, bossy dirty talkers.

That was more than he needed to know about TJ Bennett.

"Oh, here." Hailey bounced up from her seat and went to her purse for her phone. She came back to Bryan, running her thumb over the screen. "You should read this one. It's one of Tessa's favorites."

She showed Bryan her phone. A book cover took up the entire space. A book cover that was bright pink and white, with an up-close photo of a couple nearly kissing. It looked harmless enough. But then he read the title.

"*Erotic Research*?" he asked.

"Mari Carr writes hot," Hailey said. "Tess is a huge fan."

"So can I borrow this or what?" Bryan asked. He was absolutely reading something called *Erotic Research*. Especially if it was one of Tessa's favorites.

"Give me your phone," Hailey said.

He leaned to pull it from his pocket. "Why?"

"I'll put it on your phone," she said. "Then you can read it wherever you are and not worry about who's wondering about *your* erotic research."

"Okay." Sounded good to him. In fact... "Can you show me how to put more books on there?"

Hailey winked at him. "You got it. Just need your credit card."

Five minutes later, Bryan had *Erotic Research* and several others on his phone and ready to go.

"Now," Ty said to his brothers. "What are we going to do about Mom and this book club?"

"Completely forget any of this ever happened," Tucker declared.

"Amen," Travis said.

"You mean the *quilting* club she goes to each week?" TJ asked. "I think the *quilting* club is great."

Ty nodded. "Great. I'm totally down with quilting."

All the girls burst out laughing at that.

"What?" Ty asked Hailey.

"Just that we all really like *quilting* with all of you," Hailey said, coming over and putting an arm around his waist.

Ty tucked her under his arm with a sigh. "It's not a euphemism."

"You're right. Sorry," Hailey said, not looking a bit sorry.

"Okay then, I think it's great Mom goes to a *cooking* club each week," Tucker said.

"Oh, me too," Delaney told him, running her hand up his thigh. "Her German chocolate cake is my favorite thing."

Tucker groaned. "You can't make that dirty."

"If I remember correctly, *you* made it dirty," Delaney said with a laugh.

It was well known in Sapphire Falls that if Kathy Bennett made you a German chocolate cake—with extra frosting—it was a cake for two. And meant to be eaten in private.

"Dammit. Then Mom's going to a *painting* class," Travis said.

Lauren nodded. "I'm going to have to ask her to show me some new *strokes*."

"Oh God, please stop," TJ grumbled. "This is my *mom*."

"And your mom and dad most definitely—"

TJ clamped a hand over Hope's mouth. "Sunshine, I know you're all into being open and out there about everything, but how about we not go there."

Bryan grinned at the group. They were all madly in love and open about their hot sex lives.

He wanted that.

And, obviously, it was possible. Not everything about being in love and in a relationship needed to be sweetness and roses. Romance could be about teasing and laughing together.

And big, bossy dirty talk.

Yeah, he could do this relationship thing Tessa's way.

He just had a little research to do.

8

If it was *anyone* else in town, Tess would have just ignored the whole thing.

When the "request" had first come across her desk, she'd smiled, shook her head, and filed it in the I-don't-think-so pile.

But then another request had come in. And then another. And then Kathy Bennett walked into her office with the town's comment box under one arm and a pan of cupcakes in the other.

As if she would have been able to say no to Kathy anyway. Kathy's cupcakes could get the leaders of the free world to binge watch *The Girlfriend's Guide to Divorce* on Netflix together.

"We've been getting a lot of requests to—"

"Play the Newlywed Game one of the evenings during the festival," Tess filled in.

Kathy smiled and nodded. "How did you know?"

"I have three requests right here. And I should have known he'd get you involved."

Because no one said no to Kathy Bennett.

Because Kathy never said no to anyone in Sapphire Falls. If someone in town needed something, Kathy would get it done.

Which made her impossible to turn down, even if she wasn't one of the sweetest, most level-headed and honest people Tess had ever met.

"All he did was submit a comment," Kathy said.

Tess lifted an eyebrow.

"Okay, a *few* comments," Kathy admitted.

Tess knew exactly where the conversation was going to go from there.

Kathy Bennett was in charge of the town comment box because she knew the town and people better than anyone, and could objectively separate what was actually needed and which ideas were just silly. Well, mostly objectively.

And because she'd come up with the idea.

Her oldest son, TJ, was the mayor and after he'd complained about the ridiculous requests he was fielding all day long on his personal cell, at the gas station, even at church on Sunday mornings, Kathy had come up with comment box idea. She did not think Sunday morning church was an appropriate time to gripe at the mayor. Nor was dinner time when he was sitting down with his new wife. Nor was dinner time when he was at his mother's house with his family. So she'd implemented the plan, had her daughter-in-law, Delaney, build five big wooden boxes with slots on the top and put one at the diner, one at the bakery, one at the gas station, one at the bar and one at City Hall. Twice a week she rounded all the comments up and went through them, discarding the complaints— she didn't think TJ needed to see those and maintained that City Council meetings were the appropriate time to bring forth concerns—and the jokes. Like the one that had suggested putting a stripper pole in at the Come Again. At least Kathy had chosen to believe it was a joke.

It had actually turned into a great plan. City Council meetings were faster and more efficient because they weren't spending time discussing things like adding cappuccinos to the hot cocoa stand in the winter or debating whether to repaint the goal posts on the football field solid blue or with blue and white stripes. They could spend time on much bigger, more important issues. And since there weren't usually a huge number of those in Sapphire Falls, the meetings were short and sweet.

The City Council and the Mayor were all big fans of the comment boxes.

What TJ didn't know—or was possibly choosing to ignore —was that Kathy would occasionally confront some of the complainers about what they put on comment cards about her son. The cards could be submitted anonymously, of course, but Kathy recognized the handwriting of a surprisingly large percent of the population in Sapphire Falls.

However, for the most part, the comment boxes worked.

"And you think we should do it?" Tessa asked Kathy.

"I do. And I know just the four couples who should be a part of it."

Yep, this was exactly where Tess had figured this would go.

The four couples Kathy was referring to were not necessarily the most recent weddings in town, but they'd been the most entertaining. The four couples had all been married on the same day, at the same time, after competing to see who would win the big Christmas wedding. They'd all tied.

The whole town had been in on the competition and had shown up for the ceremony, so they felt more invested in those four marriages maybe than most. It also didn't hurt that three of the grooms had been Bennetts—one of the most beloved families in town—and that the other had been Levi Spencer, a transplant from Vegas who just happened to have millions of dollars at his disposal and who loved to shower those dollars on his new hometown.

Yeah, it was pretty safe to say that the three Bennett boys—

Tucker, TJ and Ty—and Levi were some of the most popular newlyweds in town.

And they were certainly some of Kathy's favorites.

Tess sighed. It wasn't that she didn't think the newlywed game with those guys could be entertaining or that the town wouldn't like it. It wasn't that she thought any of the couples would say no. It was more that any one of those guys could be a handful and a half by himself. Putting the four together and trying to maintain some level of control—and keeping things PG-rated—could be a challenge.

But Tess was in charge of festival entertainment. And she really liked Kathy Bennett.

Dammit.

Ten minutes later she pulled open the door to the Come Again.

Her eyes went immediately to where the bartender was supposed to be standing.

But Bryan wasn't there. No one was.

She looked around and spotted him across the room. He was sitting at a table with four of his regulars—Tucker, TJ, Ty and Levi. It looked like they were finishing up a late lunch of burgers and beer. They were also the only four patrons in the bar at three in the afternoon. Which she thought was a good sign for Sapphire Falls in general. Though the fact that one of them was the mayor might not have been.

"I think it will be great," Ty was saying as Tess approached.

There was only one man in the room that noticed her arrival it seemed.

Bryan lifted his head and made eye contact with her. Tessa's steps faltered for a second, then she rolled her eyes. Really? She couldn't walk when he was looking at her? For fuck's sake. She straightened her spine and lifted her chin. She needed all the bravado she could get right now. Not just because of Bryan either.

There was so much charm and testosterone and b.s. in that room at the moment, that she wasn't sure she was going to make it out alive.

"Of course you think it will be great," Tucker said. "You're the most competitive person who's ever lived."

Ty grinned at his brother. "Thank you."

Tucker rolled his eyes.

"I'm not doing this," TJ said. He was sitting back with one ankle propped on his opposite knee, an arm draped over the back of the empty chair next to him. He looked relaxed and casual, but his deep voice was firm and he was giving his youngest brother a don't-mess-with-me look.

Ty, as usual, seemed unfazed.

"You don't have to do it, but everyone's going to think it's because you don't know Hope as well as the rest of us know our wives," Ty said.

TJ scowled. "That's not what they'll think."

"I agree with Ty," Levi said, lifting a shoulder. "It looks like you know you're the least attentive of the husbands."

Come on, TJ, don't rise to the bait, Tessa thought, watching her boss. TJ was one of the most self- assured people she'd ever met. He liked things his way. And he often got them. But, as was the case with younger brothers throughout the ages, his siblings could get him going.

"Of course you agree with him, this was your fucking idea," TJ said.

Tessa started to breathe out, but then TJ added, "And there's no way in hell you're more attentive to your wives than I am to Hope."

Tessa sighed. Dammit. They had him.

"Why do you want to do this anyway?" Tucker asked Levi. "We're not the newest newlyweds in town."

"Because it's a *game,*" Levi said, as if the answer should have been obvious.

And, really, it was. Levi had been born and raised in Las Vegas of all places. He'd grown up in the gaming and entertainment industry. His family's millions had been made amusing the masses—and taking their money for it. The Spencers owned several casinos and touring shows across the country and even though he'd firmly put roots down in Sapphire Falls, Levi still traveled between Nebraska and Nevada on a regular basis.

"It doesn't matter if we're the newest newlyweds," Levi said. "The TV show had people on who'd been married for all different lengths of time. The fun was in pitting them against each other."

Tess didn't think that was exactly true, but she knew that Levi's objective here was not to compete against the brothers. It was to get them competing against each other. Because that was always entertaining. Levi loved to entertain. And to be entertained.

"I'm not doing this," TJ said again.

But Tess knew better. So did everyone around the table.

"Oh, come on," Ty said. He pulled his phone out. "Tell you what—we'll play right now. Five questions. If you win, it never goes beyond the bar. If I win, we do it for the festival."

"What if I win?" Tucker asked.

"You get to pick which way we go," Ty said.

"We're going to play the Newlywed Game right here and now?" Levi asked, looking like someone had just offered him candy.

"Yeah," Ty said. "This way if TJ really doesn't know Hope very well, then we don't embarrass him publicly."

TJ made a low growling noise.

Bryan caught Tessa's eye and gave her a grin. She returned it. She had to admit that this actually had some promise as far as fun went. Bryan pushed a chair out next to him and she sighed. She might as well stay and see what happened here. If the winner decided to go ahead with the game for the festival, she was going to need to know.

And her boss was here. She could make a good case for being here *for him*. In case he needed anything. And this was festival business. Kind of.

Of course, she had a million things to do. The festival was coming up quickly and Hailey was making good on her promise to make this the biggest, best festival Sapphire Falls had ever seen. There were supposedly people coming from all over. The bed and breakfast was already completely booked and all of the businesses in town were gearing up to be slammed with visitors. And they were all thrilled about it.

Tess took the seat next to Bryan. He leaned in and the air around her warmed and she became acutely aware of how big his biceps looked in the t-shirt he was wearing and how nicely the worn denim of his jeans looked molded to his thighs. Which reminded her of how great those biceps and thighs had felt last night.

She worked on not breathing in deeply. She wanted so much to take a huge whiff. He smelled so good and the scent reminded her of how he'd smelled... and felt... and tasted...last night on her couch. But she held her breath. She didn't need to be squirming on her chair and distracted—particularly in *this* crowd, because they would notice, comment and tease. And she didn't need him to know that she was squirming and distracted over him. He'd had his chance and he'd blown it. It was over.

"Did you know about this?" Bryan asked her.

He'd kept his voice down but TJ overheard and pivoted to look at her. "Did you?" he asked.

His tone suggested that if she had, and hadn't mentioned it to him, she was in trouble.

"Not until I got forty seven comments in the comment box suggesting we do it." She shot Levi a look.

"Are you sure there weren't fifty?" Levi asked.

"There were forty seven slips in the boxes and three formal requests that came across my desk," she clarified.

"Wow," Levi said. "That's a lot of support. I'm thinking with anything over, what, twenty, you have to just do it."

"It is a record," Tess agreed. "And when they come in on gold embossed Spencer Enterprises letterhead, they're pretty hard to ignore."

Levi grinned and lifted his glass.

"You put forty seven comments in the comment box that said we should do the Newlywed Game?" Tucker asked.

"I'm simply looking out for the happiness of my hometown," Levi said with a hand over his heart. "And nothing makes people happier than seeing four young couples madly in love. Am I right?" Levi asked Tess.

She shot a look at TJ and pressed her lips together when he frowned. "No comment," she said.

"So let's go," Ty said to Levi. "You and me, man. We're playing for the happiness of the whole town." He swiped a finger over the screen of his phone and read, "My spouse's first kiss made me think..." He looked up. "You fill in the blank."

"And you have to keep it PG," Tess said quickly. "If you're going to do this at the Community Center, it has to be family friendly and you should all start practicing that now."

The guys seemed to think that was funny... and flattering. Tess predicted she would be rolling her eyes a lot during this game.

"Kate's first kiss made me think..." Levi angled a look at Tess. "That I hoped it snowed nonstop for the next three months so we couldn't leave the house."

Tess narrowed her eyes. That was certainly insinuating things but she doubted any kids would really get it. And if they leaned over and asked their mom why two grownups wouldn't want to leave the house for days on end, that was their mother's problem.

Tess's thoughts skittered to the man next to her and the idea of being cooped up with him, just the two of them, for several days.

"That's not how you play," Bryan said.

Tess jerked upright, realizing she'd been leaning toward him slightly.

Ty held his phone up. "I looked up Newlywed Game Questions."

"Yeah, but you have to play with the girls here," Bryan said. "You write your answer down and then see if it matches what she says."

"Not a problem," Ty said, swiping his phone screen again. "Hailey will be here in two minutes."

Tess didn't doubt it. Hailey was almost as competitive as her husband.

"You expect us to call the girls and ask them to drop everything and come down here to play some stupid game?" TJ asked.

Levi already had his phone to his ear. "Hey, if you think Hope wouldn't be willing to do that for you, I understand."

TJ growled again, but he shifted so he could pull his phone from his pocket.

Yep, these guys definitely knew how to push his buttons. Tess couldn't help but giggle softly.

"Honestly, I'd pay good money to watch them play this game," Bryan said, again leaning in close and dropping his voice.

The low baritone made goosebumps trip up and down her arm and Tess had to clear her throat. "You think it's a good idea?"

"I think it could be fun to watch," he said. "But I think we should consider having it here instead of at the Community Center. There won't be any kids that way. There's no way these guys are going to keep this PG."

Tess had to admit that was a good idea. "You'd do that?"

He gave her a look that was somehow affectionate and hot at the same time. "Tess, when are you going to figure out I'll do anything for you?"

Dammit. That was exactly the kind of thing that she needed him to *stop* saying.

"Bry—"

"Sunshine and honey."

Everyone stopped talking and slowly turned to look at TJ.

"Excuse me?" Ty asked.

"Kissing Hope the first time made me think of sunshine and honey." TJ looked anything but embarrassed by his answer. In fact, he looked downright smug.

And he should, because that was damned good. In Tessa's opinion at least.

"And here I was thinking about sex."

Everyone turned, again in one synchronized movement, to look toward the front of the Come Again. Hope had just come in. She was grinning as she crossed to TJ and slipped into his lap.

TJ's hands went around her possessively and Tess had to tear her eyes away. That was pretty hot. He wasn't doing anything but *holding* her, but it was hot nonetheless.

"So, you did just say that *kissing* made you think of—" Ty paused for emphasis. "Sunshine."

"And honey," TJ said, looking very pleased with himself.

Ty looked at Hope. "Is that what you would have answered for him if you were really playing this game?"

Hope laughed. "I probably would have said tequila and jalapenos." She looked at her husband. "There wasn't anything sweet about that first kiss."

Tess couldn't help but watch them again and she saw TJ's fingers curl into Hope's hips. Tess had to clear her throat. Why was that hot?

But she knew the answer instantly. It was because of the way TJ was looking at Hope. Like he wanted to cover her in honey—and spend all day licking it off. And maybe like he was remembering doing that at some point in the past.

Tessa's gaze went to Bryan and then instantly snapped away when she discovered he was watching her. She felt her face flush and wished she could fan herself. But she could not get the idea of drizzling honey over Bryan's abs out of her mind.

"So you would have lost then," Ty said, smugly. "Your answers have to match."

TJ gave his brother a lazy stare and ran his hand up and down his wife's hip. "Maybe your idea of winning and mine are different," he said.

Ty frowned. "Winning is having more points than the other people."

"Yeah," TJ said with a little nod. "Definitely different ideas."

"Why?" Ty asked. "What makes you think you would have won with that answer?"

TJ looked up at Hope. "You want to tell him about the points I scored with that romantic answer and what my prize will be, Sunshine?"

Hope gave Ty a mischievous smile. "Do I really need to?"

Ty narrowed his eyes. "First of all, you're not supposed to answer the questions to get points with *Hope*. You're supposed to answer them to get game points."

"Maybe I don't care about game points," TJ said.

"It's no fun to beat a guy who's not even trying," Ty told him. "And besides, is it really a prize if you get it every single night no matter what you say?"

"Be still my heart."

Tess looked over to find that Hailey, Delaney and Kate had just walked in. Hailey's dry reply got a grin from her husband.

"Hey, babe."

Hailey pulled a chair between Ty and Tucker and sat,

crossing her legs and her arms. "Babe," she said to Ty. "You better kick *ass* at this game or you're not getting a prize anywhere."

He didn't seem concerned. He put his hand on her knee and leaned in, whispering something in her ear. Hailey's cheeks got pink and she couldn't fight her smile. "Fine," she said, agreeing with whatever he'd suggested.

And again, Tess found herself jealous and, a little turned on, watching the other couples.

Kate slipped into the chair next to Levi and he put an arm around her, pulling her closer. Delaney leaned in and gave Tucker a kiss before taking the chair beside him.

Tess definitely found herself tempted to cuddle up closer to Bryan. She wasn't turned on by the other men, just the public displays of affection—and desire. She wanted that. And Bryan was definitely the type of guy to do that.

"So are we playing or what?" Ty asked his brothers and Levi. "The girls are here. I say we find out who's really got the married thing going on."

"We need paper," Hailey said, bouncing up. "Bryan, you have pens and paper somewhere?"

"Office," he said.

Hailey retrieved a notebook and a handful of pens. She tore a few of the pages into strips and then handed the extras to Bryan.

"Okay, let's go," she said. She looked around the table. "No cheating. Girls, you come over on this side, guys on that side."

Everyone shuffled their chairs until the girls were sitting across the table from their husbands.

"Okay, now go," Hailey told Ty.

"Name the most interesting place you've ever had sex."

"Family show," Tess reminded him, trying to act admonishing, but fighting a smile.

"This is just for now," Ty said.

"You're just being a perv, wanting to know where we've all gotten lucky," Tucker told him.

"We all know about you and Delaney's addiction to the barn," Ty said.

"Hey, I never told you that," Tucker said, glancing at Delaney.

"You didn't have to tell us," Hope said with a giggle. "The last time you had a family picnic at your place, Delaney had hay sticking out of the back of her jeans."

Delaney didn't look embarrassed. "I do love that barn," she agreed. "But you don't know that it's the *most* interesting place," she told Ty.

"Well, I'm all ears," Ty said, pointing to her piece of paper. "Write that down."

"You all *definitely* need to practice the PG answer thing," Tess said. But the R rated version would be *very* entertaining. If they did it at the Come Again and let people know that it would be candid, it would be standing room only.

Levi laughed. "Then we'll ask the most interesting place we've ever kissed," he said. "The grown-ups will know what we really mean."

"Fine," Ty said. "Most interesting place you've ever kissed your wife."

They all bent their heads and wrote on their paper scraps. When they were all done, Ty said, "Okay, Kate, you go first."

Kate blushed as she held her paper up.

There was a beat of silence and then Ty said, "Does that say pinky toe?"

Kate nodded.

"Your answer is pinky toe?" Ty clarified. He looked at Levi. "What's your answer?"

Levi held his paper up. It said, "Backstage at a burlesque show."

Ty looked back to Kate who was reading Levi's paper. "Oh," she said softly, her cheeks getting even redder.

Ty started laughing. "Yeah, I was thinking of a *place*. Like a location. Like something that would come up on GPS."

In spite of her embarrassment, Kate started laughing too. "And I had to think to come up with pinky toe. I mean, there are only so many places to kiss somebody and most of them aren't *interesting*."

Levi's eyebrows rose. "Is that right?"

"Well, they're not *unusual*," Kate said. "I'm sure everyone here has kissed each other on the—" She stopped talking and pressed her lips together.

Ty started laughing harder and everyone else joined in.

"Oh my god, this is going to be amazing," he said, wiping one eye.

"And I have the perfect question to use during the public game," Tucker said. "The most interesting way any of us have used German chocolate cake frosting. People will love that."

Tess had to admit he had a point. Kathy Bennett was famous for her German chocolate cakes. She made one for all anniversaries and engagements—or just prior to an engagement she saw coming. And she frosted them extra thick. Many a Sapphire Falls couple had enjoyed that frosting... on things other than cake. But that would definitely not keep the game family friendly.

It was definitely going to have to be held at the Come Again.

"But we'd all have the same answers, wouldn't we?" Hope asked.

They all looked at her with surprise. And amusement.

She looked back at them. "What? You're telling me there's a *more* interesting way to use it than spreading it all over your husband's cock and licking it clean."

Everyone's eyes widened and Levi and Tucker started choking. Delaney started laughing and Tess felt her entire body get warmer.

"We are having this game here at the Come Again," Tess said loudly over the amazed reactions to Hope's comment.

Levi was still laughing. "Why is that, Tess?"

"Because Hope just said... that word... in a group conversation as if she was talking about the weather!"

She kind of hated that *she* couldn't say cock quite so casually. But she felt fairly certain that ninety-eight percent of the population didn't use the word in general conversation.

Hope was grinning at her. "Sorry, Tessa. I sometimes like to test Ty's bladder control."

Her brother-in-law leaned over and gave her a high five. "Nicely done, Sunshine."

TJ gave him a little growl at Ty's use of *his* nickname for Hope.

"Okay, but seriously we can't come up with the questions ahead of time," Levi said. "There's no studying for this. It has to be off the cuff. That's what makes it fun."

Tessa tried to focus on what they were talking about but she was having a hard time ignoring images of Bryan covered in German chocolate frosting.

Dammit.

"So can we say those words if we're here at the Come Again?" Tucker asked.

"What words?" Tess wasn't following him. Probably because ninety percent of her brain cells were honed in on Bryan. And how she hadn't had frosting of any kind in over a year. And how much she loved frosting. Of any kind.

"The words that answer the question about the most interesting place we've used German chocolate cake frosting," Tuck said with a grin. "You know, like co—".

"Right, got it," Tess cut him off. "And..." She looked at Bryan, then TJ, then Hailey. "I don't know. What do you think?"

"Of course not," Hailey said.

"But there won't be kids," Tucker said.

"No, but your *mother* will probably be in the audience."

Tess bit her bottom lip. She knew some of the erotic romances that Kathy Bennett read. They were in book club together. *She* would likely scandalize her sons.

"Your *grandmother* might even be there," Delaney said.

It was actually a pretty good bet Kendra Bennett would be there. She'd never missed a Christmas program, ballgame or anything else one of her grandsons had done. Put all three of them on a stage somewhere and she'd be there.

"So what kind of questions then?" Levi asked.

"Stuff that shows how well you know each other but won't make anyone blush," Tess said.

TJ stretched his long legs out and propped his arms along the back of Levi's chair. "Bring it on."

Hope looked at him with a smile. "You think this will be easy?"

"Sunshine, I know everything I need to know," TJ said confidently.

"The questions are things like 'What drink best described your wife on your wedding night'," Delaney said.

Her husband looked at her with surprise. "You've been studying Newlywed Game questions?" Tucker asked.

Delaney nodded. "Always be prepared."

"You're a boy scout now?" Ty asked with a grin.

Delaney shook her head. "Something much more serious and strenuous... and more likely to leave me stranded in the woods by myself with no supplies," she said. "Mother of four boys."

Ty chuckled.

"How about what movie your wife last watched?" Tucker suggested.

TJ shook his head. "Can't answer that one."

Ty shrugged. "Someone's gotta get last place."

"What I meant," TJ said. "Is that I can't answer that one if Grandma is going to be in the audience."

Ty looked from TJ to Hope. Hope gave him a sweet smile.

Ty sighed. "Seriously? Porn?"

Hope glanced back at TJ. "I'd call it "an highly erotic independent film"."

"Do *not* tell me that you guys recorded *yourselves*," Ty said.

"Well, we—"

"No!" Ty said, stopping her. "I said do *not* tell me."

"Okay, then," Levi said. "Name the last book your wife read."

Everyone bent their heads to write. Except TJ. Which Ty noticed.

"What now?" he asked.

"Not answering that with Grandma around either."

Ty looked at Hope. "For God's sake, Hope."

"What?" she asked. "A healthy sex drive is something be proud of."

"But you clearly need movies and books to get going," Ty said.

Hope leaned in and patted his hand. "It's okay if you think that." Then she glanced at Hailey. "Sorry for you though."

"Stop being so judgey," Hailey told Ty with a laugh. "You like when I wear that pirate-slave costume."

Ty nodded. "Yes, yes I do."

Tess felt her cheeks heat. She had a teeny tiny—okay, really big—pirate-slave fantasy herself. She stole a look at Bryan. Oh yeah, he could pull off the rugged pirate thing.

"Fine," Levi said, clearly feeling put upon. "Last time you kissed your wife so passionately, she was breathless afterward."

"Nice," Kate told him and bent her head to write.

Everyone else did the same without commentary and Tess

found herself interested in the answers, and the commentary that would no doubt follow.

Okay, this was a good idea.

Once everyone had looked up, they went around showing their answers.

Levi said last night and Kate agreed. Tucker was more specific and answered two a.m. and then went on to add "when I woke her up for some fun". Delaney confirmed it, and Tess felt a definite stab of jealousy at the satisfied smile she wore. Then TJ gave his answer.

"An hour and a half ago?" Ty read out loud.

Hope nodded. "It's true. It's when he was saying goodbye to come here."

"Let me see your paper," Ty said.

She held it up. It also said "an hour and a half ago".

"You were *breathless*?" Ty asked.

"Definitely."

"Come on. Like every time he kisses you goodbye you get *breathless*?"

She looked at TJ. "Yep."

"The trick is grabbing her ass," TJ said. "That does it to her every time."

Hope grinned. "And grabbing my—"

"Okay!" Tess broke in. "What did you say Ty?"

He crumpled his paper. "Doesn't matter, he wins."

"How does he win?" Hailey asked.

"His was most recently," Ty said.

"That's not how it works," Levi said. "You get points every time your answer matches Hailey's. Your score isn't about TJ's points."

Ty nodded. "Hey, that's right." He uncrumpled his paper and held it up.

"*Three days* ago?" Tucker read.

Ty frowned. "Hey, she's been really busy with the festival stuff."

"*You and Hailey* haven't had sex in three days?" Tucker said, clearly unable to believe it.

"That's not the question," Hailey said, holding her paper up. It also said three days ago. "You asked when he'd last kissed me breathless."

"You don't get breathless when you have sex?" Delaney asked.

Hailey shrugged "Sure. But not always from kissing. The other night we kind of blew past the kissing and got to the really good stuff."

"But you were breathless?" Delaney confirmed.

Hailey gave Ty a hot look. "Oh yeah."

Tess felt the temperature in the room climb and for the first time thought maybe kissing could be overrated.

"Okay, so you all got the points on that one," Tess said before anyone could elaborate on their answers further. Not so much because she was worried about the R rating now and more because she was afraid her jealousy would start showing.

"Let's do another one then," Ty said. "We need a winner to determine if we're even going to do this thing publicly right?"

They all looked at one another.

"Where did you *first* kiss your wife?"

Tess turned to Bryan. That was a great—and surprising— suggestion. As distracting as he was, she was glad he was here and glad they were doing this at the Come Again. For one, he would help control these guys. For another... she'd kicked him out of her house last night. She felt a little bad about that. Especially since his words at the door had kept her awake for hours. *If you didn't care about me, my world would be a very different place.*

And that was the thing. She did care. A lot.

"Hey, that's a good one." Ty looked down at the paper he was holding and wrote something down.

Tessa's mind went to the first time Bryan had kissed her. Stupidly.

But she couldn't *not* think about it now.

She'd been eleven and she'd fallen out of the tree in his backyard. She'd broken her arm and she remembered the horrible pain and the fear—until Bryan came running and knelt beside her. He'd picked her up and carried her into the house. She still remembered how white his face had been and how gently he'd handled her. While his mother called her mom, he'd gotten her a cherry popsicle—her favorite—and told her that he would bring her popsicles every day as long as she had a cast on. And then when her mom had pulled into the driveway, he'd picked her up in his arms again—and kissed her. Right on the lips. Before carrying her out to the car.

Her lips had tingled for a week after that.

"Okay, Hailey, you go first," Bryan said, pulling Tess back to the present.

"February tenth, sixteen years ago, Hallway outside of her history class," Ty said.

For a second, it was completely quiet. Tess stared at Ty. He knew the exact day?

"Hailey was supposed to answer," Tucker told him. "Then we see if it matches up with what you wrote down."

"It would have," Ty said. "Totally memorable day and moment for her."

Hailey rolled her eyes.

"But that's the point," Tuck said. "*You* assume she'd remember, but the rest of us don't know that for sure."

Hailey held her paper up.

February tenth.

Tucker sighed.

"Okay, let's see how you did," Delaney told Tucker.

"Okay," he agreed, shifting to face her. "Where did I first kiss you?" He glanced at Hope. "And we're not talking body parts on this one either, right?"

Hope laughed. "If we are, I need to change my answer."

"Okay." Tucker looked back at Delaney. "Nothing naughty. Where, as in place."

"Yes, dear, I got it," Delaney said. "It was on your porch swing."

Tucker turned the clipboard so everyone could see that he'd written PORCH SWING on his piece of paper.

Delaney leaned in and kissed him.

"Our turn." Hope looked at TJ. "In your yard by your garden."

TJ held his paper up. "Nailed it."

Kate grinned. "This wasn't a good tie-breaker, I guess," she said. She looked at Levi. "Under the mistletoe at the hot cocoa stand in the square."

Levi leaned onto the table, put his hand at the back of her head and pulled her in. "Damn right," he said, holding his paper up as he kissed her. It read *hot cocoa stand*.

By the time he finally let her up for air, Tessa was about ready to call the rehearsal off. The heat, and love, in the room was getting suffocating.

"Okay, let's try one more," Kate suggested, looking into Levi's eyes.

"Okay, fine." Tess said. "Who has a question?"

"How about *the biggest surprise your spouse has ever given you*?" Bryan asked. "Guys answer about the girls."

Everyone started writing.

A minute later, they all put their pens down.

"Tearing my kitchen apart when I just wanted some cobbler," Tucker said with a huge grin.

Delaney laughed and held up her paper. Her answer matched.

"Bringing me brownies when I moved in next door," Ty said of Hailey.

Hailey looked at him. "Really?"

"Yeah. Why, what did you say?"

She held up her paper. It read *showing up in Denver after he turned me down for money for Sapphire Hills*.

Sapphire Hills was the tiny strip mall on the edge of town that Hailey had tried to get a number of Sapphire Falls alums to support when they were first building it. Ty had given her the run around for months.

Ty grinned at her, even though they'd gotten it wrong. "Oh, babe, I wasn't surprised by that at all."

Hailey rolled her eyes.

Everyone looked at TJ.

He held his paper up. It said *Naked Yoga*.

They all laughed and Hope held her paper up. *Everything for the first six months.*

TJ nodded when he read it. "That's actually a great answer."

She winked at him and they all turned to Kate and Levi.

Levi held up his paper and read it out loud, "Falling in love with me in the first place."

Kate gave him a soft smile and put her hand to his cheek. "That's sweet. And crazy."

"So what was your answer?" he asked.

Kate licked her lips and took a deep breath. Then she handed her piece of paper to Levi.

He opened it. And stared.

For several long seconds.

"Uh, hello?" Ty said.

Levi looked up. He looked at Kate. "I love you."

She nodded. "I know."

He pulled her in for a long, deep, hot kiss. Tess wasn't the only one shifting and clearing her throat a moment later.

"What is going on?" Ty insisted.

Levi let Kate go and turned to them. He held the paper up. It said, *I'm pregnant.*

There was a long moment while that sunk in.

Then everyone seemed to spring out of their chairs at the same time. Hailey and Delaney grabbed Kate off of her chair and wrapped her in a huge three-way hug. Hope was crying by the time they let Kate go so she could hug her. Meanwhile the guys were all congratulating and hugging Levi. Tucker took Kate from Hope and hugged her, then passed her to TJ, who lifted her off her feet.

Everyone was laughing and most had watery eyes if not actual tears running down their cheeks.

Tess was one of the ones with tears by the time she got to hug Kate.

It was several more minutes before everyone settled down enough to agree that the Newlywed Game at the Come Again was a must-see event for the festival.

Bryan promised that the place would be set up perfectly and Hailey asked Tess if she could handle flyers and an announcement in the paper and on the website.

"Of course," she said. "This will be a lot of fun."

"I'll handle getting a host for the show," Hailey said. "Do you think Kyle would do it?" she asked Bryan of his friend.

"I actually do," Bryan said.

Kyle was a good choice. He was charming and funny and single. He'd have a great time putting questions to the married couples.

They all filed out, still talking excitedly about Kate's news and the game and the festival in general. Even TJ seemed happy about the whole thing.

It was suddenly strangely quiet when the door bumped shut behind them and Tess realized she and Bryan were alone.

"So, that was—"

"Fun," she filled in.

He grinned, clearly glad that was the word she'd used. "It was. And—"

The phone in his office started ringing before he could finish what he'd been about to say.

She smiled. "It's okay."

He pushed himself up from the chair, grabbing the crutch he'd laid on the floor next to him. "Be right back."

He headed for the office and Tess started cleaning up. She gathered the dishes and carried them to the bar. Then she returned to the table and collected the pens and the scraps of paper. She stopped when she saw that there were several pieces of paper that had writing on them by Bryan's chair too.

She picked them up and read one.

When she was eleven and broke her arm.

Tess gasped.

She looked for another.

When she said she didn't want to date me.

Clearly the first one was in answer to question about when he'd first kissed her. The second was apparently the time she'd most surprised him.

She shook her head. Of course he'd been surprised by her turning him down.

With a deep breath, she reached for the last piece of paper.

Last night against her door.

The last time he'd kissed her breathless.

He'd gotten them all right.

That didn't shock her. What shocked her was that he'd answered the questions about her in the first place.

But what shocked her even more was how much that touched her.

The sound of him laughing in his office caught her attention. She glanced around. Crap, she couldn't deal with him alone right now.

Not after last night. Not after being smacked in the face by the deep and hot and *tempting* forever love that the couples here had for each other. Not after reading his answers to the newlywed questions.

Tess carried all of the scraps of paper the group had used to the trashcan. She tossed them all in and then turned toward the door.

But when her hand hit the door, she turned back, crossed to the trash and pulled out the three Bryan had written on.

She read them again, then tucked them into her pocket, and hurried out into the bright afternoon.

9

"Cornhole."

"Horseshoes."

"Lawn darts."

"I'm not sure lawn darts are even legal anymore," Bryan inserted.

Or tried to insert. No one was listening to him.

He was sure that at least one of these men had a lawn dart set stored somewhere in his garage from the sixties and that they didn't care a bit about the legality of the game. This was serious competition time in Sapphire Falls, and the game chosen for the annual Lawn Yawn—the unofficial name of the tournament where a bunch of the older guys got together and played lawn games—was a serious decision. Most of the time it was decided by rock-paper-scissors. Sometimes a flip of a quarter. But never before had the players argued and bitched for at least an hour.

Of course, the players were the same every year. As were the spectators. The Lawn Yawn was not for the faint of heart. It required a comfortable place to sit, a full cooler and some good sunscreen.

And a sense of humor.

There was a bracket for the teams and everything.

But the most entertaining part was watching the old guys argue. Something that happened every five minutes. Rather than betting on the brackets, most of the people who showed up bet on which of the men would lose his cool and storm off first, which would use the most F-bombs, and who would pretend to strain something first. There was also always an under-the-table drinking game going. Everyone drank whenever Frank blamed a poor shot on his bad rotator cuff—which switched sides every year it seemed. Everyone drank whenever Conrad claimed that Larry was cheating—and about ninety percent of the time he was right. Everyone drank whenever Albert told the story about winning ten bucks playing cornhole when he was only eight years old at the county fair. And so on and so forth.

No one ever remembered who won the tournament, but many people remembered their own Lawn Yawn hangovers from years gone by. For Bryan, the granddaddy had been in 2013.

This morning, Bryan was listening to them, flashing back to that horrible morning-after, and wondering how in the hell he'd ended up in Dottie's *meeting* with these guys about the tournament.

Oh, yeah. Tessa.

He'd gone to her house last night after finishing *Erotic Research*, but she hadn't answered the door. Or her phone. So he'd called TJ to find out where she was supposed to be first thing this morning. He'd thought about camping out on her front porch, but he could admit that he was thinking maybe he didn't know her as well as he'd thought. Before the last few days, he would have guessed that he was far more stubborn than she was and he could easily outwait her on the front porch.

Now he wasn't so sure.

If the romantic, starry-eyed girl he'd known all his life had really read *Erotic Research* eight times, then he didn't know her very well at all.

And he was thrilled.

Not that she was more stubborn than he'd thought, but that she was interested in some—or all—of the naughtiness in that book.

It was one of his favorites now too.

He needed to get this meeting over with.

"How about beer pong?" he asked.

It was something new. That's what this needed. Something no one had won before. Time to shake up the routine—and, yes, he did realize that the same would be applied to him and Tessa.

"Beer what?" Frank asked.

"Beer pong. You set up ten cups in a triangle shape on both ends of a long table. There are two teams. You take turns trying to bounce a Ping-Pong ball into a cup on the other end of the table. If your ball lands in a cup, your opponent has to drink that cup. Then it's removed. You play until one team eliminates all of the other team's cups. But," he said, thinking fast, "we do it bigger. We use buckets, or even trashcans, and big rubber playground balls."

"We're going to drink an entire trashcan full of beer?" Albert asked.

"No, you'll just drink from a cup, but it's a bigger game this way," Bryan said.

"I don't know if I can throw with my bad rotator cuff," Frank said.

"It's underhanded," Bryan said. "More tossing than throwing. Just like horseshoes or cornhole."

"Can we drink whatever we want?" Conrad asked.

"Well, if you drink iced tea and we're drinking beer, you

have an advantage, don't you think?" Larry asked.

"I'll drink beer," Conrad told him. "I was just wondering."

"You were just wondering about something that doesn't make a damned difference to you?" Larry asked.

"This is why we never get anything done," Albert declared.

"Guys," Bryan said loudly. "How about we pick a number."

Frank looked over at him. "Pick a number for what?"

"I'll think of a number. You all pick. Whoever gets closest gets to pick the game." This had to be what kindergarten teachers went through.

"Fine," Frank said. "A number between what and what?"

Bryan had no idea. "One and fifty," he threw out.

"Eight," Frank said.

"What if I was going to say eight?" Albert asked. "Who says you get to go first?"

"Were you going to say eight?" Frank asked.

"No," Albert told him. "I always pick thirty. But that's not the point."

"Okay," Frank said. "You go first."

"Thirty," Albert said.

Jesus. Bryan rubbed a hand over his face.

"Why should he get to go first?" Larry asked.

Oh, for fuck's sake. "What would Tessa do?" Bryan asked loudly over the bickering.

The men all looked at him, then each other.

"She'd probably have us all write down our vote and then put them in a hat and pull one out," Conrad said.

"Then let's do that," Bryan told them. Whatever got this over with. So he could go find Tessa and find out why she'd ditched the meeting.

And why she was avoiding him.

The men all grabbed napkins and wrote down their votes, while Bryan contemplated his life choices. This was Sapphire Falls. These were the pillars of the community—arguing over lawn games and having to be supervised like five-year-olds. But he couldn't help but grin as the men wadded the napkins up, threw them into Frank's cap, and held it out to Bryan.

He loved this crazy place and he was staying—for better or worse.

Bryan reached in and pulled out a napkin. He smoothed it out and read, "Beer pong it is!"

All but Albert cheered.

Bryan tucked the napkins into his pocket and rose from his chair.

"Okay, gentlemen, I'm out of here."

"Who's going to do the bracket?" Larry asked.

Bryan looked at him. "Does Tess usually do the bracket?"

They all nodded. Of course she did. Tessa did everything that kept things running smoothly around here.

He and she were so alike in so many ways. He loved the behind-the-scenes stuff. He'd never begrudged Ty or the other athletes the spotlight. Bryan could have trained and competed like they did. But it wasn't in his nature. He competed against himself—improving his times and distances—but he'd always been out for the pleasure of the activity, to absorb and appreciate the moment. He was a great motivator because he helped people focus on their goals and motivations and making themselves better before they worked on being better than someone else. He loved watching other people accomplish things.

Tess was like that. Behind the scenes, making things work, making things great and letting others enjoy and shine.

"Then I'll be sure she gets that bracket done," he told the men. "I'll see you all later."

"But what about—"

"Dottie?" Bryan called out. "A round of coffee and cinnamon rolls for the boys, on me."

That quieted them down—just like snack time in a kindergarten classroom—and Bryan said a final quick goodbye and escaped.

He pulled the wadded napkins from his pocket and looked them over. Sure enough—they all said beer pong but one. The one he'd chosen. He ripped them all up and tossed them into the trashcan by the streetlight in front of the diner on his way to his truck. He didn't want to be caught with that one-off vote that read LAWN DARTS.

There was no way he was letting those guys play with lawn darts. It was his public service of the day.

———

Tessa knew she shouldn't be surprised to see Bryan on her front porch steps, but she was.

What she wasn't surprised by, at all, was the way her heart leapt when she saw him.

Damn. Old habits really died hard.

Of course, it wasn't an *old* habit to flash to the memory of being on Bryan's lap with his hands and mouth all over her body. No, that one was definitely newer.

Tessa swallowed hard as her body flushed. Which was amazing, considering her body was already hot and flushed from her run.

And then there was the memory where she'd told him that she thought he should find another girl.

Yeah, definitely new.

"Hi," she said as she approached, aware that she was sweaty and dressed in fitted workout clothes.

Then again, it seemed whenever Bryan was around, she was very aware of things her body was doing.

"'Morning," he said, his eyes tracking over her from head to toe.

"Everything okay?" she asked, lifting a shoulder to her temple to wipe a trickle of sweat.

Typically, she liked the feeling of being sweaty and hot and out of breath. It meant she'd worked hard and pushed herself. She liked the feeling of energy that pumped through her and the feeling of accomplishment. She could distinctly remember the first weeks and months after she'd decided to start running. She'd hated it. She'd hated the sore muscles, the blisters on her feet and the gasping for breath, the sweat, the realization that she couldn't even make it a mile. But it was the end of the run that kept her going back out. The way she felt standing under the shower spray after she'd finished, after she'd refused to quit no matter how much she'd wanted to, had kept her putting those shoes on.

She also remembered the feeling the first time she'd doubled her distance. Then the day she'd beat her personal time. Then the time she'd gotten brave enough to sign up for a 5k. And she'd not only finished, but finished in the top ten for her age.

Yes, typically, she liked how she felt after a run.

But today, with Bryan's eyes on her, taking in every detail—from her tomato-red face to the hair escaping her ponytail to her bright pink socks that didn't go with her bright blue running tights—she felt self-conscious and gross.

"No, Tess, everything is *not* okay," he finally said.

It was probably the socks.

"What are you doing here?" It was just after eight in the morning. She knew Bryan was more of a night owl—one of the very few reasons the bartending gig made sense—and that he tended to not see daylight before about ten. She also knew he'd worked last night.

It seemed she knew details about him without even meaning to. Once a stalker, always a stalker. Even if it was unintentional now.

He was sitting with his forearms resting on his thighs, the picture of casual and laidback. But she sensed a strange tension in him.

"You missed our meeting this morning. Thought I'd stop by and fill you in on the details."

Meeting? She thought quickly. Ah, the Lawn Yawn. "You went to the meeting at the diner?" she asked, unable to fight the smile. She'd been to exactly one meeting with that group. That had been more than enough. For the last few years, she'd left them to all the decision making, and bickering, and simply drawn up their bracket after they were done.

"I did. TJ said that was on your agenda this morning, and I'm here to help you."

"That meeting is completely pointless, even for the men involved. They make the same arguments every year even though they all have a great time no matter what game they play, and no one shows up—including *them*—because of the game. I gave up meeting with them four years ago or so."

"Smart girl. So you probably don't need a rundown about the change to beer pong then."

"Beer pong? Seriously?"

"My suggestion."

"Really."

"They were bickering about everything else. I thought maybe changing things up a little would be good." He looked at her directly. "You know how sometimes you take things for granted until something shakes you out of the routine?"

Tess shifted uncomfortably. They weren't taking about beer pong. "Yeah. Change can be good. Give you perspective."

He nodded. "Change can make you really appreciate what you had before too."

She cleared her throat. "So you think changing to beer pong will help them appreciate cornhole?"

"I think seeing you naked and giving you an orgasm has

made me appreciate having a long history of friendship with you."

Naked. Orgasm. Words like that from Bryan's lips hit her hard—and low. Her body responded as if he *had* said fuck and suck.

Naked wasn't a dirty word. Orgasm wasn't exactly naughty. But from him, they had the same effect on her. Interesting.

And very inconvenient, considering she was trying to avoid all of this.

"A long history?" she asked. "How is the other night related to our history?"

"You really don't know?" he asked. "You don't realize that whether you want romance and sweetness or not, our history as friends and your crush made that orgasm even better?"

She sucked air in through her nose. She did kind of know that actually. But that didn't mean she didn't want the dirty stuff.

"So because of our history as friends, you getting me off with just your fingers on my couch is as good as if you'd bent me over and fucked me?" she asked, purposefully being blunt and graphic.

He was making her face the other night? Fine. He'd face it from her perspective too.

He looked at her for a long moment, heat and electricity zapping back and forth between them.

"Yes," he finally said. "Because watching your face the other night was the hottest thing I've ever seen, in part because of our long history and all the memories of all the times I've seen different looks on your face. And if I was fucking you from behind, I wouldn't have been able to see that."

Tess barely resisted squeezing her knees together. Okay, so *fucking* from Bryan was really hot.

She swallowed. "So yeah, beer pong. Good move."

He nodded, as if the change in topics was totally expected.

"Thanks. I'm getting more into the idea of changing things up, in the context of the familiar things I've always loved."

Definitely not talking about beer pong.

"You've always loved the Lawn Yawn?" she asked lightly. Or tried to. It seemed like her chest was too tight to even take in much air.

Because if *fucking* was hot from Bryan, then *love* was equally so.

She was such a sucker.

"The Lawn Yawn is something I've appreciated more than I realized. Being gone and coming back makes you realize how much you depend on some things to always stay the same. When things start changing, you understand how much it means to count on certain things that you've taken for granted."

Tess looked at him closely. Meeting his eyes was tough because she felt the impact all the way to her toes. But she saw more than heat and seduction in his eyes.

"Sapphire Falls was what you could count on after your accident," she said. "Everything in your life changed suddenly, and you needed Sapphire Falls to be the same."

"And you. You and Sapphire Falls go hand in hand for me."

She could tell he meant that, and it made her heart flip, in spite of herself.

"So for a year and seven months, you just needed to assume everything was how it always was," she said.

"Until I got on top of the other changes, in my body and routine and job."

Tess nodded. That made sense. "And now?"

"Now I'm ready for the next change. The change in our relationship. Going from friends and crush to more."

"And I—"

"I'm sorry I assumed you were exactly who I thought you were and that you were still waiting for me," he interrupted. "Who I *assumed* you were because it was easier for me. I just *needed* you to be that girl as I adjusted. That girl helped me get through a lot of it."

She frowned, her chest feeling tight. "How? I didn't do anything."

"You thought *I* could do anything," he told her. "Or I assumed you thought I could do anything. And it helped me think it too. I've seen over and over how much it can matter just to have someone believing in you."

"But—" Tess started, thinking that through. She loved the idea that she had somehow helped him through everything. "You must have suspected I wasn't exactly who you thought, since you never really came to me with any of this."

He nodded again. "Maybe. Or maybe I was worried about not being who *you* thought *I* was. I couldn't lose godlike status with you while I was working my way back."

She couldn't help her smile. "I didn't think you were godlike. Exactly."

He lifted a brow. "Didn't you?"

Tess propped a hand on her hip. "Ego intact."

"Thanks to you."

She took a breath. If she'd really had something to do with his recovery—that meant something. A lot. He'd changed her by inspiring her to try running. If she'd done the same for him...yeah, that was big. "And now you're not worried about losing godlike status?"

"I'm back." He gave her a grin. "I'm new and improved."

"I may not survive," she said drily.

Though she couldn't argue. Bryan was still him—funny, optimistic, self-deprecating while totally confident. As if something had sanded the sharp point of his ego to a more subtle edge. It was still there, but it was as if he now knew he could back it up. His cockiness before the accident had partly been an act as he'd been figuring himself out. Now he knew himself.

"I'll help you through it," he told her. "Need you to survive it —and thrive. With me."

Even after the other night, when she'd turned him down and given him a pep talk about finding someone else, he was here on her porch, wanting to be with her.

A trickle of sweat between her breasts suddenly brought her back to her messy post-run condition.

"I've changed some too," she told him honestly.

He nodded. "I'm getting that." He looked her up and down. "You're jogging?"

There was something funny in his voice, but she couldn't put her finger on it. She nodded. "Yeah." Though the word *jog* made her cringe. That was far too easy a term for the way she'd tortured herself this morning. Thoughts of mountains and beaches had been on a constant reel...interspersed with pictures of Bryan.

But *yeah* was all she was going to say about that. She wasn't ready to talk about her running with Bryan. Which was so crazy, considering she wouldn't be doing any of it if it wasn't for him.

"How long have you been running?"

How could she tell him without him assuming he was the reason?

Okay, it was a straightforward question. She could answer it casually, not give anything away and move on to another topic. "A little over two years."

He hesitated. "How far did you go this morning?"

Crap. She paused again. She knew other people who ran for exercise and because they enjoyed it. Or so they could keep eating cupcakes or drinking beer. But most of them went no more than five miles and most did more like one or two.

She coughed and looked at the ground.

"Hey," Bryan said gently. "It doesn't matter. I'm just curious. No judgment."

Her head came up. He was used to coaching high-level, serious athletes, and she could tell from the look he was giving her that he thought she was embarrassed to tell him because she hadn't made it very far.

Tess straightened her spine and met his gaze. "Ten."

He gave her a little confused frown. "Ten?"

"Miles

His eyes traveled over her again, more slowly this time. "Ten miles?"

"Yep."

"How fast?"

She was proud of her pace. Very proud. She'd worked hard to get there. But the minute she told Bryan her time, he'd know that she'd been training. Hard.

Tess took a deep breath. "An hour and thirty-three minutes."

She just couldn't lie about that. She'd worked for every one of those minutes. And no one else, besides Ty, would understand that was a great pace.

Bryan looked surprised for a blink. But his expression quickly morphed into something else—almost anger.

"It appears there's even more about you that I don't know," he said tightly.

She snorted at that. Which didn't make him look *less* irritated.

"Really, Bryan?" she asked, in the face of his annoyance. "You really think there *aren't* things you don't know about me?"

"I thought you were a pretty open book, I guess."

Tessa put a hand on her hip. And he'd counted on it. He'd just told her that. He'd wanted her to be the same. But he'd also just said he was okay with change in the midst of the familiar. Well, she was still her, but, yeah, new and improved too.

She needed water. And a shower. But she didn't feel like they were done here. Or that she could just walk away this time. She'd done that a couple of times with him already. She'd made *him* walk two nights ago.

Her running wasn't pathetic. Her twenty-plus years of loving this man who barely knew her was. And maybe starting running because of wanting to bond with him was. But what she was doing now was something she was proud of.

"I run," she said. "A lot. I'm working up to fifty miles a week."

That made him sit up. "Fifty?"

"Yes."

"You're training," he said. It wasn't a question.

"Yes."

"For what?"

"The Colorado Marathon."

Bryan gave her a little frown. "You already missed it."

"Next year."

He nodded, clearly processing that. "Have you done a half?"

He didn't seem quite as stunned as she would have expected. She shook her head. "That's the plan this year. There are a few I'd like to do."

"Such as?"

Okay, fine. She could tell him all of this. Why not? He couldn't change her mind. She had a plan, she was well into it, in fact, and she loved it. Bryan Murray was...everything she'd always wanted. *Before* she gotten a life of her own. She didn't need to live vicariously through him anymore. She had done the training, she had—or would have—the money to enter and travel to the races, and to pay Jake Elliot to get her to the next level.

"There are a couple of Rock 'n' Roll halves," she said. "And an oceanfront run. And a covered-bridge half marathon in New England I've got on my list."

He still looked irritated, but he also looked...amazed. "I had no idea you were into this."

She nodded, not trusting what else she might confess.

"Is this what Denver is about?" he asked.

Tess pressed her lips together and nodded.

"You want to go out there to train for all of these."

She swallowed. "Running the flat countryside here isn't challenging me anymore," she said. "I need to do more if I want to keep getting better."

He nodded, though he did still seem amazed. "You're really serious about this."

"I am."

Bryan stretched to his feet on the second step of her porch. From there, he was looking down on her from a significant height. He didn't look happy. He didn't look shocked either. And he wasn't laughing at her. "If I still lived in Denver, would you have asked me to train you?" he asked.

For some reason, the phrase *train you* made her stomach flip. He didn't mean it sexually. She knew that. But she couldn't help but respond to the low timbre of his voice. And there was something about how he was watching her now.

Tess cleared her throat. "Maybe," she fudged.

He shook his head. "I wouldn't have let anyone else do it," he said. "If I found out you were in Denver and hadn't been in touch, and were letting someone else train you, I would have tracked you down and not left you alone until you let me do it."

"You—" She had to clear her throat again.

There was something about Bryan being so insistent that made her stupid heart swell. And it *was* stupid. This was just about his ego. He was widely known as one of the best trainers. He would have definitely wanted to be involved with someone from Sapphire Falls. She'd like to think that *she* would have been the reason, but honestly, this was Bryan's passion. He would have wanted to train anyone he personally knew.

"I guess I hadn't thought about it," she finally said. Flat-out lied, actually. She'd thought about it but had quickly dismissed it. She couldn't have Bryan involved in her running—anymore than he already was. She needed to do this on her own. Well, with Jake. But that was different.

Bryan knew she was lying. She could tell. He didn't laugh in her face, but he definitely looked plenty skeptical.

"No? I didn't occur to you for one second in the process of thinking about going to Denver to train for marathons?" he asked.

"Well, okay, I might have thought about it once or twice. But I wasn't ready for it when you were living there and then you... moved home."

"Right. I moved home." As if it was a simple life change—moving home like lots of people did.

But all of the real reasons he was here were right there between them.

"Right."

"And now you're ready? For the training?"

She nodded. "I will be. I, um—" She coughed.

She was completely nervous and excited about the news she'd gotten via email just that morning. She'd figured it would be a couple of weeks before she even heard back, but Jake Elliot's answer had been in her inbox that morning. He had agreed to meet with her and discuss taking her on as a client. He wanted her to run the half marathon in Steamboat Springs in two weeks, and then they would meet while she was there.

Jake wanted to see what her time was in the half and where she placed before he accepted her. She kind of hated that. She wanted to improve compared to herself. But she understood that the race would be an objective measuring stick for Jake.

So she was going to Steamboat Springs. The same weekend the festival was supposed to start.

She *really* hated that.

"You what, Tess?" Bryan asked, his voice low.

She lifted her chin when she realized that she was focusing

on the middle of his chest instead of meeting his eyes. "I'm running the Fourth of July half marathon in Steamboat and then I'm meeting with Jake Elliot."

Bryan's eyebrows slammed together. "You've talked to Jake?"

She nodded. "He emailed me and I talked to him last night."

"And he's taking you on?"

She shrugged. "Maybe. He's interested. I need to perform well in Steamboat and have a solid plan together. But I think I can convince him."

Bryan rolled his eyes. "You're not going to have to convince him."

Her heart sped up at that. "Really? You think he'll take me?" she asked.

Bryan scowled again. "Of course he'll take you. Unless you stop halfway through the run or take three hours to finish, he'll take you."

"Really?" She stepped toward him. "You think my time will be good enough? He made it sound like he wanted it faster."

"For fuck's sake," Bryan said. "That's *his* job."

"But—"

"Tess, he'll take you. And he'll train you and you'll run the marathon and you'll probably qualify for Boston if that's what you want."

Tess felt her eyes widen. She wasn't sure she *wanted* Boston. That wasn't on her list exactly. She'd much rather run in Paris or Alaska. But *qualifying* for Boston would be amazing. "You think so?"

Bryan's frown deepened. "Yeah, I think so. That's what he does."

"So...great," she said. She was sure her smile showed how much this meant to her. "Then...that's great."

"Yeah, great," Bryan muttered. He ran a hand through his

hair. "I can't believe you've been running all this time and I didn't know."

Tess felt her smile die. She shrugged. "Why would you know?"

She paid attention *him*. Not the other way around.

Bryan didn't say anything for a long moment.

"What?" she asked him.

"I'd love to know what made you start running. I don't remember you liking it in high school."

"I never did it in high school," she said. She still wanted to avoid telling him exactly what had inspired her. Because she really had left that girl and her obsession behind. Mostly.

"So what made you try it?"

"A couple of things," she hedged.

"I'd love to know," he said sincerely. "For one thing, this is clearly big in your life. I really thought I knew you. This is great, but I'll admit it's a surprise. A great surprise. You know how I feel about running. I had no idea we shared this passion."

Passion.

He was referring to running, but there was really something about hearing that word from him that made parts of Tess clench. Not that the whole couch scenario was ever very far from her mind, but *passion*...yeah, she wasn't sure she'd ever really felt that before. The only thing that came close was the running. Which was also because of Bryan.

"I read a blog," she confessed. "It was very...inspiring. I was...going through some stuff and I knew I needed a change. That seemed like the answer."

He was frowning again, but it wasn't the angry scowl from before. Now he looked concerned. "What were you going through?"

Loving you from a distance for far too long. Realizing that the thing I loved most about you was the way you threw yourself into everything with your whole heart. Realizing I wanted that. For me.

That had been the enlightening she'd needed. To realize that she wanted things for herself, not things that would make Bryan take notice.

She'd wanted to experience the *joy* and abandonment that was so evident in Bryan whenever he did a blog post or a video. She'd wanted to live life the way he did. Because he was really *living* life, while she sat in Sapphire Falls and did the same things over and over, in the same places, with the same people.

Tess chewed the inside of her cheek. She didn't want to lie to him. Not really. They shared a passion now. That's what she'd always wanted.

"I was feeling restless. Like I needed a change," she said. "Like life was passing me by and I wasn't fully experiencing it. The running started out just making me appreciate nature around me and getting to know my body and my...spirit." She had to remember this was *Bryan*. He was the one who had written about all of this first. "I wanted to know how hard I could push myself. How hard I would work for something I wanted. I wanted to feel...triumphant."

Bryan was nodding. He got it.

Of course he did. Those were practically his words.

"And you got what you wanted from it?" he asked.

"I figured out that I can do more than I thought, if I want it bad enough," she said. "I learned that I can get better. I learned to be patient with myself and kind to myself. And I let myself start thinking bigger—bigger than what I've always known, bigger than this town and...this life."

She felt ungrateful when she said that. She didn't mean that she didn't love her life, her family, friends, home. But there was a big, big world out there that she'd really first seen through Bryan's eyes. Now she wanted to see it up close. She wanted to be *in* it.

"And so now you're getting ready to go and conquer it all," Bryan said.

Getting His Way

Tess nodded. "Yeah."

Bryan pulled a long breath in through his nose. "Okay. So I'm actually thrilled to learn it."

"You are?"

He shrugged. "Of course. Someone I've known so well for so long, someone I care about, has discovered the joy and pain of something I've loved. Something that made *me* a better person. Yeah, I'm very happy for you."

Happy for her. *O-o-o-kay.* So maybe the whole let's-settle-down-and-live-happily-ever-after-together wasn't set in stone for him.

Tess couldn't believe how devastated she suddenly felt.

Had she wanted Bryan pursuing her and derailing all of her plans? Making her entertain the idea of throwing it all to the side just to have him? Tempting her with the one thing that could change her mind about everything?

No.

But did she want him pursuing her and telling her that he wanted her and needed her, kissing her and touching her and fulfilling so many of her fantasies?

Well, she wasn't dead or an idiot.

"Okay, so then I guess that's that," she said, starting up the steps. Damn, she should have told him about the running before.

Before he'd given her an orgasm, seemingly effortlessly. Before she'd learned, for sure, that he had no physical issues with his erections. Before she'd known what she'd been missing.

Dammit.

Bryan caught her arm as she passed him. "So let's talk more. The half is in two weeks."

She looked at him, his face only inches from hers. "I know."

"I can get you ready."

He would coach her. At least short term. He was offering.

God, talk about getting everything she'd always wanted. An orgasm *and* training from Bryan? How could she say no?

"Really?"

"Of course. I'd love to."

"Well—" If she agreed then she'd *really* be committed to Steamboat. And Jake. And everything.

Like leaving Bryan.

And the fact that she was even hesitating made her finally nod. "Okay."

"Go shower," he told her. "I'll make you some breakfast. And we'll talk."

Shower. Eggs.

Well, eggs hadn't been on her list of things she wanted from Bryan, but knowing him, he was great at those too.

10

She was a runner. Damn. He had not seen that coming. And he had not expected it to hit him with the strength that it had.

He'd known a lot of female runners over the years. Strong, tough, beautiful women. He'd even dated a couple, slept with more than a couple. But their shared love of the sport had never been as important, and as much of a turn-on, as it was with Tess.

Bryan moved around her kitchen, pulling together the perfect after-workout breakfast. Ten miles was nothing small. She needed a refueling with the right balance of protein and carbs that would nourish her body quickly and well.

If she was doing it right, she would have fueled and hydrated before her run and partway through. And he had the definite impression that she was doing it right. Tess was the girl who kept the mayor's office running, who was organizing most of the festival, who dotted I's and crossed T's for everyone else. So he was sure that Tessa was taking care of herself with her running. She'd looked really good walking up her front sidewalk that morning. Bryan wasn't sure even Ty looked that healthy after a ten-mile workout.

That still meant she needed a good breakfast, and there was something about doing this for her that felt really good. Intimate even.

Coaching her would have felt the same way. He cracked six eggs, whisking them harder than he needed to. Fuck, he hated the idea of Jake Elliot coaching her.

Jake was a good coach. One of the best. He'd do a great job with Tess. If she was really ready to work hard, Jake could get her there.

But Bryan was completely, irrationally jealous of the idea. Coaching was a relationship unlike any other. You had to be a friend, a psychologist, a teacher. You had to know your athlete well enough to know when he or she needed an empathetic ear, or a kick in the ass.

Bryan knew that Jake was meeting with Tess not to judge her talent or dedication, but to see if there was chemistry between them. Not sexual chemistry—necessarily—but chemistry that would allow Tess to trust him, allow him to be fully, brutally honest, and allow them to maintain a mutual respect even when she hated him and when he said hard-to-hear things.

Then again, Bryan knew Jake wouldn't rule *out* sexual chemistry.

He poured the eggs into the pan to scramble them and started the whole-wheat toast.

He really wanted to train Tess.

It was the damnedest thing.

He'd given up coaching. Moving to Sapphire Falls meant changing what he did for a living. Ty was still competing, and Bryan was able to coach him to an extent—the extent that he could tell Ty that he needed to step it up or help him through the inevitable mental blocks that happened to any athlete at times. Bryan knew Ty, knew how he trained, knew his competition history and cared about his success, so he could help Ty out. But they weren't establishing a relationship from square one, and Ty didn't need Bryan out with him on the trails or beside him in the gym anymore.

New clients would.

Ty had offered Bryan a place with him in his new training program that he was establishing in Sapphire Falls, and Bryan had agreed to help out. But not full time.

Athletes who were just getting to the point of high-level competition were Bryan's specialty. Not beginners, but not the elite who already had Olympic medals or world champion status or even multiple marathons behind them. He was the transition guy—taking those who had started, who knew what they wanted, and needed help getting to the next level. Like Tess. Evidently.

He'd stumbled upon his gift to push and motivate by being Ty Bennett's best friend all his life. He'd figured Ty out by knowing him since they were five. He'd watched Ty grow, listened to him talk about his sport, gotten into his head because he was in every part of Ty's life. He'd known about Ty losing his virginity, the first fight he'd had with his father, the biggest disappointments of his life and the greatest victories. Watching an Olympic athlete develop—not just through his sport, but through his *life*—had given Bryan unique insight. Then he'd gotten to know other athletes through Ty and had figured out they all had things in common.

Bryan's career had started beside swimming pools, on tracks and trails, and in bars postrace, talking to—and listening to— athletes of all backgrounds, at all levels. And he'd figured out that his love for sports, his outgoing, charismatic personality and his undying optimism was a perfect combination for coaching.

But he'd known a move to Sapphire Falls would make

continuing that path difficult. So Bryan had accepted that it was time for something new. He'd work with those athletes as needed, but he couldn't be in the trenches with them. He couldn't be hands-on with them, the way he was used to being. He had run, biked and swum with his clients. He'd literally worked out their muscle knots, made them their smoothies, started and stopped the stopwatches. He'd been beside them, with them, through the transition to serious, every day, eat-sleep-breathe athlete.

But he had been looking forward to the change. To hanging out with people who were less intense—and less crazy—than high-level athletes. He was happy to be spending time with people who were happy with the simple things in life, farming and family, rather than those who worked their bodies to the peak, and sometimes beyond, for a little bit of gold and glory.

Athletes were nuts.

A case could be made for people in Sapphire Falls being a little nuts too, of course. But they were good nuts. Happy nuts. *Satisfied* nuts.

Athletes were never satisfied. At least not the successfully competitive ones. They always wanted more. That was what kept them training.

Satisfaction was what he wanted—in a nutshell. The ability to look around and say, "I'm where I'm supposed to be", instead of always looking ahead and pushing for more. Whereas it looked like Tess was doing the opposite. She'd just discovered that she wanted more.

He suddenly missed the coaching.

He honestly hadn't. Not in eighteen months. For one, he'd been the one needing coaching at times with his rehab. For another, this was a new chapter. He knew looking back and wishing for things from the past would keep him from being able to move forward and accepting his new life.

But he wanted to coach Tess.

Just Tess.

He felt like he was missing out. But how exactly did you miss doing something you'd never done? Hell, he hadn't even known it was an option. He hadn't known she ran.

And she didn't just run. She trained. She was looking at marathons. And she'd done it all herself. For two and a half years. She'd been pursuing this, training, getting better, and she'd done it on her own.

That said a lot about her, loudly, to Bryan. There were athletes with coaches behind them and endorsements on the line who struggled at times. Tess had been here, in Sapphire Falls, with a nonexistent running support group, training on the dirt back roads.

Damn. The internal drive and motivation that took was sexy as hell.

It was like Tess had turned a page for him that morning. A page in the book of *her*.

He'd thought he knew this story. He would have bet that he knew it nearly by heart. It was hard to wrap his mind around a competitive Tess, bent on beating everyone around her, pushing her body to the point of pain to be better than someone else. He couldn't remember her ever being anyone's rival. She helped other people. She lifted others up and helped *them* shine. She was one of the most content and happy people he knew. Or so he'd thought. Competitive runners needed a bit of...dissatisfaction. It was what motivated them—seeking that gratification. Tess had always seemed very gratified by her life.

But the pages in this book had been flipping rapidly lately. He'd learned she had a sassy, confident side. He'd learned she was a virgin. Who liked dirty talk. Who read erotic romance and got excited about being bossed around in bed. Now he'd learned that she was driven, passionate, internally motivated. Maybe she had found a competitive streak too.

And the differences in her weren't all internal. He'd noticed some of the physical changes over the past few years. She'd lost some weight, tightened up some. But he hadn't *noticed*, because it didn't matter. He'd always liked how she'd looked. He loved her curves. He loved the softness and the fullness and...

Suddenly, he straightened. She had lost some weight, but she was talking about amping up her training now. She might lose more weight if she kept training. That meant fewer curves.

With a frown, he dropped some butter into the pan of eggs. And put more on her toast.

"You're making me eggs?"

He turned as she came into the kitchen. Her hair was hanging in damp tendrils around her freshly scrubbed face. She was dressed in yoga pants and a tee and looked relaxed and sexy.

Of course, now that he knew she was leaving, he should leave her alone. And he might have. If it wasn't for that virgin thing.

Maybe it made him a jerk, but he really wanted to be Tessa's first.

Especially because she was leaving.

He wanted to *be* something to her that no one else could or would.

The ladies at the Community Center had said he needed to give her something she couldn't get anywhere else to keep her here in Sapphire Falls.

He'd thought that was good advice.

But no one else knew about Tessa's running—the intensity of it, or her goals for it. Now that he did know, he couldn't try to convince her to stay. But he could give her something that she'd take with her forever. Being made love to by the first guy she'd loved.

He wanted to set the standard.

If there were other guys—and he supposed that was inevitable, though he didn't want to spend one minute thinking about it—then he wanted her to know what it was like to have *amazing* sex with a guy who really loved her.

Hopefully then she'd hold out for that every time, forever.

Bryan realized he was gripping the spoon tightly and frowning at her. And that he hadn't said a word to her yet. He made himself relax and smile at her. "It's almost ready."

"I hope you're planning on helping with that," she said, eyeing the skillet as she took a seat on one of the stools at the center island. "I can't eat that much." She picked up the glass of orange juice he'd poured and put it next to one of the two place settings he'd put out.

He set a plate in front of her. Tessa studied the eggs like they held the meaning of life.

Bryan sat next to her and dug in.

"So tell me about your nutrition program," he said after they'd both taken a few bites.

She coughed and squirmed on her chair. Bryan took a long swig of his coffee and waited.

"I've been using the RF10 program," she said, naming a line of supplements that he personally loved.

"That's awesome," he said. "Who's working with you?"

He hadn't even been aware there was someplace local that sold the program. Of course, anyone could walk in off the street and buy the RF10 stuff from any health store, but the best retailers helped their customers make the right choices based on their goals.

"I just get it online," she said, squirming again and stuffing her mouth with toast.

He frowned. "How did you know what to start with?"

There wasn't exactly a wrong way to use the supplements— they were completely natural—but there was definitely a *right* way to use them as a part of a running training program.

"Did a bunch of reading," she said. She cleared her throat. "There are some really great websites and stuff out there."

He couldn't argue with that. He had a blog of his own and hoped that people found it a good resource if they didn't have a local person or coach. He hadn't blogged for a long time, but he'd left it set up. "Let me look at what you're doing. I can make some tweaks."

"Okay, sure." She waved her fork in the direction of the cupboard over her coffeepot. "In there."

An hour later, Bryan had all of her supplements laid out, had made her write out her workout plan, had looked at her workout tracking over the past six months—something else he strongly encouraged his clients to do—and had looked over her stretching program.

He sat back and lifted his second cup of coffee. At some point, she had loaded their dishes into the dishwasher and wiped off the island as he'd pored over her information.

Not only was she serious about her program, she was doing everything right.

"I'm impressed," he told her. "This is almost exactly the program I would have set up if I'd done it."

She gave him a little smile and lifted her shoulder. "Told you there are a lot of great resources out there."

There were. But Bryan knew why this program seemed so perfect.

It was his.

Well, not *his*. He hadn't personally put it together. But she'd applied his principles.

He knew there were other resources, other coaches, other approaches that would get a serious runner to the ready-to-compete level. In fact, he was *very* aware of those other coaches and programs. He kept up on what others were doing. But that was the thing—there were other *different* approaches.

What Tess was doing was applying *his* principles. Things that set him apart from the others.

"Are you in touch with anyone about your program? Ever

emailed anyone? Called them?" he asked casually, feeling anything but.

The truth was, she could have emailed him a question—or questions—over the years and not used her real name, and he never would have known. He enjoyed answering questions here and there and had gotten dozens of messages a week before he'd moved back to Sapphire Falls.

But if she had, why keep it a secret? In fact, why keep any of this a secret?

"Oh, once or twice," she said flippantly. "Mostly, I just figured things out. It's not rocket science."

He almost laughed. No, it wasn't NASA-level stuff, but there was absolutely some science to running. At least to running well. And she damned well knew that if she was doing the reading that would lead her to information about supplements and protein/ carb balance and the principles of hydration.

"I would have been happy to answer questions for you," he said. "It's what I do, after all."

And he did it very well, thank you very much.

If she *had* messaged him anonymously, he wanted to know why. If she *hadn't*, well, he wanted to know why.

They could have been sharing this all this time. He hated that he was just learning about this.

"I didn't want to bother you," she said, looking into her coffee cup instead of at him.

He scowled at that. Was *that* why she hadn't told him who she was? Because he was growing more and more certain that she *had* emailed him over the years.

"You have never, ever bothered me, Tess," he said. He reached over and lifted her chin. "I mean that."

She sighed. "You have to say that because you want to sleep with me."

He gripped her chin a little harder. "Yes. I do."

She took a deep breath. "I don't think I can have sex with you."

"Oh, yes, you most certainly can."

"I'm leaving."

Yeah. That sucked. And as he thought about it more, he knew that he'd get even more disappointed.

But he'd never try to keep her here.

And no way was he passing up the chance to make love to her.

He'd missed out on being a part of her running dream. Now she was going to go to someone else for that. But Bryan could be a part of her sexual fantasies. He was going to be a part of those dreams for sure.

"You're not leaving today."

She pressed her lips together and studied his eyes. "We can't have amazing sex."

He reached out and ran a hand up her arm to her neck. He stroked his thumb up and down her throat. "I think you know better."

She shook her head slightly. "I mean, I don't want to."

He frowned. "Tess—"

"We can have sex. But we can't have *amazing* sex." She shook her head quickly, actually looking worried. "I'll never want to leave then."

He would have had to be dead to not have his ego react to that. But his heart reacted as well. She really wanted Denver. She wanted to run, to see how far she could go—literally and figuratively. And she'd picked the one guy who would get that and who would want it *for* her.

"I'm not going to let you stay," Bryan said, feeling his heart clench.

He couldn't believe this. His plan had always been to come back to Sapphire Falls, to stay. With Tess.

Now he was here, and not only did she want to leave, but he was going to push her to do exactly that.

"You won't try to get me to fall in love with you?" she asked.

"You mean fall in love with me *again*?" He simply couldn't let that go.

She frowned. "What?"

"You've been in love with me most of your life, Tess. Maybe you got over me, but don't pretend that I couldn't have had anything I wanted from you for a really long time."

That was an asshole thing to say, he knew. But it was true. And he needed to hear it. And more, it was going to turn her on.

He'd read *Erotic Research*.

Twice.

She liked bossy and in your face. So to speak.

"Well, I most *definitely* got over *that*," Tess said, sliding off her stool. "And thanks for reminding me of how stupid I was. No worries about *that* happening again."

"How long have you been reading my blog?"

She froze in the process of pushing the stool out of the way so she could step around it—and him.

"Wha—what do you mean? You have a blog?"

He huffed out a laugh. "I know you've been following my blog, Tess. You've said a few things lately that sounded familiar. Now the RF10, the progressive program. It's all me." He took her hips in his hands and turned her to face him. "How long?"

She really didn't want to tell him. He could see it all over her face. So a long time then.

Finally, she looked at his collarbone and said, "Two and a half years."

"That's how long you've been running."

She pulled away and paced across the kitchen. "Yep. Come on, Bryan, you're not actually shocked to know that I started running because of you, are you? You're the sun in my solar system. *Of course* a huge life change like that would come because of you, right?"

Bryan stared at her. She'd started running because of him? It was one thing to give nutritional advice, to give inspiration and stretches to runners. But she'd *started* because of him?

"I—I didn't know."

"Makes sense though, right?" she asked.

"I'm...honored."

She laughed at that. "Honored? Is that how you've felt about my silly crush all these years?"

He knew he should correct the silly part but he also knew she wouldn't believe him. "Yes," he said honestly.

She winced so he went on. "Tess, you are the most generous, kind, caring person I know. For you to give me the attention you've always given me has been an honor, yes."

"Oh, I humble you?" she asked sarcastically.

"Uh, no. The opposite of humble," he said with a grin. "You made me feel like a million dollars. And now I'm amazed. This is what it's always been about with coaching."

She braced her hands on the counter behind her. The center island and a couple feet of floor were between them but Bryan saw every one of her emotions. She was embarrassed. But she also liked knowing that she was building *him* up with this truth. And that was just like her. It was about everyone else first.

"I'm not running because of you," she said. "I ran the first time because of you. But then I loved it and I couldn't stop."

"How did I get you out running that first time?" he asked.

She pressed her lips together for a moment. "I missed you and was worried about you after the accident. Your mom said something about you in yoga one night when I was filling in and—"

"My mom takes yoga?" Bryan interrupted.

Tess nodded.

"And you teach yoga?"

"I fill in when Hope needs help and took over a couple of classes when she got too busy."

Of course she had. "Filling in" and "help" were big words in Tessa's world.

"Okay, go on." The yoga thing with his mom was interesting. Turned out there were more than a few things about Sapphire Falls and the people here, even other than Tess, that he didn't know.

He needed to go see his mom. She had had a tough time accepting his injury and disability after the accident. She'd been in a deep denial that had strained their entire family, especially his sister. But they'd worked through it, and now his mom was his biggest supporter. He saw her at least twice a week. But suddenly, he wanted to take her out to dinner. And hear about yoga. And anything else he didn't already know about.

He did not like having the women he loved keeping stuff from him.

Now that his shit had stabilized, there was a lot he needed to pay more attention to.

"Anyway, hearing her talk about you made me—" she blushed and looked at the floor, "—miss you."

Bryan's heart clenched hard in his chest. "Tess." He waited until she looked up. "Don't ever be embarrassed about thinking about me or missing me."

"It's pathetic how much I thought of and missed you."

He really hated the word pathetic.

"Well, I was pretty pathetic then too, because I missed you all the time."

She took a deep breath. "Your mom had said how much she liked reading about your recovery and rehab on your blog. I went home and googled it, because I wanted to know about your recovery and rehab too. And then I got into the archives—

the running stuff. And the travel stuff. And *pathetically*," she said, as if trying to prove that of the two of them, she would easily win a pathetic contest. "I read every word of every post."

"So you started and loved it," he said, feeling...cocky. More so than he ever had. He'd been important to Tess. This was real stuff. This wasn't shy, sweet, awkward Tess. This wasn't his smile or his flirting or his abs impressing her. This was big stuff. His passion, his words, things that gave him a lot of pride.

She nodded. "I loved it. And after about a few weeks, I couldn't stop."

A streak of what Bryan could only call satisfaction went through him. She'd done it on her own—he was still impressed by that—but she hadn't been totally alone. She'd had him. He'd helped her discover this love and work through it and improve. He'd coached her. Without knowing it, and from a distance, but he'd still been a part of this.

And if eggs had felt intimate and important, this felt a million times more so.

He got off the stool and went to stand directly in front of her.

"Thank you."

Her eyes widened. "For what?"

"For making me a part of *this* passion. I want to be a part of *all* of your passions, Tess."

———

T ess had no idea what to say to that. He was thrilled. She could tell.

How could she tell him that he *wasn't* a part of this?

This was the stuff Bryan lived for. She couldn't tell him anything but how great he was. Dammit.

"I guess—" Her phone rang before she could complete that

thought. Which was for the best. She wasn't really sure what she was going to say anyway. "Sorry."

He shook his head. "Lots of people need you."

She crossed to her purse to find her cell and pulled it out. TJ was calling. "Hello?"

"Tess? Need you down here. The racing guys are here, and I can't find any of the forms they need. The guys who are doing the pig roast called, and they need to know where to bring all the ice. Hailey says we need more chairs in the square, and I need you to let everyone know that I am not going to be able to pre-sample all the pies for the bake-off."

Tess listened to it all, feeling a familiar urge to roll her eyes and laugh. She did love her hometown, and she loved watching TJ Bennett be the mayor of it. He wanted to be short and to the point, effective and efficient. That wasn't really how Sapphire Falls did things.

"I'm on my way," she told him. "Give me twenty minutes."

"I'll give you ten and four pieces of pie."

She did laugh then. "I'll settle for twelve minutes and two pieces of pie."

"Deal." And he hung up.

"I need to go," she told Bryan. But simply looking at his mouth made her long to take her clothes off, crawl into bed with him and not come out for about...forever.

Wow. She never would have guessed spilling her guts to him would be a turn-on. But she felt closer to him. And she also realized she was for *sure* running the half marathon in two weeks. She was tempted to stay. But she'd hate herself if she didn't do this.

Talk about a roller coaster—she'd wanted him home, he'd come home and she wanted to leave, he wanted her to stay, now he knew everything and wanted her to go.

It was so ironic that *he* had been everything she'd thought she wanted for so long—until *he'd* intervened in her life. Even if the intervening had been unintentional.

And by ironic, of course she meant a big fucking mess.

"Okay. What do you have after TJ's issue?"

"The kids' fun run."

"Fun run?"

"Yeah, it's an obstacle course with various stations set up where they can get healthy snacks and learn about their hearts and—"

Bryan cut her off by pulling her close and covering her mouth with his.

When he finally let her up, she felt a little dazed. "What was that for?"

"Because I'm a fucking idiot."

"The kids' fun run reminded you of that?" she asked, giving him a small grin.

But he didn't smile back. "Yeah."

"How?"

"It just proves, again, that you're amazing. But you've always been amazing. And I've always known it. But I'm not sure *you* have, and I wasn't doing a damned thing to help you know it."

"You don't have to say that," she told him, stepping back. But she wasn't saying it to be self-deprecating or coy. She meant it.

"Te—"

"I know you've always *liked* me, Bryan," she said, stopping whatever apologetic or reassuring thing he'd been about to say. "Not in the wild, passionate way I'd wanted you to, but I knew you liked me. But you haven't really *known* me. You haven't really always known I'm amazing. In fact, I haven't always *been* amazing. I've been nice, sweet, likeable. I've been helpful and organized and generous and willing—those things are what have made people like and appreciate me. But I haven't been *amazing*. Yet."

He stood staring at her for several long seconds.

"What?" she finally asked.

"I think you hit amazing a long time ago. It's too bad that you haven't had anyone here telling you that."

She took a deep breath.

Then he gave her a grin and let her go. "It's all about making others better. Love the fun run. I want in. I'll meet you wherever you're setting it up," he said.

"The park. Between the ball diamond and the pool."

"Got it. I'll be there." He tipped her chin up. "Do me a favor, okay?"

She nodded.

"Don't let anyone tell you when you're amazing. *You* tell you when you're amazing."

She felt tears welling up and blinked quickly. "Even you?"

"Hell, Tess, especially me." He pulled her in and kissed the top of her head. "Look how long I missed it. I clearly don't know what I'm talking about."

She swallowed hard as she watched him make his way to her front door.

And she felt a little less pathetic about how she felt about him. Not because it had dimmed, but because how could a girl *not* feel that way about him?

11

"You are a sadistic bastard."

"Then I must be doing my job."

Tess looked up from where she'd collapsed on the grass next to her front porch steps.

Bryan was sitting there, totally casual, sipping lemonade, for God's sake, and grinning at her.

He turned the stopwatch to face her even though she couldn't see it from where she was working on not dying.

"You're two minutes faster than last time."

She fell back in the grass. Two minutes. That was less time than it took to listen to the new Chase Rice song. It was less time than a commercial break on TV. It was less than the time it took her to make a sandwich. And yet...she grinned.

It was a nice improvement in a week.

"You need to stretch," Bryan said a moment later. "And you need to get some water in."

"Yeah, yeah, hang on. I'm trying to decide if life is still worth living if this is how I'm going to spend my time."

He chuckled at that. "Wow, I *really* did my job today then."

Tess knew it was a weird thing to feel happy about, but

truly, running had changed for her in the past week since Bryan had made it his mission to get her ready for the half marathon.

Running had always been a solitary thing for her. Other than Bryan's blogs and vlogs, Tess had been self-disciplined and motivated. She'd had no one cheering her on. Or to complain to. Or about.

Now, not only was Bryan waiting for her at the end of her run, but she had him in her ear via Bluetooth on her phone through the workout.

He shared his playlists and he talked to her. Sometimes it was inspirational-pep-talk stuff, sometimes he talked about his trips, sometimes he just talked. He told her stories she hadn't heard before about other athletes he'd worked with, his favorite farmers' market in Denver, stories about his family, and even current events like the giant beer pong game practice in the park.

And there was more. He was cooking for her, keeping her on a specific eating plan. He had her working weights and had put her through a combo of core training and yoga that he'd put together himself.

All of that was making her feel stronger and more confident about the running. She'd already been able to complete the thirteen miles, but now her time was improving and she just felt better in general.

She also knew it was not about her electrolytes or her carb-protein ration or improved core stability.

It was Bryan.

But instead of pathetic, she felt good about that too. Because this wasn't just making her better—it was making him happy. He was truly enjoying coaching her, and Tess had finally accepted the truth that it wasn't the coaching as much as it was coaching *her*. She could tell it mattered to Bryan that *she* meet her potential. So, of course, her time had improved.

She lifted up on her elbows to look at him, the threat of death having passed for the day.

"You know, you're pretty good at this," she said.

He didn't say anything. His gaze was locked on her face though.

"The coaching thing," she said, in case he didn't know what she was talking about. "This is really your thing. Why the bartending?"

He swallowed but still said nothing.

"Bryan?"

"Yeah?"

"You okay?"

"You need to stretch and eat."

"Okay. In a second. I want to know why you're bartending instead of coaching now."

"The Come Again is the main place people here go to laugh and let go and celebrate," he said. "I love being a part of that."

She frowned. She'd never thought of it that way. But it fit Bryan. He liked to make people happy, to make things work.

"We do have a lot in common," she said. He'd mentioned it the other day, and she had to admit he had a point. They were both people who met other people's needs and got a lot of satisfaction from that.

"Tess?"

"Yeah?"

"I'd really like to have a normal conversation that makes sense, but with you lying there like that, in your running clothes, I'm having a hard time keeping my eyes on safe subjects, not to mention my thoughts."

Tess looked down. She was stretched out in the grass, in a pair of short running shorts and a fitted top that left her stomach bare. Because it was hot. And wind resistance. She certainly hadn't thought about them being *sexy*.

She was also sweaty with no makeup on and her hair up.

But Bryan was now letting his gaze roam over her, and he definitely seemed to like what he saw.

"Really?" she asked. "This is a turn-on?"

"My two greatest passions together?" he asked. "Oh yeah."

She sat up the rest of the way. "Your *two* passions?"

"Running," he said.

Yeah, she knew that one.

"And you."

That one was a little harder to believe. Especially considering they hadn't had sex, or even talked about it, since he'd discovered she was a runner.

She'd assumed he'd gone into coach mode, and that had shut off any boyfriend stuff. He'd been all in on the coaching. She'd been okay with that. She saw him for her workouts, her meals and all the festival activities he was helping her with.

The fun run—the obstacle course set up with running in between stations with other fun activities and learning centers —now had a few additional stations, including a hula-hoop stop, a chicken-dance station and an entire section where contestants had to use crutches for part of the course and a wheelchair for another section. They'd put those in to increase awareness about the physical challenges people faced when they need those devices to move.

The whole course was also now handicap accessible, with ramps in place and volunteers willing to help anyone who couldn't propel themselves. There were two boys they knew of from Sapphire Falls and one from nearby Chance who would need partners to push them and help with activities. Tucker's boys, Henry, David and Charlie, had volunteered to be their partners.

So Tess and Bryan had been spending a lot of time together, but they'd been busy and focused on other things. Hearing that he was turned on now and having trouble with appropriate thoughts seemed odd.

"Me?" she finally asked. "I'm a *passion*?"

"More so every day."

"Because I'm running and you know it started because of you and your ego is puffed up about it?" she asked.

He shook his head and then stopped. "Yeah. Okay, my ego is puffed up about it," he admitted. "But you've always done that to me."

She grimaced.

"No, it's good. Great even. Do you know what it does for a teenage guy to have someone think he's amazing? You told me that for so long, I believed it. You gave me this huge head—that I needed to talk to athletes and kick their asses and think I had something to say that mattered. You're the reason *so* many people can do the great things they do—you helped me push them."

She opened her mouth but nothing came out. That was all...wow.

"*But*," he went on. "Seeing you every day, spending all this time with you, has made me want you even more than your sweet smile and gorgeous breasts did before."

She looked down at her chest. "Gorgeous?"

He groaned. "Girl, you're killing me."

Well, that only seemed fair. He'd been trying to kill her with the running for a week now.

She got up slowly, trying for sexy, though the cramp in her hamstring and the resultant grimace and limp probably ruined it. Then there were her neon purple and green shoes with her blue socks.

But this was Bryan. The man who had, amazingly, become even more the object of all of her affection and lusty thoughts over the past few weeks.

"Do you think of that night on my couch?" she asked as she approached where he was sitting.

"Every damned time I see you," he said, his voice gruff.

"We were sitting on that couch two nights ago when we were going over the list for the pie-eating contest."

There was also going to be a salad-eating contest because some parents thought that sent a better message to the kids. Not surprisingly, they only had three contestants signed up for the salad. The tavern-eating contest was more popular with eight contestants. The loose-meat sandwiches were a local favorite, and the current record was ten sandwiches in fifteen minutes.

But the pie was definitely the most competitive with fifteen contestants, including the reigning king, Jason Gilmore, the local boy turned doctor extraordinaire who had moved to California to be with the love of his life. Everyone missed him, but Jason and Tara made a point of making it back to Sapphire Falls a few times a year, and Jason had declared he'd never miss a festival.

"We *were* sitting on the couch just the other night," Bryan acknowledged.

"And you made no move."

"My hand is getting sore from all the *moving* I've been doing," he told her, his voice dropping lower as she stepped up on the step just below where he sat.

She moved between his knees. Tess felt her pulse quicken. "You've been doing *that* and thinking of me?"

Bryan put his hands on her hips and drew her closer. "It's not like that's a brand-new thing, Tess."

She looked at him skeptically. "Come on."

"I have loved these curves," he said, running his hands over her hips and around to her butt. "And that sweet smile and that easy blush and those eyes that light up for me, for a very long time."

Her breath was coming a little faster now. "I thought you were a breast man."

"Oh, honey, my fantasies about your breasts are *really* naughty."

Her eyes widened. "Tell me."

He laughed. "No way. That will start something we can't finish."

She leaned in. "Then let's finish it. You haven't even talked about sex in a week."

"Because you've been tired and we've been busy."

"So we're *not* going to have sex? Because I'm leaving?" she asked. She had to tamp down the thought—and urge to say out loud—that she could stay.

No. That was exactly what she'd been afraid would happen if she got involved with him.

And she did feel involved.

They hadn't slept together, but between festival stuff and the coaching, she felt closer to him than she ever had.

She'd always liked him, knew him better than anyone because she paid attention to him—lots of attention. But now the things she knew and observed were things he shared with her and let her in on.

Turned out that having a real relationship with a guy was even better than stalking him.

Who knew?

"We are going to have sex," Bryan finally said. "I am going to make love to you all night long. I'm going to give you so much fantasy fulfillment you'll have to get a much bigger diary."

Tess swallowed, her body going hot and melty. "When?"

He shook his head in wonder. "Damn, you wanting me like this does amazing things to me."

"I've wanted you for a long time."

"I didn't know you really knew what you wanted from me though."

"Oh, I know what I want. The biggest fantasy involves the

shower. Just so you know. And I happen to need a shower right now. Just so you know."

He let out a quick breath. "Showers are a little tough. My ankle is unpredictable at times, even on dry, even ground."

She nodded. "I was thinking about that. I'm going to order a tub bench."

She didn't care if they were standing or not. She just wanted to see Bryan naked and wet, steam rising around him.

He gave a choked laugh. "Those aren't really built for that."

"If we get the heavy-duty one, they hold up to four hundred pounds."

"You researched this?" he asked.

"Yes."

"That might hold our weight," he said. "But they're not really made for movement."

She sighed. She liked the idea of *movement* with Bryan. "I'll be gentle."

His fingers gripped her butt a little tighter and he pulled her in until he could kiss—and quickly lick—her stomach just above the top of her shorts.

She sucked in a breath.

"I want to spread you out on my bed where I have plenty of room to do *that*, all over your body, all night long," he told her.

She looked down and took in the sight of his mouth on her skin. "Okay, fine." She gave in. "But there better not be flowers or jazz or champagne involved."

He grinned up at her. "It'll be your first time. You don't want *any* romance?"

She took his face in her hands. "Most people lost their virginity in the backseat of a car or camping at the river in sleeping bags when they were still teenagers. I had fantasies of losing mine in the bed of your truck. I don't need romance."

He nodded. "Okay. Got it."

She straightened, accepting the fact she was showering

alone again. But that didn't mean his *thoughts* couldn't be with her.

"I'm glad I thought to get the waterproof version when I shopped online." She stepped back and watched Bryan try to get his mouth to work.

"Online shopping?"

She smiled and moved around him, heading for the front door. "Well, it's not like there's a sex shop in York or something," she said. "You could run in to someone you know on the sidewalk. How embarrassing if you had one of those bags in hand."

She pulled the screen door open and stepped through.

"Tess!" Bryan called after her. "You better not get yourself off in that shower without me."

"You're free to come watch."

She could hear his groan from several feet away. But, unfortunately, he never joined her. In spite of the fact she left the bathroom door open. Instead, she found her breakfast on the counter with a note that read, *"I'm getting you a rose for every time you tease me like that from here on."*

She sighed and picked up her bowl of quinoa and strawberries.

Damn him. He always got his way.

———

"So she's going to Colorado?" Ty asked as Bryan refilled his iced tea.

"Yep." Bryan coughed and turned away before his best friend caught the look on his face. He had never felt this crazy sensation of being torn right down the middle. He wanted Tess to go to Colorado. She wanted it. She'd worked for it. And truthfully, she deserved it. She was good. He could keep pushing her here to a point, but the next step was really to go up against other runners—some at her level and some who were better. That was how an athlete got better—by being challenged.

"I can't believe she kept this a secret," Ty said. "It's crazy that she's been *training* all this time and none of us knew."

"We knew she ran," Hailey said. "But I guess we assumed it was just a little jogging. We had no idea she was this serious."

Bryan swung back. "Right?" he said. "I mean Ty never stops talking about his training."

"Hey," Ty protested.

Hailey gave her husband a look. "He's right. It's a part of everything—how you eat, drink, sleep—"

"But she's not trying for a world championship," Ty said. "Is she?" he asked Bryan.

Well...that was something that had been bothering him. "Right now it's a series of half marathons."

"She's going to work up to halves?" Ty asked.

Bryan decided he needed to talk out his concern. "I don't know."

"So halves might be as far as she wants to go?" Ty asked.

There were runners who specialized in halves. "She's strong at that distance," Bryan said.

"Maybe she'll stay there. Or at least for a while." Ty lifted his glass of iced tea.

Bryan leaned a hip on the custom built counter behind the bar. It was the perfect height for him to mix drinks and fill orders when he was in his chair. He didn't work in his wheelchair much anymore, but it was nice to have the option. And it worked well for leaning against even when he was out of the chair.

"Here's the thing," he said. "I don't think she's really a runner."

Ty and Hailey both lifted eyebrows.

"You just said she's a strong runner at thirteen," Ty said.

"She can do the work. Her times are good. She's trained her body. She's a *runner*," Bryan said. "But she's not a racer. She's not competitive enough."

"You didn't tell her that did you?" Hailey asked.

"No," he admitted. "But maybe I should."

Besides Hailey and Ty's reaction, he heard a cough come from the end of the bar. From Peyton Wells.

Bryan glanced at her. She was pretending to study her beer, but he included her when he said, "You know Tess. She's all about everyone else. She runs this town—no offense," he said to Hailey.

"None taken," she told him. "She kept me on track. And she does even more for TJ. And she really seems to love it."

"She's practically putting the whole festival together," Bryan said.

"Good thing," Hailey said. "I've been out doing promotions like crazy. This is going to be the biggest one we've ever had. Our advertising is covering a huge radius, and I got an insert in the *Omaha World-Herald*."

"Well, she's amazing," Bryan said. "She's handling the festival, she fills in at the yoga studio and the bakery."

"And with Delaney," Peyton added.

Bryan sighed. "Exactly. She's all over Sapphire Falls. Helping, making things better. And she does love it. She's energized by supporting everyone else."

"Sounds like someone else I know," Ty said. "That's you, buddy."

Bryan nodded. "Yep. I know her. I always rode and ran for the love of it. Never had the desire to compete. I know competing and racing aren't going to make her happy." He sighed and looked from Ty to Hailey to Peyton. "But I can't tell her that, can I?"

Ty started laughing, Hailey looked appalled, and Peyton said, "Fuck no."

Yeah, that's what he'd thought.

"I can't try to convince her to stay."

"No," Peyton told him firmly. "You can't. You can sit your ass here in Sapphire Falls and wait for *her* for a change."

That was exactly what he could, and probably should, do.

He leaned in, forearms on the bar. He needed someone to agree with him, so he had to make this point. "She's been saving money for a year. She has four jobs paying her. There's no way she didn't have enough money a long time ago to move and start racing. She never talked about running to anyone. Even Ty or *me*—two people who could have and would have helped her with anything. And," he went on, "she could have done a dozen halves by now. She has the distance, no problem, clearly has for a while."

He made that last declaration dramatically and waited for the three people listening to start nodding.

"So why is she just now doing it, when you're here and interested in a relationship?" Ty asked. Like the jackass he was.

Bryan sighed. "I don't know."

"Men are so stupid," Peyton muttered.

Bryan looked at her. "Anything you'd like to share, Miss Wells?"

"You going to make me pay my tab tonight?" she asked.

Bryan narrowed his eyes. "Whatever you're going to tell me better be good."

"Deal." She swiveled her bar stool so she could look at them all. "Here goes. You think she's still madly in love with you. You think the casseroles she brought over after you moved home and organizing the volunteers that helped you and your family out while you were still in rehab and the cards she sent were because she was in love with you."

Bryan frowned. Yeah, he had thought that.

"But that's just Tess, Bryan. And if you think about it, now that you've been around her for a while, every day, here in

Sapphire Falls, you know that. She would have done the same for anyone."

Bryan stared at Peyton. Damn. She was right. He couldn't argue that.

"And you also think that she's done all the running because of you. Everyone who hears about it will. So she needs to get away from you and do it without you to prove to you—and herself—that she can be her own person."

"She told me the other night she did start running because of me," Bryan admitted. That had been huge.

"No. She went out the first time because of *me*," Peyton told him.

"You? You don't run," Bryan said.

"No, I don't," Peyton said adamantly. "I fucking hate running. But when I told her I wanted to clean up and get healthier, she talked me into running with her. That lasted about a month. But by then, she was hooked."

"So she didn't start because of me." Bryan felt definitely deflated at that. "Why didn't she say that?"

"Because you liked thinking it. Tess would rather make you happy than worry about getting credit for something herself. And you did have a little to do with it." Peyton shrugged. "She thought of it for me because of the stuff you'd written about. But the point is, she did it for me—the way she does everything for someone else. She thinks *you're* the one she revolves around, but she actually revolves around anyone who needs something. She doesn't get taken care of—she does the taking care."

Bryan looked at the younger girl who was well known as a hellion. She was an attention seeker and loved to push boundaries and buttons.

But damn—she knew Tessa. And obviously cared about her.

"You've been paying attention," he said.

Peyton gave a small laugh. "Tess and I are a match made in heaven. I need taking care of, and that's her specialty."

And *that* was why she was leaving now. The truth hit him hard.

Peyton nodded as she saw the truth dawn on his face.

"She's been waiting to take care of *me*," Bryan said, his voice raspy with emotion.

"And now that you don't need that and are, in fact, pushing her to let *you* take care of *her*, she's leaving."

"She's leaving *because* I rehabbed and got better," he said, rolling it all around in his head. "She didn't leave before this because I came back hurt, and she had to see if I needed her."

"And she wants to go out into the world and be independent because you're here being sweet and gentle and caretaker-ish, and she isn't comfortable being on that end of things. And, no, she's not competitive enough to race. But running is her only way of going to Denver without feeling guilty for leaving everyone here," Peyton said.

Bryan was floored. "How do you know all of this?" he asked, while acknowledging that every bit of it made sense.

"It's obvious," Peyton said. "If you're not all caught up in *her* paying attention to *you*, that is."

He gave her a dirty look. But she was right.

"So now what?" he asked the group.

"You gotta give her what she wants," Ty said with a shrug.

"I need to let her take care of me?" Bryan asked. "I don't do that any better than she does."

"Except when it comes to Tess," Hailey said. "You've always been okay with *her* paying extra attention to you."

She had been taking care of him all these years—her thinking he was amazing, being his secret admirer and sharing all her thoughts and feelings with him, waiting and saving herself for him—had all taken care of him because it had fed the part of him that wanted to be important to her.

"So I need to—"

"You read *Erotic Research*?"

Bryan turned slowly to his right as the main subject of conversation stomped into the Come Again, much as she had the night she'd announced to the whole town that he had no say in her love life.

He grinned. So much for that.

But he stopped grinning when he really looked at her.

She was ticked. Tessa Sheridan was ticked at him.

Tess stopped in front of him, the bar separating them. "Hope just told me that Hailey told you to read *Erotic Research*. And you *did*?" Her voice rose on the last word.

"Of course. Why wouldn't I?" he asked. "It's basically a guide book to your imagination and fantasies."

"So you read about him tying her up and using sex toys, and you *still* think that romance and flowers and everything is the way to go?"

He looked at the three people sitting at the bar and the three guys at the nearest table.

Tessa's eyes followed his as she seemed to realize for the first time that there were other people paying attention to the conversation. She blushed a pretty pink and pressed her lips together.

"I thought Ross was romantic in certain parts," Bryan said easily.

Tess looked Bryan directly in the eye. "I need to see you in your office."

Bryan didn't know what exactly was going through her mind, but there was *something* in the air between them.

He looked at his customers—the three at the bar and the four tables of patrons in the room.

"Closing time, guys," he called.

The three at the bar just grinned. The rest of the place would be harder to clear out. It was only nine p.m.

But Tess turned on her heel and headed for his office.

"If you leave now, you don't have to pay your tab for the night!" he called.

Chairs scraped as everyone suddenly got to their feet and started for the door.

Peyton was the last one out. "Don't mess it up," she told him helpfully.

"Thanks so much," he said. "Now get the hell out."

She went with a grin, and he turned the lock on the door the moment it shut behind her.

He looked at his office door from across the bar. He knew exactly what to do. He just needed to rein in his desire a little before he got to her. He was definitely going to take care of her, exactly the way she needed him to, but she was a virgin—a virgin with a dirty mind, but a virgin nonetheless. That would require at least *a little* care.

He opened the door to his office. Tess was standing next to his desk, her arms crossed. "I'm not into butt plugs."

Bryan took a second to let that hang in the air between them. Tess had just said butt plugs to him. "Okay."

"Just because I like reading about some of that stuff, doesn't mean I'm into doing it all," she told him.

"Okay."

"But I can't believe that you read that, knowing it was one of my favorites, and you still want to romance me. I don't want sweet. I like the bossy thing."

Bryan's body tightened. "Okay."

"And the blowjob stuff."

Blood rushed south. "Okay."

"And the pirate-slave stuff," she added.

"Tess," he said firmly. He needed her to stop talking. And start doing.

"Yeah?"

"Take your clothes off."

12

S he blinked at him. "Excuse me?"

"I said take your clothes off."

Her eyes flashed, partly in anger—and partly with heat.

"Just because you said so?"

He nodded. "Yeah."

"You think that's enough?"

"I do," he said honestly. "But if I add I want you to get up on the desk so I can lick you until you come, I think you'll definitely do it."

Her eyes widened and her lips parted.

"Don't make me say it again. If I have to undress you, I'm not going to let you come until you beg."

Her breathing was faster now, and she wet her lips.

Should he do this? Of course he should. Would it make it harder for her to leave for Colorado? Maybe. Hopefully. He'd feel like shit if it was *easy* for her to leave, even without the sex. After he rocked her virgin world, he really needed it to be hard for her leave.

But she would. He'd make sure of it. He was a fantastic

coach. He'd gotten far more stubborn people to do far more than leave him and Sapphire Falls behind.

His heart ached again with that idea—that Tess had a dream he *could have* been a part of if not for his fucking accident.

He didn't let himself spiral down that path very often. The accident had happened. He couldn't change it, and it had changed him—mostly for the better.

But there were times when he got pissed off at Fate.

And with Tess, he was as close as he'd ever been to feeling sorry for himself.

Thankfully, she chose that moment to take off her shirt.

He'd been grateful for naked breasts in his life. Multiple times. But probably never more than he was in that moment.

If he had to contemplate the injustice of his situation, at least he could look at Tessa's naked breasts while he did it.

"Keep going, darlin'," he told her, gripping the edge of the desk to keep from reaching for her...yet.

She reached behind her, unhooked her bra and let it drop.

Her breasts were full, soft and round, exactly the way Bryan liked them. Her nipples were already hard, perfectly pink, begging for attention. But he needed *all* of her.

He looked back to her face. "I didn't say stop."

Tess hooked her thumbs in the top of her pants and she pushed them to the floor and stepped out of them. She either hadn't been wearing panties or she'd slid them off too. It didn't matter. She was bare now, and Bryan wasn't looking at anything except all of that delicious, kissable skin.

"Now up on the desk. Where I can reach you."

She looked at the desk. And hesitated.

"Your safe word is pickle," he told her. Then he reached for her.

He grasped her wrist, tugged her close and then grabbed her waist with both hands and lifted her onto the desk.

He felt her surprise—not because he hadn't warned her, but because she hadn't thought he'd be able to lift her. He grinned. He bench pressed more than she weighed in the gym three days a week. He also easily outweighed her, and propelling himself in his wheelchair and with his crutches was no breeze.

He looked at her sitting on the desk, gripping the edge with white knuckles.

"What's your safe word?" he asked.

She licked her lips again. She didn't like the idea of butt plugs, but she liked the blowjob scene in *Erotic Research*.

Julia had been good at it—the author had said so, but Bryan could admit the description did sound like the book's heroine had done a good job.

He wondered how many times Tess had read that section.

"Pickle," she finally said softly.

"Right."

"Am I—" She swallowed hard. "Am I going to need a safe word?"

"If there's *anything* you want to stop doing, you use it," he told her. "Or, you know, tell me to stop."

She returned his smile with a small one of her own.

"So what are you—"

He knocked the one pile of papers and a couple of pens to the floor. His desk was thankfully pretty bare. He preferred to do his paperwork at one of the tables in the bar.

"Lay back and spread your legs."

She didn't want romance. She didn't want sweetness. She loved *Erotic Research* and had definitely responded the few times he'd been firm with her.

And he was determined to make this *amazing* for her.

So, yeah, he was going to boss her around.

He waited for about ten seconds. Then he lifted an eyebrow.

She lay back.

One eyebrow. Nice.

"Good girl." He grabbed the arm of his office chair and pulled it around so he could sit directly in front of her knees. "Now feet up on the edge."

She bent her knees, bringing her heels up to the desk.

Bryan ran his hands up and down the backs of her calves. Tess wiggled her butt but otherwise didn't move.

She looked gorgeous. Her hair spread out on the pale wood, her breasts rising and falling with her rapid breaths. Her legs trembled and her fingers curled into the top of the desk as if trying to ground herself.

That was good. That was very good. He wanted her off-kilter and spinning. God knew, he was. The trembling thing was apparently contagious.

Tess was incredibly coachable. For him. She thought she was a pushover, but the truth was she wasn't malleable for anyone but Bryan. She was tough and confident and driven. She knew what she wanted. No one could derail that.

Except for him.

He'd claimed her as his in kindergarten—whether either of them had really understood any of that dynamic then or not. He was the guy who could change Tess, who could make her want more, see the world differently, push herself.

That meant that he had an obligation. Just like a coach, he had to be sure this woman who had put her trust in him, who believed that he would always do right by her, got the very best of him.

And that meant he was going to have to say goodbye to her.

He could convince Tessa to stay in Sapphire Falls with him. He knew that, and the gravity of that truth weighed on his heart. He could have her. But if he kept her here, it wouldn't really be *her*. Not the her she really could be.

They had a history, he knew her, she trusted him. She could throw him out of her house, tell him he was being an arrogant ass, confess deep, intimate secrets and cry in front of him, and she would still climb up on his desk and let him into her body —and her heart.

That meant he could help her be everything she wanted to be.

Even if it meant making her go to Colorado. And to Jake.

"Bryan."

Her soft pleading pulled him back from wondering how in the hell he was going to be able to do this and then let her go. That's why he'd been waiting. He could have been making love to her for a week, but he'd known it would make it harder and harder for both of them when she left if they established any habits.

He'd planned to wait until her last night in town, when things were set in stone, when she couldn't change her mind, to make love to her.

But, again, things weren't going as planned.

He couldn't really say he was upset here though.

He leaned in and kissed her knee. "Open up, Tess."

She let her legs fall open, and Bryan took a moment to love everything about being a heterosexual man. He ran his hands up her inner thighs. She arched her back as he neared the apex.

"Gorgeous," he said gruffly. "Fucking gorgeous."

He couldn't see her face from his seated position, but he could see how much she wanted him. And for the first time ever during sex, Bryan felt humbled.

Not a common emotion in the heat of the moment, for sure, but with Tess it really worked. She was amazing. He'd been such a jerk, assuming so many things. He'd selfishly assumed everything about this was about him. And in spite of that, she was here, offering him everything.

He could take it all. He wanted it all. He could tell her he was in love with her. He could convince her that he could coach her here and get her ready for the marathons. He could persuade her that she didn't need Jake.

All of that was true.

But that was why he couldn't do it. He had to make her go.

This wasn't just about training and running. It was about Tess being *more* than she'd ever been.

Bryan ran his hands over her smooth inner thighs, loving how the muscles reacted to his touch. Again he stroked her, making her squirm. Then he brought his thumbs together at her center, opening her and stroking over her clit. Her neck arched and she moaned. Swirling over the nub, Bryan lost himself in the sounds of her climbing need.

His name on her lips was perfect, her body spread out for him the most beautiful thing he'd ever seen. But he needed to see her face.

"Prop up, Tess," he said, sliding his hands under her ass and pulling her to the edge of the desk. "Watch me."

She moved up onto her elbows, almost eagerly. He grinned.

Her cheeks were flushed, her lips parted with her ragged breathing. He made eye contact, then purposefully dragged his eyes down to her incredible breasts, over her stomach, the perfect curve of her hips, then to the pink folds his tongue tingled with the need to taste.

"Watch me," he told her again, moving a finger over her clit.

Her attention focused on his hands as she whimpered softly.

He circled the sweet spot, then slid lower to her hot, slick opening.

"When you're in Colorado, I want you giving all this sweetness plenty of attention," he told her. "I want your fingers here, pleasuring yourself, and I want you imagining *my* fingers and tongue." He slid one digit into her silky heat, only to the first knuckle.

She gasped, and Bryan had to pull back on the need to

thrust—even if it was just a finger. Her body was so ripe for lots of hot, dirty sex. There were so many things he wanted to show her, to do with and to her, so many positions, so many ways to make her scream.

"And I'm going to send you a vibrator. Maybe one a month. We'll start a vibrator-of-the-month club. Just you and me," he told her. He slid his finger in to the next knuckle. "I'll send them to you and you'll send me dirty videos of you using them and calling out my name each time you come."

She whimpered softly as her body clenched around his finger.

"So greedy," he said gruffly. "You want this so much. There are so many things you want and don't even know about."

The things he could do with a king-size bed, Tess and no time limit.

She arched closer to his hand and made a soft, needy sound.

No time limit. That was the one thing he didn't have.

He slid his finger into her fully, almost groaning at how tight she was.

"Love your body, Tess," he said. "You're so damned sexy like this. All mine. So hot." He stroked his finger in and out and felt the way she shivered at the friction.

"But you don't want the flowery words, right?" he asked. "You don't want to hear sexy and beautiful. You don't want to hear about how much it means to me that you'll let me be here like this with you, or how much I want to make this good for you." He stroked in and out again before adding a second finger.

With the added stretch, she moaned and pressed closer to his hand, taking him in easily.

He stroked deep and a little harder now, sensing her growing need. "You want to hear things like you're *fucking* killing me and how I intend to suck your clit 'til you beg me to take you, and how I want to feel you coming so hard around my cock the neighbors will hear me shouting."

He curled his hand, rubbing over her clit with his thumb as he continued to thrust.

"Or do you need even more than that, Tess?" he asked. "Do you need to just flat-out hear that I'm going to fuck you until the walls shake, and that your pussy is the sweetest I've ever had and that I want to take you in every way there is for a man to take a woman?"

And that did it. Tess flew up and over the summit into a beautiful orgasm, calling his name, her body milking his fingers.

"Sit up," he ordered her.

He kept his fingers deep in her body as she put her legs down and sat up. He stroked her as he took her mouth in a deep, hot kiss, relishing the ripples still going through her. Then he dropped his lips to her right nipple and sucked hard.

Tess's fingers tangled in his hair, holding his head in place. "God, Bryan, yes."

"You're going to come for me again before I fuck you," he told her. He flicked over her clit with his thumb, his eyes locked on hers.

Her body shuddered and she grabbed his shoulders. "I can't—"

"Yes, you fucking can," he growled. He leaned in and licked over her clit, swirling his tongue around the sensitive spot and making her cry out. He kept pumping in and out of her with his fingers as he curled his other hand into her ass cheeks and then sucked on her clit.

She pressed closer to his mouth even as she said, "Bryan, I can't take it."

"You can take it and you will." He looked up at her, keeping his tongue on her clit. She was watching him raptly. "Beg me."

She wet her lips and shook her head.

He sucked and then stopped. He stopped his fingers too, just holding everything on edge.

"Beg me, Tess. Beg me to make you come again."

She bit her bottom lip.

He started to pull his fingers out.

"No!" she protested, trying to close her thighs and trap his hand.

"Beg me. Say please and tell me that you've never wanted anything as much as you want me right now in this moment."

Not even running. Not even Colorado.

But he couldn't add that. He couldn't deny her pleasure, period. If it was dirty talk and reenactments from her favorite romance novels, or if it was letting her go so she could pursue her dream, he'd do it. Whatever Tess needed.

She took a deep, shuddering breath. Then she said, "Please, Bryan. Please make me come. I've never wanted anything as much as I want you right now in this moment."

And damn if he didn't see the truth of it in her eyes. They were playing. It was part of the demanding persona she wanted in her lover. It was part of the hot, dirty talk. But more—it was true.

Bryan had a million things he wanted to say. And he couldn't manage even one of them.

Instead, he bent his head, slid his fingers deep and made her come, made her cry out his name and grip his shoulders as if she'd never let go.

But she would.

And that's why as soon as she went over the edge, he stood and gathered her to his chest. He let her slide to the floor. When her feet touched the hardwood, he turned her, unzipped, rolled on a condom and grasped the desk on either side of her hips. "Hold on, honey," he said gruffly next to her ear. "I've wanted to bend you over for so long. Now I'm going to think of you every time I come into this office."

With that thought, he pushed her forward until her breasts rested on the desk and then thrust forward, sliding into her from behind. She gasped and instinctively arched her back, allowing him to get even deeper.

He kept one hand on the desk, lest his ankle wobble on him, but he grasped her hip with the other, holding her still for his strokes. Deep, hard, fast. He took her with the passion of a man trying to make his mark and stake his claim.

Tess pushed against the desk, pressing back into him with each thrust, and soon she was clamping down on him deliciously and crying out his name *again*.

Satisfaction streaked through him as he pumped in and out until he couldn't hold back any longer and came with a shout, gripping her hip and the desk, hanging on for all he was worth.

But it wasn't his legs that were threatening to make him fall.

That was all his heart.

———

Tess knew she should feel awkward after all of that. She'd been as exposed and vulnerable as she ever had. But she hadn't felt vulnerable. Not even when she'd had her legs spread wide for Bryan and he'd been tormenting her with fingers and tongue.

Yeah, that should have been awkward.

Turning to face him after he'd made her come for a *third* time and looking at those lips that had done incredibly, amazingly intimate things to her, should have made her blush. The fact that he was even *able* to make her come three times should have maybe embarrassed her. In the novels, the women often had multiple orgasms, seemingly easily, but she knew better than to think that was real-life stuff. But this was Bryan, and she had been waiting for him forever. Coming easily for him, begging him and pleading, doing whatever he wanted her to do, should have been expected.

It had been, if she was honest.

She'd known he could make her do anything he asked.

But instead of embarrassed or awkward, she felt beautiful. Sexy. And powerful.

She had affected him too. Deeply. She could see it. And feel it. And it was a heady experience.

Tess put a hand against his cheek and looked into his eyes, and for the first time, she sensed that the tables had turned.

She wasn't the only one overwhelmed here. She might not even be the most overwhelmed of the two of them. And she knew that Bryan knew it too. She'd had no idea that making herself vulnerable to someone could make *her* feel powerful, but that was exactly what had happened.

Bryan didn't look away though. He seemed to be drinking her in. He cupped her face in his hands and said, "Thank you."

"For what?"

"For letting me be the one. For waiting for me."

Her heart turned over in her chest. A bit painfully. She never would have thought it would be painful to hear something like that from Bryan Murray.

She also never thought she would have to choose between Bryan and something else.

Until that first day she'd put on running shoes and huffed and puffed her way over a quarter of a mile of country road, Tess would have picked being with him over *anything* else. Hell, for *months* after that, she still would have picked him. She'd hated running for at least four months. She'd barely liked it for a lot longer than that. It still hadn't gotten to where she liked it *more* than Bryan. And that had been before he'd put his head between her legs.

She would never like anything more than *that*.

But how she felt about herself after running was better than how she felt about herself falling head over heels for Bryan again simply because he'd turned his attention on her.

Now that he lived—literally—four blocks away from her, she was leaving. Because if she didn't, she would hate herself.

But...

"It never could have been anyone but you," she told him softly.

He leaned in and kissed her. It was deep and hot, not hungry, but sweet and...thorough. He kissed her as though he was soaking her in and trying to become a part of her.

But he already was a part of her.

He always had been.

13

"This is going to be great," Tessa said, looking at the ladies gathered on the stage at the Community Center.

They'd completed their final fashion show rehearsal and were beaming at her from under the stage lights.

It was crazy, but Tess felt tears stinging. But it wasn't the outfits or the perfect turns—which had been about sixty-percent of the turns—or that the music had matched up exactly. It was the familiar faces of the women she'd known her entire life, and the sexy voice of the emcee who had been equally charming, funny and informative during his narration.

She was going to miss the show.

She couldn't believe it.

The festival officially kicked off on Sunday, but she was leaving for Denver tomorrow at seven a.m. The plan was to get there a week ahead of the race, get settled in the apartment that a friend of Bryan and Ty's had helped her secure and train for a few days, just to get used to the altitude.

So she was going to miss the festival. Something she hadn't done ever. Bryan was heading up all of the activities he'd helped her with over the past few weeks, and Hailey was handling everything else. It was all set, and she was sure it would go off without a hitch.

But she wanted to be here.

Tess turned away from the stage before she started to cry. It was so stupid. She'd seen every fashion show, every Lawn Yawn, every Founder's Day play, every everything in Sapphire Falls. She didn't really expect this festival to be dramatically different. But the giant beer pong game would be fun to see. Frank was the favorite, but she thought Albert could surprise everyone.

And of course the fun run. That was new and her baby. But Bryan was an excellent second-in-command and had already added so much to it.

She had nothing to worry about. She needed to be focusing on *her* run.

"Tess, don't rush off," Dottie called as Tess gathered her bag.

She was working on composing herself before she faced Bryan. He would hate thinking that she didn't want to go to Colorado now after all her big talk.

Tess took a deep breath and turned to the stage again. "What's up, Dot?" she asked.

"We just wanted to say thank you."

Tess swung toward the doorway as a deep voice answered her question.

All of the guys from the Lawn Yawn were walking in.

"Wha—"

"Miss Sheridan!" A little girl ran into the room, dodging the older guys. It was Molly Petersen, one of the girls from the talent show. Her two sisters were right behind her, and they were followed by the other kids from the show.

Molly threw her arms around Tessa's waist. "We'll miss you!" she declared.

Tess returned the hug, still startled by the people who kept coming through the door.

"What's going on?"

"My mom said you're leaving," Molly told her.

Tess hadn't told many of the people involved with the festival that she was leaving. It wasn't like they'd signed up for things because of her. The festival would go on as planned. No one would know the difference.

But people kept coming. After the older guys and kids was a group of her friends, including Hailey, Delaney, Hope and Kate and their guys, as well as Travis and Lauren Bennett, Phoebe and Joe Spencer, and Mason and Adrianne Riley. The gals from the book club were there, as was Peyton and several bakery regulars. Three families she'd worked on home remodels for came in behind several girls from Tessa's three yoga classes.

The room was soon full of people Tessa knew and had worked with. Of course. This was Sapphire Falls. There wasn't anyone here she *didn't* know.

Even Derek, Doctor Kyle Ames and Officer Scott Hansen were there.

And then Tess was caught up in a hug by Caitlyn Murray, Bryan's little sister. Her boyfriend, Eli, might pitch in the major leagues, but Eli and Cait were from Sapphire Falls and had promised to make it to at least part of the festival. Eli had even brought some friends from the team, which promised to make this festival even more memorable—at least for the baseball fans in town. And since Eli had signed with the Friars, *everyone* in Sapphire Falls was a baseball fan.

Tess felt hands on her shoulders and instantly knew who was behind her.

"Hey." Bryan's low voice in her ear made the tears that had been threatening finally slide down her cheeks.

"You did this, didn't you?" she asked.

In true Sapphire Falls style, when any gathering of more than two people occurred, food and drink was appearing like magic. A cooler of lemonade and beer was set up beside a long table covered with chips, sandwiches, fruit salad and cupcakes, where power tools and poster board and markers had been five minutes ago.

"All I did was casually mention to a couple of people that you were heading out in the morning."

She turned and looked up at him. "When you ordered the cupcakes or asked Dottie to make sandwiches?" she asked with a smile.

"Seriously. All of them did this after hearing you're leaving." He dipped his knees slightly to look into her eyes. "You're surprised?"

"Uh, very."

"Tess, you're very loved."

She laughed lightly. "This town loves—and takes—any excuse for a party." But she felt her heart warming as she looked around. They were all here for her. She knew that. Felt it.

"While I'll admit that it's not *difficult* to get people together to eat and drink," Bryan said, "you have to know you're important to them."

Tess could tell it was very important to him that she acknowledge that. "I know." She put a hand on his cheek. "Thank you."

They were broken up a moment later by friends and family, and Tess was passed around the room as everyone wanted to tell her how wonderful the festival was, how wonderful they thought her running was, how wonderful they thought Colorado would be for her and how much they would miss her.

About an hour in, Tess was completely overwhelmed. She wasn't used to being the center of attention, or being showered with love and being praised.

Bryan knew that.

She was walking past the doorway that led out to the lobby of the center when someone grabbed her wrist and pulled her around the corner.

Bryan backed her up against the wall just on the other side of the room full of people, rescuing her.

"You ready to get out of here?"

"You think I can just disappear?" she asked, hoping for exactly that.

"You want to make a speech or something?" he teased.

She shook her head adamantly. "Definitely not."

"Up on stage? Spotlight? Microphone?"

He was kidding, she knew, but she still shuddered. "I think I'll pass."

"Good." He leaned in and kissed her. "I knew this would be a lot for you, being the woman of the hour, but you deserve it. I want you to know you're loved and wanted."

She nodded, her throat thick. "Thank you."

"Ride the Ferris wheel with me."

Her heart thudded. It was so stupid. She was thirty years old, for God's sake. But his look, his tone, and her reaction were all far too serious for a simple spin on a carnival ride.

Because there was nothing simple about taking a girl on the Ferris wheel in Sapphire Falls. Everyone here knew that when a guy invited a girl into one of those swinging bucket seats, it meant he was serious about her and was staking a claim.

It was Friday. The festival didn't really kick off until Sunday, but the carnival ride company was already in town setting up.

"Do you think they'll let us ride?" she asked as Bryan took her hand and they snuck out of the Community Center and headed for the square.

"I already set it up," Bryan said. "We'll be the first riders of the festival."

She liked that. It was even...romantic. And she didn't mind at all.

There was no one else at the ride but the operator. He gave them a big grin as they walked up the slight ramp to where the seat stopped to load and unload. They got in, and the man clicked the lap bar into place. Then they began their ascent.

They didn't talk as they slowly made their way to the top. As they climbed, Tess looked around, taking it all in. It had been a few years since she'd been on the ride, and she'd never done it at night.

"It's so beautiful," she whispered, not sure why but feeling like the moment called for quiet contemplation.

The town of Sapphire Falls spread out below them, glowing with the soft yellow lights of the street lamps in the residential areas and the taller lights farther out that stood in the yards of the farmhouses. On Main and around the square, it was quiet, the lull before the festival. Soon, the streets and sidewalks would be covered with people, multicolored lights and booths, stands and games.

But this was the real Sapphire Falls. Peaceful, comfortable, happy.

Everywhere her gaze landed, she had a memory. Dottie's Diner, the gazebo, the grocery store, the bakery—it was all visible from up here.

"You're a part of this town, Tess. It's partly the place it is because of you."

She nodded, accepting that truth for maybe the first time. "I'm going to miss it so much."

"It will always be here. Whenever you're ready to come home," Bryan assured her.

She turned to him. "All of it?"

His gaze roamed over her face before meeting her eyes. "Tessa Sheridan, are you asking me to wait for you?"

Her heart gave such a hard thump she couldn't breathe for a moment. Because she not only wanted to ask him exactly that, but she had a feeling he was going to say yes.

"Well, if I kiss you on this Ferris wheel, it means you're mine," she told him.

"Well, if you don't kiss me on this Ferris wheel, I'm going to kiss you."

But she did.

"Wait for me," she whispered against his lips.

"Always."

———

Eight days later

S ix miles. She was six miles in and it felt good. Running in the mountains was tougher than the Nebraskan plains, but Bryan had pushed her over the past two weeks and she could tell she was ready. She could do this.

Tess pressed up the hill. She could see the top and she was moving well.

She was really doing it—she was running a half marathon in Colorado. Like she'd always dreamed.

She kept Bryan's voice in her head as she pumped her arms and legs, determined to finish the hill strong. *You know what this takes. You're completely prepared. This is all you. You've got this.*

And suddenly she was at the top. That was the hardest hill of the run, the biggest incline, and she'd just finished it. Happiness burst in her chest, and she knew she was grinning stupidly. But surely she wasn't the first or last runner to pass that point and want to leap for joy—if their muscles weren't burning and their lungs weren't screaming.

Leaping could come later, she decided.

Then she turned the corner. And pulled up short.

The gray rocky mountainside rose on her left, but the tree line that had been on her right suddenly broke here, and the edge of the road seemed to drop off suddenly into nothing but clear mountain air right below it.

But she wasn't looking right below it. She was looking out over the mountain range that rose up majestically and filled the view as far as she could see.

The rocky and jagged mountainsides were dotted with the deep green points of evergreens that faded to lighter green and then to gray and then white, where snow capped the peaks. The sun shone down between the puffy white clouds, breaking up the shadows on the mountains into varying shades of gray.

Tess moved to the edge of the road to tentatively look down. A girl who'd grown up in Nebraska had only been up off the ground like this if she climbed to the top of the water tower.

There was a low fence barricade on the edge of the road, and Tess expected to see nothing but jagged rocks below her. But instead, the mountain sloped very gently, and she found the ground continued immediately below the barricade for at least another twenty feet before it really dropped off.

There was a flat rock about five feet from the edge. The view from there had to be spectacular.

Tess looked up the road she was supposed to be running. The finish line was still a little over seven miles away. She had to get back on pace if she wanted to finish with a decent enough time to email to Jake Elliot.

But then she looked back at the view before her.

And she knew she wasn't finishing this race.

She'd just gotten what she'd come for.

She'd run in the mountains of Colorado. She knew she could finish. But finishing wasn't nearly as important as taking in this view and *being* in this view for a while.

With that thought, she threw a leg over the barricade and carefully made her way to the rock. The incline was slight and the ground not as uneven as she'd expected. She crawled up onto the rock and looked out over the Rocky Mountains.

She took a deep breath of mountain air, lifted her face to the sun and realized that *this* was what this run was about. To get to this spot. On her own. For herself.

This wasn't about Bryan. He'd never even know she'd done this. This wasn't about Jake or getting a trainer or improving her time or even finishing her first half marathon.

It was about finding a spot in the world that could only be appreciated by getting to it all by herself, on her own two legs, and only because she wanted to.

She'd done that.

She wasn't sure how long she sat on that rock just looking and breathing and feeling and thinking. No other runners had passed by the spot in several minutes when she finally checked her watch.

No way.

Tess jumped to her feet. The race had *ended* some time ago. Even the slowest runner would have finished at least fifteen minutes ago. She was six miles from the start and seven from the finish and all she had were her shoes and cell phone.

"Tess?"

She froze.

It couldn't be.

She turned slowly to find that Bryan was, indeed, coming toward her from a car parked along the side of the road. She could see someone was still sitting in the driver's seat, but Bryan was making his way toward her by himself, a crutch under each arm and a frown on his gorgeous face.

"*Bryan?*"

"Jesus, girl, I've been waiting down there forever. The last runner—besides you—crossed the line like twenty minutes ago. I was worried."

He'd been waiting for her?

Bryan was here. And he'd been waiting for her. Tess let that sink in.

Wow, she liked that.

"Sorry, I..." She turned back to the view and waved a hand in the direction of the mountains and trees. "I got waylaid."

He nodded from where he stood just off the pavement, watching her. "Okay. So you're...fine?"

She sighed. Bryan was here. She'd figured out why she was running and that she could keep doing it without being in Colorado with Jake. She'd seen the mountains. Yeah, she was better than fine. "I'm good. I've figured some stuff out."

"Oh?"

"Yeah. Like that I *really* like that you're here. And I really like that you were waiting for me at the end."

"It was going to be a really romantic, amazing moment," he said with a nod. "I even had flowers."

She smiled. "You know I don't want flowers."

"Yeah, but what you *do* want, I can't do at the finish line of a half marathon in front of a crowd of people."

She giggled. "I'm glad you're here."

"I couldn't be anywhere else. How god-like would I be if I didn't surprise the love of my life by being there for one of her biggest moments?"

She went completely still, then turned more fully toward him. "I'm the love of your life?"

"Yeah," he said with a nod. "And if you don't already know that, then I'm a jackass. Which I've long suspected is the case. Hence, the being here and the flowers and the renting a hotel room with a gigantic shower and built-in bench."

Tess couldn't breathe. She was the love of Bryan's life. That was...good. So good.

"That shows incredibly good taste on your part," she finally said.

He gave her a slow grin. "Just promise that you'll keep telling me what you need and want. I'm not sure my guessing and instincts can be totally trusted."

Tess felt tears welling up. "Oh, I don't know. I didn't tell you to come here, but here you are. And there's a sturdy tub bench in the shower at the hotel." Yeah, she hadn't missed that part. Or the implication. She was going to get to have shower sex with Bryan Murray. "It's perfect."

"Well, turns out, I'm still really good at being the guy behind the greatness, and you, honey, are greatness."

She watched as he moved closer, carefully placing his crutches on the uneven ground. She almost felt bad about making him come up here. Then she remembered—she hadn't made him do anything. He was here of his own free will. And he was doing fine. Bryan Murray had left Sapphire Falls and come up into the mountains after her.

God, she loved him.

"How did you know where I was?" she asked as he settled in next to her on the flat part of the rock.

"GPS on your phone."

She lifted an eyebrow.

"Hey, you're not the only one with stalker skills. You just try to get away from me."

She grinned as her heart turned over in her chest. He was here. He was really here. He'd come for her. He'd been waiting at the finish line for her. He'd come to find her.

Yeah, she liked this turn of the tables.

"So what's going on?" he asked, laying his crutches to the side.

"I talked to a girl at the starting line," Tess said. "She was really nervous. Said she just wanted to finish and all of that. So I gave her the Bryan Murray special." He cocked an eyebrow at that. Tess laughed. "A *pep talk*. I told her a bunch of stuff straight off the blog."

He laughed. "Of course you did. Because heaven forbid you be focused on *you* before a big race and giving *yourself* a pep talk."

"I didn't need a pep talk," she said. "I was there. At the starting line to a competitive half marathon in Colorado. I'd already done what I came to do."

"Really?" he asked. "That was all?"

"Until I rounded that curve back there," she said. "And saw this." Again, she swept her hand across the view.

It looked like a picture postcard. Except she was *in* it. She could *feel* it, smell it, hear it. The deep green of the trees on the mountainside, the bright white of the snow on the peaks, the sunlight streaming through the puffy white clouds and the endless blue sky—it was all gorgeous. But the smell of the air was so different here too. Even the feel of it on her skin. The energy in the mountains, the sounds of the birds and insects…it was all fresh and new and she simply hadn't been able to resist stopping to take it all in.

"I stopped," she told him. "I realized in an instant that I didn't care about the race. I'd come for this."

"So you crossed your finish line early," he said.

He wasn't teasing her. He didn't look at all disappointed. He understood.

"I got a text from the girl I'd given the pep talk to a little bit ago. It was a photo of her crossing the finish line," Tess said. "And I was so happy for her. And for me. Because that wasn't the view I wanted for myself at all."

"But you got your view," he said.

His tone was so affectionate, she looked over at him and her heart flipped at the look in his eyes.

"Yeah. And I realized that all the hard work has paid off. Two years ago, heck, even a year ago, I wouldn't have been able to run these six miles in this altitude to this spot. All of that training got me to this place. Every bit of it was worth it."

"I love you."

He said it so suddenly that she blinked three times before it really sank in. "You really do, don't you?"

He gave her a smile that was part affection and part exasperation. "I really do."

"That's a good thing," she said with a nod, totally nonchalant as she pressed a hand to her chest, trying to still the wild racing of her heart. "That shows not only that you've grown up and learned a few things, but you're never going to be able to walk into your office again and not think of me. That would be sad if we weren't together."

He nodded, looking completely serious. "Why do you think I'm here? I can't get a damned thing done at my desk."

She finally grinned at him. "Thank you for coming after me."

He put a hand to her cheek and rubbed his thumb along her jaw. "Well, it's definitely my turn. I owe you about twenty three years of pursuing."

"Twenty two. If you want to be exact. But—" She covered his hand with hers and looked into his eyes. "It's a deal."

"Then it will be your turn again." He lowered his hand and braced himself on the rock. "This wooing thing is hard work. I'll be ready for a rest."

Tessa laughed and leaned into him. "Your twenty-two years will be better than mine. You'll be getting to have sex the whole time. And, you know, *not* having to write in a diary and wondering if I even know you exist."

"*That* is a really good point," he agreed. "I definitely took the best shift."

Tess shook her head, but she slipped an arm around him and hugged him close. Somehow, in spite of it all, they'd managed to get it right. She really did feel like she was on top of the world. "I love you too, by the way," she said.

And, right on cue, he said, "I know." Then he kissed the top of her head.

Eight months later

"That was pretty good."

"Pretty good?" she huffed. "Seriously?"

"You didn't have the kick at the end I expected," Bryan said with a shrug from where he was sitting on the front porch steps, waiting for her.

"It's a freaking *hill*," she said between gulps of air.

"So?"

"You're a sadistic bastard."

"Must be doing my job then."

He gave her the grin that usually made her heart kick, but at times like this—when she'd just finished ten miles and was hot, sweaty, tired and sore—made her want to punch him.

Tessa doubled over, resting her hands on her knees and focusing on breathing. Damn, the inclines were still tough.

"That view was pretty awesome though," he said after she'd regained her breath slightly.

She straightened and wiped her hair back from her forehead. She grinned. "It was, wasn't it?"

She'd stopped partway up to admire her surroundings and had snapped a photo for him. Like she always did.

"But you just had to rent the cabin the farthest up the mountain, didn't you?" she asked, moving to sit next to him on the steps and look out over the Smoky Mountains.

He handed her a cold bottle of water.

"Your time was better than you ran in Arizona." He held the stopwatch to show her. "But not as good as Hawaii."

"It was ninety degrees in Arizona," she reminded him. "And you know beach running is my favorite."

He nodded. "You stopped and gawked around a lot at the Grand Canyon too," he said.

She elbowed him. "I took in the view on Maui too," she said.

"Yeah, but you preferred *that* view from the massage table they set up on the sand," he teased.

"Well...yeah." She took a swig of water.

This was their third trip. Third of many. Once she'd realized she didn't want to actually race and compete, and that Bryan did want to travel if it was with Tess and involved seeing some back roads, they decided to make the trips without even looking at race schedules. Tess did a ten-mile run in each place, on her own, competing only against her own time. And always taking time to stop and look around. They spent the rest of the time sightseeing—though usually self-led, since tour guides drove Bryan a little batty—taking in the local culture and food, swimming, tandem biking, canoeing and other activities Bryan could do, and having hot, dirty sex. As well as making love.

"So the top of the mountain wasn't the only thing I asked about when I rented this place." Bryan stretched his legs out and leaned back, propping his elbows on the step behind him.

"Oh?" She took a long swig of water.

"The shower is enormous. And has a built-in bench."

Tess felt her mouth curl into a smile and she looked over at the man she'd loved for almost twenty two years. Okay, honestly, twenty five. She'd never really been over him. "I saw that bench. You think it's sturdy enough for two?"

"For sure."

"Even with a lot of...motion?"

"Absolutely."

Tessa felt her heart accelerate faster than it ever did running. "Did the reservation people wonder why you were asking?"

"Why I was asking for a sturdy built-in bench in an enormous shower?" he asked. "I have a spinal cord injury. They can't ask questions like that."

She laughed. "But you probably told them anyway."

Bryan certainly hadn't gotten any shier in the eight months they'd been together. In fact, if it was possible, he was *more* outgoing than before. He was big on public displays of affection, as well as public displays of pride in Tessa. He loved to talk to the people they met traveling, explaining about his injury and his crutches, and how he was following the love of his life around while she ran in all the places she'd dreamed about. And when he found someone interested in running or biking, it was impossible to shut him up. He loved the personal consulting via email and Skype that had organically popped up from those conversations. He'd taken up blogging again and did video blogs when he wasn't working with Ty's athletes, running the Come Again, and working on the multitude of community projects and committees he kept signing up for.

Frankly, keeping up with him was exhausting.

And Tessa had never been happier.

"So my mom made me swear that we weren't going to get married spontaneously on one of these trips," he said casually.

The water Tessa had just sipped went down the wrong pipe and she had to hack and cough for a moment before she could speak.

"*What?*" she squeaked a moment later.

He grinned at her. "I told her about this tandem bike race in Spain in June. I was thinking we could do that, and that the finish line would be the perfect place for us to get married."

Married. Holy crap.

But it didn't take that long for the idea to sink in. It actually would be kind of perfect. Except...

"June is festival time. We can't miss that," she said. She'd vowed to never miss another summer festival in Sapphire Falls ever again. It had almost killed her not being there for the last one.

"Okay, then town square during the festival it is," Bryan said agreeable. "We could do the tandem bike in Spain thing anytime."

She laughed. "Oh, sure, anytime."

But they could. That was the wondrous thing.

Then she stopped. "Did you just...you want to get married during the festival next year?" she asked.

"Well, yeah," he said as if it was the most logical thing in the world.

Married.

To Bryan.

That didn't take *any* time to sink in. She breathed out and slumped back on the step. "Well, it's about damned time," she said and tipped her bottle up to empty it.

A moment later, he yanked the bottle away, tossed it onto the ground and hauled her into his lap.

She laughed as she straddled him. "I don't smell very good."

"Say it, Tess," he told her in that low, firm voice she loved.

"I don't smell very good."

"The other thing."

She smiled. "That it's about damned time you married me?"

"Say yes."

"You didn't ask a question."

He looked up at her for two beats, realized she was right and muttered, "Dammit."

She laughed again and wrapped her arms around his neck. "Good thing I know you so well and that I don't want all that romantic, sweet stuff."

"Yeah, well, you're going to keep getting it anyway," he told her.

She knew that. And she didn't *really* mind at all.

"As long as you have Delaney put in a built-in bench in our new shower, you can be as sweet and romantic as you want," she said. Delaney was helping them build their house, right on the outskirts of Sapphire Falls. "*Outside* of the shower. And the bedroom," she added. "And your office. And the kitchen. In those places you better be naughty."

"The shower is already in the plans," he told her, cupping her butt and pressing her down against his growing erection. "And maybe I'm starting to come around to your way of thinking about the shower and the bedroom and my office and the kitchen."

She shook her head. "Everything always goes *your* way," she said, her heart full of love and happiness.

"Are you kidding?" he asked. "You've made me work harder than any girl, coach, doctor or physical therapist ever did."

She grinned, and he laughed.

"Which is exactly as you'd intended, right?" he asked, his smile and eyes full of the same love and happiness and satisfaction she was feeling.

"You've always said that hard work pays big dividends," she told him. "That's straight off your blog."

"Hmm...it's no wonder you love me. I'm quite brilliant."

She scooted off his lap and held out her hand. "You are indeed. So let's go get some dividends."

"Dividends as a code word for sex. I like it." Bryan took her hand and she pulled him to his feet.

Then they headed straight for the shower with the built-in bench.

And everything, absolutely everything, went exactly her way. Twice. Then his. And then hers again.

———

Thank you so much for reading *Getting His Way*! I hope you loved Bryan and Tessa's story!

And up next from Sapphire Falls is **Getting Into Trouble** with hot cop Scott Hansen and Sapphire Falls bad girl, Peyton Wells!

Sapphire Falls cop Scott Hansen is big, he's hot and he's also the source of Peyton Wells' dirtiest daydreams.

He only has one fault...he's crazy about her.

She'll do absolutely anything Scott asks if he obeys three simple rules: they're both naked; there are lots of hands and lips involved; and they absolutely do not call it a relationship.

The R word gives her hives. Why can't the guy just be happy with no-strings sex?

Grab Getting Into Trouble now!

———

The Sapphire Falls series

Getting Out of Hand
Getting Worked Up
Getting Dirty
Getting Wrapped Up
Getting It All
Getting Lucky
Getting Over It
Getting His Way
Getting Into Trouble
Getting It Right
Getting All Riled Up
Getting to the Church On Time

And more at

ErinNicholas.com

———

Join in on the fan fun too! I love interacting with my readers and would love to have you in the two places where I chat with fans the most--my email list and my Super Fan page on Facebook!

Sign up for my email list! You'll hear from me just a couple times a month and I'll keep you updated on all my news, sales, exclusive fun, and new releases!
http://bit.ly/ErinNicholasEmails

Join my fan page on Facebook at Erin Nicholas Super Fans! I check in there every day and it's the best place for first looks, exclusive giveaways, book talk and fun!

ABOUT ERIN

Erin Nicholas is the New York Times and USA Today bestselling author of over thirty sexy contemporary romances. Her stories have been described as toe-curling, enchanting, steamy and fun. She loves to write about reluctant heroes, imperfect heroines and happily ever afters. She lives in the Midwest with her husband who only wants to read the sex scenes in her books, her kids who will never read the sex scenes in her books, and family and friends who say they're shocked by the sex scenes in her books (yeah, right!).

Find her and all her books at
www.ErinNicholas.com

And find her on Facebook, BookBub, and Instagram!